CIJ00829091

THE GIFT OF GIRLS

I sat as if I were wearing clothes, the seatbelt emphasising the shape of my breasts, making them more prominent, my face half-hidden by my hair. It was embarrassing to be sitting there like that; actually, it was shameful, but I felt protected as if in the hands of fate. I didn't have to make any choices or decisions. My credit cards, keys and mobile phone were in the plastic bag with my clothes in the back of the car. I was like a child in some ways, totally free, free of my clothes, free of responsibility. I just had to do *anything* demanded of me. In thirty-one days I would be free and, at that moment, it seemed an eternity away.

'Sit still,' he said. 'You're wriggling about.'

'That's because it hurts,' I replied.

'That's nothing, Magdalena. That was just a little bit of . . . foreplay.'

He saw my face screw up in trepidation and patted my knee.

'You can do this, Magdalena,' he added, his voice almost kindly. 'Like all things in life, if we accept new experiences with equanimity we learn and grow from them.'

'What do you learn from having your bottom spanked?' I asked petulantly.

'What do you think?'

I wasn't sure. It would never in a million years have crossed my mind that a man one day would smack my bottom – I mean, like that, naked over a sofa. I didn't know such things went on.

By the same author:

BEING A GIRL

THE GIFT OF GIRLS

Chloë Thurlow

This book is a work of fiction.
Always make sure you practise safe, sane and consensual sex.

Published by Nexus 2009

2 4 6 8 10 9 7 5 3 1

Copyright © Chloë Thurlow 2009

Chloë Thurlow has asserted her right under the Copyright, Designs and Patents Act 1988
to be identified as the author of this work

*All characters in this publication are fictitious and any resemblance to real persons, living or
dead, is purely coincidental.*

This book is sold subject to the condition that it shall not, by way of trade or otherwise, be
lent, resold, hired out, or otherwise circulated without the publisher's prior consent in any
form of binding or cover other than that in which it is published and without a similar
condition, including this condition, being imposed on the subsequent purchaser.

First published in Great Britain in 2009 by
Nexus
Virgin Books
Random House, 20 Vauxhall Bridge Road
London SW1V 2SA

www.virginbooks.com
www.rbooks.co.uk

Addresses for companies within The Random House Group Limited can be found at:
www.randomhouse.co.uk/offices.htm

The Random House Group Limited Reg. No. 954009

Distributed in the USA by Macmillan, 175 Fifth Avenue, New York, NY 10010, USA

A CIP catalogue record for this book is available from the British Library

ISBN 9780352345202

The Random House Group Limited supports The Forest Stewardship Council [FSC], the
leading international forest-certification organisation. All our titles that are printed on
Greenpeace-approved FSC-certified paper carry the FSC logo.
Our paper procurement policy can be found at www.rbooks.co.uk/environment

Typeset by TW Typesetting, Plymouth, Devon
Printed and bound in Great Britain by CPI Bookmarque, Croydon CR0 4TD

For Jim Arnold

CONTENTS

nexus Symbols key

 Corporal Punishment

 Female Domination

 Institution

 Medical

 Period Setting

 Restraint/Bondage

 Rubber/Leather

 Spanking

 Transvestism

 Underwear

 Uniforms

1

The Interview

Sitting across the desk from Simon Roche in his office was worse than sitting A level French; worse than being sent to Sister Benedict to be reprimanded. My armpits were dripping and my knickers were so damp they had ridden up into the crack of my bottom. I was wearing a lacy blouse that revealed rather more bare flesh than was probably appropriate and my cheeks turned pink with embarrassment as I followed Mr Roche's eyes down to my throbbing breasts.

My flatmate Melissa had said, if you've got it, flaunt it, and the thing with clichés is, while they are usually true, they don't always apply.

With the push-up bra shamefully tipping my breasts out of my top, I had chosen a pink suit and cherry-red heels high enough to give a girl a sense of presence. That was the plan. My clothes were neat, pretty, feminine and tight enough to ensure that my bones could be seen to be exactly where they should be, pressing through my lightly tanned skin and brushing the inside of the pink fabric.

I was wearing the uniform of a girl with confidence, although I couldn't help wondering as I gazed back mesmerised into Simon Roche's deep-set eyes if I had got it all terribly wrong. He looked like Heathcliff in *Wuthering Heights* with wavy black hair and those probing dark

1

eyes that had remained for an age on my breasts before panning slowly upwards over my chin and my nose. As our gaze met once more, I got the impression that he was looking into my soul, into my hidden desires and secrets. Desires and secrets I didn't even know I had.

The office was cool and dark with pale wooden planks underfoot and floor-to-ceiling windows cloaked by vertical blinds. The blinds were partially drawn and bars of light patterned the room in such a way that for a moment I felt as if I were a bird in a gilded cage, there of my own free will to have my wings clipped. Roche-Marshall was one of the top accountancy firms in the country and a month's work experience at their London office would give me a feeling for the profession before I started my degree at the London School of Economics.

'Aren't you going to find accountancy a little dull, Miss Wallace?' Mr Roche began.

'Not at all, I adore figures.'

He cast his eyes over my neck and shoulders, over that reckless display of cleavage.

'As do I,' he finally said, and I felt the flush on my cheeks burn more brightly. 'How old are you?'

'Eighteen.'

'So, no gap year?'

'No,' I said and paused. 'I want to get ahead. I like to succeed in what I set out to do and taking a year off now would slow me down.'

'You seem very . . . disciplined.'

'Yes, I am.'

'That is something I like in a girl.' His eyes in the refracted light seemed to sparkle like black stars. 'Unlike art or literature, that can be bent to the shape that pleases the practitioner, the purity of numbers demands our subjugation to discipline.'

He clearly expected a reply and I wasn't sure what to say. 'Yes,' I said. 'I think that's probably right, Mr Roche.'

'You can call me Simon, and I shall call you –' he paused before saying my name '– Magdalena.'

My name sounded oddly sensual in his deep voice. 'OK,' I said with a little shrug.

'We are a very old firm. Some of our clients have been with us for a hundred years. Dealing with other people's money requires complete trust. I like to reward those who respect that trust. Those who betray it I punish. I punish with extreme severity.'

As he spoke, he lowered his voice and I felt a shiver run up my spine. 'Of course,' I said, filling the moment's silence.

He looked down at my application and continued. 'I see you received the maths prize at school.'

I nodded.

'And your hobby is gymnastics?'

'Yes.'

'I'm sure you look very fetching in a leotard?'

Was this a question? Was this the sort of thing employers asked? I wasn't sure what to say. 'Well ...' The flush on my cheeks must have been turning from pink to crimson. My throat was dry. I tried to swallow.

'Magdalena, you're not embarrassed, are you?' he asked.

'No, not at all.'

'And?'

Now what did he mean?

'I said, I imagine you look very fetching in a leotard?'

'Well, yes, I suppose.'

'Good. We try not to be too dull, even if we are accountants.' He pushed the papers into a folder and smiled. 'I'm sure you're going to fit in at Roche-Marshall very well, very well indeed. I shall look forward to seeing you on Monday.'

That was it. I was in. I was so thrilled my knees felt wobbly as I got to my feet. Simon Roche pushed back his chair and stood, tall in his charcoal suit, a few curls of

3

dark hair climbing over the top of his blue-and-white-striped shirt. He wasn't wearing a tie.

He walked with me out to the lifts and stood there studying me in my pink suit, my slender waist and prominent hipbones, my full breasts of which I was secretly rather proud, the neat cut of my dark hair which Sister Bianca had once described as the colour of temptation. I had never been sure if the little nun from Napoli had been flirting with me.

The lift bell rang and Simon Roche touched my arm as if to guide me between the silver doors as they whispered open.

'Until Monday,' he said.

'Thank you, thank you so much,' I replied.

The doors closed and the lift whisked me down seven floors to the glass entrance of Roche-Marshall, a temple to the divinity of numbers, the altar for the sacrificial lamb.

2

Learning the System

I arrived sparky bright in a yellow suit Monday morning and was astonished to be given the job checking the accounts for various large corporations. I imagined this was a test, that the accounts had already been signed off, but there was probably going to be some small error in each one and, if that were the case, I was determined to find them.

It may seem weird that a girl like me, a gymnast, should enjoy the cold inflexible world of numbers, but I really do.

Life when you leave the safety of school is bewildering. We have all this education and ambition and temptation, and, while you are navigating a path through the grown-up maze, numbers have a purity, an honesty. Except in quantum physics or spacetime, two plus two always equals four, and there is comfort in knowing that, even if deep down the mathematician knows it isn't strictly true.

I had been placed on my own in a small office with a view over the church spires and old slate roofs of East London. I was just along the corridor from Simon Roche and mid-morning he popped his head round the door to ask how I was getting on.

'Fine, fine.'

'Have you found any inconsistencies?'

I couldn't resist a small smile. 'Yes, a few,' I replied.

'No problems with the software?'

'No, I did IT at school.'

'Good for you.'

He seemed to be studying my feet under the desk. He glanced up, gave me one of his penetrating looks and left me with a vague sense of unease as he closed the door behind him.

Simon Roche gave me the feeling that he knew something I didn't know, that he was aware that, while I was gilding my CV working as an intern at Roche-Marshall by day, from eight at night until two in the morning I was serving complimentary drinks at Rebels Casino in Piccadilly.

The truth is, I wasn't taking a gap year and I was doing a waitressing job that wasn't entirely suitable because I didn't have any money. Well, yes, I had about £1,000 in savings, but I was sharing a flat in Camberwell with Sarah and Melissa, and £1,000 added to my meagre £3,000 student loan wasn't going to last through my first term at the LSE. Not if I wanted to eat. Actually, not eating wasn't a problem, it was not buying the clothes and creams and underwear that make a girl after seven years at boarding school feel that life's worth living.

How I had managed to get into this sorry state wasn't exactly my fault. Father made and lost fortunes with his harebrained schemes and had just lost the most recent fortune publishing English textbooks for the Chinese; only 50p a copy to print in Singapore, but, with ten million copies rolling off the press, the Chinese man who had ordered the books vanished. Poor Daddy got stuck with the bill and went bankrupt. He was now in the Middle East trying to set up a business selling second-hand aeroplanes, my Spanish mother was acting suicidal, and I was on my own.

I had taken the job at Rebels at Melissa's urging because I had once played Sally Bowles in the school

6

production of *Cabaret* and my role at the casino required a similar costume: a bowler hat and bow tie, a sleeveless girdle that nipped in the waist and, correspondingly, pumped up my breasts, black fishnets hooked to a garter belt and shiny black knickers, which alluring prospect invited punters to smack my bottom, an occupational hazard rewarded with small gratuities and, as I'm sure it says in the Bible, who among us can resist temptation?

The job allowed me to get a glimpse of the real world, or at least the real world of gamblers, who, as often as not, seemed to toss their chips across the green baize of the gaming tables so that it resembled debris vanishing on the outgoing tide. The majority of the players lost their money, and most did so with the equanimity of poor people standing in the rain at bus stops.

There were exceptions, and I often lingered over the blackjack table to watch an Australian man who wore the same creased linen suit every night and always appeared to cash up more chips than he had purchased at the beginning of the evening. He didn't drink cocktails, but took a bottle of Coke every time I passed with the tray.

On Saturday, at the end of my first week at Roche-Marshall, I plucked up the courage to ask him how come he always seemed to win.

'I have a system,' he said and he placed four £50 chips on the three of diamonds.

My tray was empty and I had to dash off to refill it. I swept back around the room. An actor named Jay Leonard, whom everyone knew from the TV soaps, shoved £5 down my knickers and smacked me so hard I nearly dropped the tray.

'Ouch,' I cried.

'She loves it,' he called.

I stumbled on, bottom burning, determined to get a first in economics from the LSE.

Men, I had discovered, were obsessed with bottoms. They want to spank them, pinch them, squeeze them like

7

ripe peaches in the greengrocer's. Men see bottoms and can't keep their hands to themselves. Even some women are lured by the same strange temptation – the nuns at my school, certainly, who dearly loved to see girls breaking the rules so they could instil a bit of old-fashioned obedience in them. Spanking may have been banned in most schools, but not in mine.

I hurried in a circle giving out drinks, wiggling without even meaning to, and, when I reached the Australian, I watched him scoop in another pile of chips.

'That's amazing,' I said.

'It's easy when you know how,' he replied.

I watched him refill his glass with Coke. As he looked up, our eyes met.

'Will you teach me?' I asked breathlessly.

He laughed. 'Listen, babe, no one gives away their system, not for anything,' he said.

'Please, I'm desperate.'

He pushed back his shaggy mop of dirty-blonde hair and his blue eyes ran over my features. 'Why are you so desperate?' he asked.

I told him that I had to support myself through university, that I was working unpaid in an accountant's office, that if he told me I'd never breathe a word to anyone. 'Please,' I said. 'I'll do anything.'

He looked at my breasts, my trembling inflamed lips, and he looked long and hard into my nervous eyes. 'Anything?' he asked.

The noise in the casino seemed to fade to silence. The lights had dimmed. There was only the Australian looking at me with sea-blue eyes in a nest of wrinkles, a smile on his leathery face. When you say to a girl at school you'll do *anything* if she'll let you read her essay, or let you borrow her new ra-ra skirt, it doesn't mean the same as when you say you'll do anything for a man in a creased linen suit in a casino at 1.30 in the morning.

'Anything?' he said again.

I bit my lip and nodded my head.

I was conscious of what I was doing but in a subconscious sort of way, if that makes sense. What I mean is, I hadn't thought it through. It just seemed as if there was something inevitable about it, there was no alternative, it was the right thing to do at that moment.

'What time do you finish?' he asked.

'Another half an hour.'

'I'll play on till then and then we'll get a taxi back to my hotel. All right?'

I nodded again.

My heart was thumping like a drum as I raced off with the empty tray. I couldn't believe what I had done, that I'd bitten my lip and nodded my head, that I'd agreed. It was absurd. It was outrageous. It was shameful. Girls like me don't do that sort of thing. They don't even think about such things. But I had been given an impossible choice: condemn myself to poverty or take a chance, nod my head, and agree to do *anything*.

I trotted back to the bar and refilled the tray. As I moved through the casino the enormity of what I was contemplating didn't seem real. It was like being back on stage in *Cabaret*. I was parading about in a corset and black stockings, my legs tapered in stilettos, my breasts pumped up like an ad for Wonderbra. I was in costume and a costume makes you feel safe, hidden. It makes you feel that you are playing a role. It wasn't me but the actress in me that had looked back into the Australian's eyes and silently agreed to his proposal.

In my head there were two voices. One was saying: I can't do this, I'll never do this. The other was saying: You must do this. You must do this. You nodded your head. You must do this.

The flush on my neck burned like a brand, my blood like fire in my veins. If anyone ever found out I'd feel mortified. And yet, and yet, I could see all the advantages, and the disadvantages reminded me for some

9

reason of Sister Benedict in chapel quoting the parable of the ten talents: the good servants who had taken the cash gift from their master and doubled their money had *done the right thing*, while the servant who had ignored the opportunity and hidden his solitary talent in the desert had the coin taken from him when the master returned.

For unto every one that hath shall be given, and he shall have abundance: but from him that hath not shall be taken away even that which he hath.

It was chilling. When opportunity comes knocking you have to be dressed and ready for it. Surely that's what Matthew in verse 25 was trying to tell me.

My armpits were tingling and damp. I felt breathless in the tight corset. I couldn't focus on anyone or see anything except the picture in my mind of a girl in a bizarre black costume in a small bare room listening to the sound of an iron knocker rapping on a bolted door. Opportunity's here. Are you going to let me in?

The last thirty minutes at work always dragged but time that night was racing, the minutes ticking me closer to the moment when I threw back the door, the sound of knocking an echo coming closer and closer.

You must do this. You must do this. You nodded your head. You must do this.

There were a few more slaps on my bottom, a few more creased bank notes shoved down my pants, and suddenly, instead of changing out of my casino clothes, I was pushing my arms into a floor-length raincoat that I buttoned up to my throat.

I can't do this, I'll never do this.

The colour drained from my face as I moved like a shadow through the casino to the main doors. The Australian was waiting outside. He didn't speak and neither did I. He stopped a cruising cab. He opened the door and stood back, gazing at me like the master judging the servant with the solitary unused talent.

I hesitated. I was on the banks of the Rubicon. Once I crossed the raging river there was no way back. This was my last chance to say no, to apologise, to rush off and find another taxi to take me home.

Kate, another girl who finished at two, ran down the casino steps to where her boyfriend was waiting in his car. She gave me a wave as if in encouragement and, as I waved back, I stepped into the taxi's dark interior. I was on autopilot. I wasn't making my own decisions. They were being made by some power outside myself. I sat in the corner of the seat trembling and silent, my fingers laced together in my lap, like a prisoner in the dock.

My companion introduced himself. His name was Sandy Cunningham. It was all very formal. Magdalena Wallace, I said. He patted my knee as you would pat a restless pony. It was all so weird and all so easy.

There was nothing, absolutely nothing wrong with making it with a sixth-former from the local grammar school on the bottom field; heavens, the third-year girls were at it like rabbits. But Sandy was a man, an adult, and I really had no idea how I had come to be sitting there in a taxi with him and how I should behave now I was there.

'You're not nervous, are you?' he asked me.

I blushed. 'No . . .' I paused. 'Yes, I am a bit.'

He patted my knee again. 'I can have the taxi drop me, then you can go home,' he suggested. He looked into my eyes. My pulse was racing. There was a throbbing in my temples. A tightness across my chest. I felt like a reprieved prisoner and, now I was free, I wasn't sure what to do with my freedom. I watched the shop lights race by, a few late-night couples wandering home, a drunk sitting in the gutter drinking from a bottle wrapped in a bag.

There are in life few moments that are of the essence, direction-making or changing, few decisions that determine who we are and what we might become. This was one of those moments, one of those decisions. It was as if sitting in that taxi in high heels and fishnets there were two girls, the me I thought I was and the me I really am. Freud says we are all someone else underneath, and the real person underneath has different feelings. The feeling I had as the black cab slowed outside a hotel in Kensington was that if I didn't take this opportunity to learn the system I would have an entire lifetime to look back and regret it.

The taxi stopped.

'We're here,' I said.

'Remember, anything,' he said.

I nodded and bit my inflamed lip.

The uniformed desk clerk gave Sandy that man-of-the-world sort of grin as we entered the soft light of the foyer. I felt like shouting, 'I've never done this before,' but that would have been childish and, anyway, the moment had passed. I was standing facing the row of three lifts watching the numbers rise and fall and trying to work out square roots as they shifted and changed.

The silver doors in the middle lift pinged and, as they whispered open, it felt as if a rock were being rolled away from the mouth of a cave. It was like the beginning of an adventure. Once I entered the cave I would be setting out on a journey.

I paused. Like the two girls I had imagined in the taxi, I was one person outside the lift. I would be another if I entered.

'Shall we?' he said.

As the lift was about to close, Sandy put his arm in the space. The doors shuddered impatiently, then opened again. There was still time to make an excuse and leave, but dire straits call for desperate measures. Sandy Cunningham knew how to beat the system and I entered the mirrored cubicle thirsting for knowledge. He pressed 7: the fourth prime number; VII in Roman numerals; the Hindus invented it and the Arabs shaped it. There was a girl at school who had the number tattooed on her

12

bottom after sleeping with seven boys in three days at Glastonbury during the rock festival. Seven is said to be a lucky number and my stomach lurched as we glided through the void, our reflections captured in the glass, a girl with pink cheeks and a floor-length raincoat, a man in a creased linen suit, a puzzled look on his sunny features.

Up through the numbers, 1, 2, 3, 4, 5, 6, 7. The doors opened and I followed him along the corridor with its dimly lit floor lights and trays of half-eaten snacks from room service abandoned outside locked rooms. The hour was late. Insomniacs listened to the soft hum of televisions; you could see a flicker of blue light below some of the doors. We turned a corner and, as we reached room 713, I felt a pang of regret that it was this room and not one of the others, although that was silly. In theory I believed in lucky numbers, but unlucky numbers are an invention of the devil.

He shoved a key card into the lock and a green light indicated when the mechanism was ready. He turned the handle and I entered a vast luxurious suite which surprised me: he clearly made a fortune playing the system, I thought. We made our way through the living room with its sofas and baskets of fruit into the bedroom with its enormous bed, leather armchairs, a television and pink lampshades that gave the room a pastel glow.

He closed and locked the door.

'I've never done anything like this before,' I said, the words escaping from me in a terrible rush.

'Neither have I,' he replied and he knew I didn't know what he meant. He smiled. 'I've never told anyone the system, not anyone, not ever.'

That made me feel better. It made me feel that what I was going to get was worth what I was going to give, although what exactly I'd be expected to give I wasn't sure. It seemed as if I was being inducted into some wonderful secret, something esoteric and divine, and it

13

didn't seem quite so disgraceful as he peeled off my long raincoat, put his arms around me and kissed me on the lips.

I was quite shocked by this, although I'm not sure why. I had pictured myself lying back on a bed, eyes pressed tightly shut, Sandy Cunningham bouncing away on top of me. I was going to give my best, I always do, but kissing just felt weird and I pressed back half-heartedly at first and with somewhat more enthusiasm when I realised it really wasn't so bad.

His fingers began the long task of unlacing the corset. It came away in his hands and I sighed with a sense of release as he placed it over the arm of the leather armchair. He kissed my neck and shoulders, my collar-bones, then bent to unclasp my stockings. He rolled them down my legs and I slipped out of my shoes. He unsnapped the garter belt and studied this strange harness before placing it with the corset. He did every-thing slowly, undressing me as you would open a surprise parcel, and it occurred to me that this was the difference between a man and a boy. Boys want to do everything so quickly they leave a girl feeling that it's all a bit of a waste of time.

Sandy was like a scientist doing research on my lips, my chin, my neck. My breasts were throbbing painfully, my nipples prickling with pins and needles. I had the odd feeling that I wanted him to bite me, bite me hard, but he didn't: he took my nipples in his mouth, one at a time, and suckled on them like an infant. They popped out and became hard and the pins and needles went away. Slowly, slowly, he kissed my rib cage and the hollow of my stomach. He went down on his knees and, as he carefully lowered my knickers, a shower of £5 and £10 notes scattered like leaves around our feet.

'Blimey, must be fifty quid here,' he said.

'That's because it's Saturday.' My voice was a whisper. I was naked, stark naked with a strange man just about

14

old enough to be my father. He was on his knees sniffing and licking at my pussy and I couldn't understand why I was so aroused, why I was so wet. What I was doing was out of character, so unacceptable, so absurd and outrageous, it was shamefully, lusciously exciting. My body was sheathed in perspiration. After six long hours trudging around the casino having my bum spanked I felt totally and wantonly alive.

I arched my back and pushed out my breasts. I cupped the back of Sandy's head and pushed his face into the wet gash of my open pussy. I sighed as the lips of my labia parted and his tongue wormed its way between my legs.

Sister Benedict had always implied that I had the potential to be wicked, and being wicked, I realised, was liberating. All through my life I had been imprisoned by views and opinions that didn't belong to me. I was a gymnast. I was a bird. I wanted to be free. I wanted to fly. I had sat through a million exams and now I was in a strange room with a strange man holding the cheeks of my bottom and lapping at my pussy.

It was so unlike me, so depraved and intimate I would never be able to tell anyone, not even Melissa, who claimed to have done it all by the time she was fourteen. But I was sure she had never done this, never stood boldly naked with a man's long tongue like a key opening the secrets between her legs, her breasts on fire, her reflection captured in the dark face of the television screen. I was an intern at Roche-Marshall in the City of London and soon I would know *the system*.

A moment of doubt pricked my mind: I remembered reading in a book by Jean Rhys or Anaïs Nin that a girl should always make sure she is paid before the act, not after. But Sandy Cunningham seemed an honourable type and I was too absorbed to do anything but enjoy the feeling of my own warm juices turning sticky on my thighs, the sharp jolts of pleasure as contractions zipped like electricity through my tummy. I was remotely aware that my sense of shame and embarrassment made the sensation more intense, more thrilling. I was a bad girl and being bad after always trying to be good was liberating.

I had an inkling that every woman fantasises about having sex with a stranger, about being taken by accident, by chance, as a prostitute, and then taking the money to perform the service. There is something logical in it all. Why else would prostitution be the oldest profession? Was it really so terrible, so shameful? What is our role, after all, I wondered? What are we supposed to do with this life? I was born with certain assets: I was good at figures and, ironically, I had become a figure, a long slender figure 8, the sign of infinity.

I took a firmer grip on Sandy's head and he pumped his tongue like a piston in and out, in and out. I could feel something fiery and mysterious moving through me, something the girls at school talked about like they talked about ghosts when the lights in the dorm were turned off, though, like ghosts, few girls had actually ever seen one, felt its touch. My ghost was coming now and, at that moment, the worst possible moment, he let go of my bottom and just stopped. He stood up. I sighed and, like a deflated balloon, all the air went out of me as he scooped me into his arms and tossed me quite roughly on the bed.

'Was that all right?' he said, and shamefully I nodded.

He removed his crumpled suit, his blue polo shirt and his boxer shorts. Only as I gazed at his cock did I realise that I had never actually studied a man's penis before. Boys always act as if they are late for a train. They whip your knickers down, push up inside you, and just as it's beginning to feel nice, that's it, they shoot their milky sperm inside you, or over your stomach, and then go all soft and silly.

Thank heavens for the pill, I thought, as Sandy Cunningham slid across the bed and pushed his hard cock inside me. I was so wet, there was no pain, no awkwardness, just a feeling of mild relief, a feeling that I had done the right thing. I wanted to learn the system and buying that privilege with the only currency available to me was the sensible thing to do. I thought for a moment of Sister Benedict and forced the image out of my brain.

My legs rose automatically and I locked them around Sandy's back, urging him deeper and deeper inside me. The contractions I'd felt before he stopped thrusting his tongue into my pussy returned once more and a few hot moments passed before that elusive climax gripped my chest, moved down in a gathering wave through my insides and burst out of me in a frenzy of unimaginable pleasure. I had been in prison and, with that orgasm, I was set free.

Sandy had held back with a gambler's instinct for self-control and when he pulled out I felt a terrible sense of loss. I didn't want it to be over. I didn't know what I wanted. This wasn't a bit of fun on the bottom field with a boy from the local grammar. This was the real thing. This was adult sex. I was still filled with shame but also an odd sort of pride, these two emotions competing for space, my mind confused, my body revelling in the moment.

He was wriggling from my locked legs and rolled me on to my tummy. He grabbed the pillows from the top of the bed, wedged them under me so that my body formed an arch and before I knew what was happening, his tongue was pushing into my bottom. I couldn't believe it. I froze. I didn't know what to do, what to think. It felt so strange, so wrong, so new, so nice. In the land of love I had been a blind person and in probing the eye of my bottom Sandy Cunningham was drawing the blinds from my eyes.

My bottom was so tight only the tip of his tongue pushed through the tiny ring, but the more he pushed, the

17

more the ring opened and drew him inside. At first I just lay there feeling guilty and embarrassed, letting him do it, but the movement set off a chain reaction. I started pushing down with my toes, rolling my hips, thrusting my bottom at him, his big moist tongue slicked with the oils leaking from my pussy, making me so wet I thought I might float away on a tide of intoxication.

When he stopped, I had that same sense of loss as when he'd withdrawn from tonguing my pussy. I wiggled my bottom like a monkey in the zoo and what happened next I had not been expecting. Of course, we had all talked exhaustively in the dorm about anal sex and we read about it in *Cosmo* and *Nuts*. But it was a step beyond my imagination, and all the pleasure of having his tongue inside me vanished with the pain and humiliation as he took a grip on my jutting hipbones and pushed his cock deep inside my virgin bottom.

'Agh, agh, agh,' I squealed, gasping for air, and he pushed harder and harder, drilling as if for precious minerals inside my body.

I bit the bed sheets to stop myself screaming and widened my legs as with each thrust my body arched further. I took a grip on the headboard, pushed my feet into the bed and, to my complete surprise, as I widened my legs the pain went away. I was horrified that I was allowing a stranger to do this, to have mounted me in this way, but through the shame the pain was turning to pleasure. Those two senses, like smell and taste, were indivisibly linked.

My bottom was drawing him deeper inside me and I used the muscles I'd made strong on the parallel bars to hold him, to clench him tighter. I was sweaty and wet. All my routines as a gymnast had shaped me for this. I wasn't made for the Olympics, for winning prizes, my breasts had grown too ripe and lush, my bottom too perky and round. I was made to be on my knees, my back arched, my breasts hanging heavily like udders below me,

18

my strong arms supporting a stranger drilling into the very heart of my being.

Anal sex. Just the words were a turn-on. *Anal sex. Anal sex. Anal sex.*

I was whispering the words in my mind like a mantra. Sex had always been fun but short-lived and far from satisfying. It was like losing at chess. The game contains its own pleasures, but winning makes all the moves and strategies and hours of devotion more meaningful.

Sandy started to moan. His grip on my hipbones grew tighter. I let go of the headboard and all but left the bed and took wing as his cock finally erupted. I felt the flood of come wash through my back passage, pumping away as if releasing some precious elixir that would now belong to me. We collapsed back on to the bed sheets in a tangled octopus of quivering arms and legs. I was panting for breath and relished the pleasure of his hot semen slipping out of my bottom into my gaping pussy and pubic hair.

This was my first time, the first time I'd done it properly. I was tingling all over as if parts of me that had been asleep had been woken like Snow White with a kiss and all that follows. I felt guilty, ashamed, but I was proud, too. I've done it. I've done it. Now, I would learn the system, I thought, but Sandy Cunningham had something else in mind.

He rolled me over and straddled my torso. He slid forward, pushed the pillows under my shoulders and presented the head of his dripping penis at the door of my closed mouth. It bobbed up and down like something alive, a little creature with its own free will, tickling my lips and nose. I could smell a blend of scents, Sandy's semen, my own discharge, my own dark places, and tentatively, like a snake, I pushed the tip of my tongue between my closed lips to lick the big mauve head.

I had never done this before. Of course boys had tried, boys will try anything and everything, but I had always

19

pulled away and told them they were disgusting. I didn't think Mr Cunningham would have appreciated any schoolgirl reluctance and opened my lips wider to allow it to slip inside.

The head of his cock filled my mouth. The trunk had grown soft, but he kept pushing it in and out until it grew hard again. Just as I'd first been unwilling to take this alien object up my bottom, all the fine tissues of my throat wanted to reject his cock. But he patiently kept pushing down into my yawning mouth and, by doing a sort of breathing trick to stop myself gagging, I started to appreciate the odd pleasure of sucking and nipping at the warm piece of flesh. I was tempted to bite down hard, it seems a natural instinct, but controlled the urge, wrapped the shaft of his cock in my tongue and contented myself with sucking as hard as I could.

Sandy Cunningham went faster and faster, deeper and deeper. He took a grip on the side of my head; my jaw was aching, my ears hurt, my mouth was stretched wider than the figure in Munch's *The Scream*. I felt a wave of satisfaction when he squirted out a speck of sperm that splashed against the roof of my mouth and tickled my taste buds with the tang of something bitter-smooth, like lemons and Greek yoghurt.

He withdrew slowly and I licked my lips. He looked down at me for a long time. The lights were dim but I could see the sparkle in his blue eyes.

'You've got a long way to go, babe, but you'll get there,' he said.

My body was electric. My palms were all sweaty. I was so happy. 'What about the system?' I said.

He grew stern and shook his head. 'You must be joking, that's a trade secret.'

I gasped. 'But ... but you promised, you ...' Tears pricked my eyes. I'd been conned. I'd been cheated. I'd let this strange man do *everything* and now, and now ...
'But I've done everything you wanted.'

20

'And you weren't bad for a beginner,' he said, and leaned forward to lick away my tears.

'You did promise.'

'Let that be a lesson to you, never trust anything but your own instincts,' he said. I sniffled and as I went to speak he sealed my lips with his finger. 'Tell me something, was it terrible?'

I shook my head.

'Was it the best ever?'

I tried not to nod and sniffed again. 'You did promise.'

'And a deal's a deal.'

He grinned. He was making fun of me. That's the problem with being eighteen, you don't know when men are really serious and when they're just pulling your leg. I sighed with relief.

He rolled off me and stretched out on his back for a moment. He was panting for breath and I was jiggling my jaw trying to get it back into place. Sex can be more challenging than gymnastics, I realised.

'Come here.'

He pulled me on top of him, kissed me briefly and, as he took my bottom lip between his teeth, he slapped the plump curve of my backside as hard as he could.

'Ouch,' I screamed.

'Shush, you'll wake the neighbours.'

'That hurt.'

He slapped the other cheek, even harder.

'Ouch. What are you doing?'

He was grinning, stroking my bottom, and I could feel ripples of pain and even a strange sort of pleasure drifting up my back and down my thighs.

'All you girls need is discipline.'

'I am quite disciplined enough, thank you very much.'

'Well, we'll see about that,' he said. 'Over there, top drawer.'

He released me from his grip and pointed at the dresser. In the drawer I found a pack of cards. He turned

21

on the bedside lamps and dressed in his boxer shorts and shirt. My bottom was on fire and I caressed my tender cheeks.

'Why did you do that?' I asked him.

'It's good practice.'

I didn't know what he meant. 'Practice for what?'

'You'll find out soon enough. Now watch.'

I should have asked him what he meant, but everything was happening so fast it didn't occur to me at the time and, anyway, all I could think about was learning the system. I handed him the cards.

There was hardly any point in my lacing myself in the girdle and for some reason it seemed perfectly natural sitting naked on the bed while he shuffled the deck. I could smell sex in the air, his semen, my girlie juices and sweat all mixed into a carnal soup, a lusty perfume. I had been on what the girls at school called 'a trip around the world'. I'd been pierced in my three openings, my mouth, my pussy and my bottom. Getting dressed now would be like closing the stable door after the horse has bolted.

'The system is actually very easy. What it requires is self-control.' He looked up into my eyes. 'How's your self-control?'

'Not that good,' I replied and we both laughed.

Now he explained that in blackjack you bet on one card before being dealt a second. The picture cards are all worth 10 and the point is to get as close to 21 as possible. If you have less than 21, you can take another card, you then either *twist*, and get that card for free, or you can buy another card, therefore doubling your stake. It's only wise to double with tens or aces. An ace is equal to one or 11, and if you get a 10 or a picture card with an ace, that's called blackjack and you automatically win – unless the dealer has a blackjack also, in which case you get your money back. After the dealer draws his cards, if you have a higher number than him, you win; if you don't, you lose.

22

The system played by Sandy Cunningham was simple. He would bet one unit of money: £1, £10, £100, it doesn't matter what the bet is, but he would play one chip worth one unit. If he won, he would take his one-chip winnings and bet again, just one chip. If he lost, he would double the stake to two chips. If he lost again, he doubled again and would continue to do so up to a maximum of five bets. So, to play the system, you needed $1+2+4+8+16$ chips, a total of 31 chips, or £31, £310 or £3,100.

I was sitting cross-legged, elbows on my knees, watching as he dealt the cards. Sandy had scooped my tip money from the floor and was using that to demonstrate.

'But what happens if you lose five times in a row?' I asked.

'You go home.'

'You mean you lose your money?'

'No one's ever invented a system that's foolproof. The beauty of this is, the law of averages dictates that you rarely lose five hands in a row. Try spinning a coin five times and see how many times you get straight heads or tails.'

He got out some more bank notes, we kept playing and, uncannily, every time I got to the moment where I might lose, on the fifth hand I won and got all my money back. It was like magic.

'I've been travelling the world for ten years and the casinos have paid for it,' he said. 'You don't make a fortune, but you should always come out ahead.'

'I can't wait to try it for real,' I said.

It was so exciting. My pussy was all sticky and the smell of sex on my bare flesh made me feel lucky. We kept playing for ages and it was fun, and even more fun when all Sandy's money was in my pile. I gave it back to him.

'No, no, no. You keep it,' he said.

'I can't do that . . .'

'You earned it, didn't you?'

He gazed from my lips to my protruding nipples, then back into my eyes. Again I recalled the books of Jean Rhys and Anaïs Nin. I was a girl being paid for my services and it was shameful and thrilling.

'Remember, good luck runs out and bad luck always changes,' he added. 'When you're on a winning streak, keep playing. If you're losing, know when to stop.'

'That's great, thank you.'

'Thank you,' he said.

3

The Fall

All that had happened that Saturday night in Sandy Cunningham's hotel room kept playing through my mind like a clip from an erotic movie. I kept pressing pause to ponder the details, the way he had undressed me like a rare and precious gift. I suppose that's just what I was. What I am!

I was getting *so full of myself*, as Sister Benedict always said. But it had only just dawned on me that I wasn't a young girl any more. I wasn't living behind the high walls of the convent. I was a woman – in every sense of the word. I filled the burlesque costume at the casino really rather well. My long body had filled out – all rounded and enticing at the top, my bottom pouting and desirable. Add to this my dark liquid eyes and protruding hipbones and I had all the accoutrements of feminine power. I was eighteen, the best age to be. Men would now be clay on my potter's wheel, butter in my hands. I was the mistress and men would be my slaves. I was free, free from the past, from childhood, from my money worries.

I knew the system.

In the video replaying through my mind I could see Sandy unsnapping my stockings from the garter belt and rolling the fishnets down my silky legs. I remembered the way the money in my knickers had scattered over the floor, sticky and sweet smelling from being pressed

25

against my bare skin. I adored the way he had caressed my body, my breasts sparkling and fizzing, as his hands, like the palms of a sculptor, released me from the prison of my self. I could summon up the feeling that had come over me when he first put his tongue in my bottom, how I had felt depraved, debased and exhilarated all at the same time.

There are millions of articles about anal sex in girls' magazines but they always focus on whether you should or shouldn't do it. They describe the best lubricants, the perfect position; they say it's the best way to keep your man interested. They describe this act as if it is a gift reluctantly given. But when it comes to describing the actual feeling, the journos aren't sure what to say because describing feelings is never easy, and one girl won't feel the same way as the next. Men take pride in the sense of violation, imagining they are explorers conquering new continents. But what they don't know is that girls want to be conquered. We are designed to be conquered, penetrated, to give up our prizes, not with reluctance but with joy.

Deep down in the subconscious of every girl is an unquenchable thirst, a hunger, a desire to be desired to a point where pleasure turns to pain and the pain turns to new, unknown, unimaginable realms of pleasure. When Sandy Cunningham made my bottom wet and slid his cock inside me I felt mortified that I was letting him do this, and yet, at the same time, I wanted him to. I had made a pact. I had known when I stepped into the mirrored lift at that hotel in Kensington that I would do anything to learn the system and that Sandy with his suntanned face and saucy blue eyes would do everything he wanted in exchange. I was ashamed but intrigued, breathless and electrified.

It hurt, it really hurt, and I was tense because what Sandy was doing at first seemed depraved and shameful. But with each thrust, the tension slowly ebbed. The anxiety faded. My muscles began to relax and the pain became tolerable, less painful than pleasurable, like something completed, something that is meant to be. With my head buried in the soft down pillows, with my eyes sealed like two steel shutters, with my pussy oozing sweet nectar over my thighs, I was overcome by a sense of wickedness and debauchery, and also a sense of wellbeing. I had discovered a part of myself that was new and had been waiting just below the surface to be discovered.

I had been on that legendary trip around the world. I had taken Sandy Cunningham in all my private places, my pussy, my bottom and my mouth. I was feeling guilty, naturally, but as I lay naked in my own little bed in my own little bedroom late on Sunday morning, with Melissa and Sarah sitting with gaping mouths on the edge of the bed, I couldn't help feeling pleased with myself.

After vowing never to tell anyone, I told the girls everything. I mean, it's impossible to keep secrets from girls you've been boarding with for yonks, and of course I lingered over every shudder and thrust, every wet sordid detail.

'How old was he?' asked Sarah.

'About forty, and really quite handsome in that Australian sort of way,' I replied.

'What's it like?'

'What?'

'You know,' said Sarah, 'in the . . .'

'In the bum?' I asked her.

'Yes.' She nodded and leaned forward.

'Mmm,' I said. 'You have to relax and just let it happen.'

Sarah hugged herself as she thought about that.

Melissa was more practical. 'Are you going to teach us this famous system, then?' she asked.

'Oh, no, you have to pay for that,' I told her.

'I bet it doesn't work.'

27

'Well, we'll see.'

I stretched my back and yawned. I was deliciously tired still and closed my eyes.

Melissa spoke to Sarah as she got to her feet. 'That's what happens when you bonk your brains out all night.'

'I wish,' said Sarah, and I opened one eye to give her a wink.

They closed the door behind them. I slept all afternoon, and that night, with the money I'd won playing blackjack with Sandy – proof if proof were needed that my story wasn't exaggerated – we went to the Funky Monkey and got thoroughly caned. I had always been the least adventurous of our little threesome and we drank endless toasts to my new-found immorality, as Melissa put it. I could tell she was dead jealous and Sarah admitted that she intended to take Saint Matthew's advice if the same opportunity ever presented itself to her.

Monday morning I woke without a trace of a hangover and had a spring in my step as I marched into the glass temple at Roche-Marshall wearing a navy-blue pencil skirt, a skinny white T-shirt and Sarah's red military jacket with the wide collar and two rows of brass buttons running at angles from the shoulder to the waist.

'Very patriotic,' Simon Roche said when he made his usual morning call. 'How was your weekend?'

'It was . . . unreal.'

'You've got colour in your cheeks, Magdalena. Did you go on a long country walk, or was it something more stimulating?'

A picture of Sandy Cunningham on his knees lapping at my pussy came to my mind and now my cheeks really did turn red. 'Well, yes it was . . .'

'Stimulating?'

'Actually, yes.'

He smiled. 'You're blushing,' he said. 'How charming. By the way, what size shoes do you take?'

'A narrow six,' I replied and looked back at the rows of numbers on my monitor.

He left, smiling still, and it was another five minutes before I suddenly thought how weird it was that he should ask my shoe size; but then, Simon Roche was a weird sort of bloke. He was tall, darkly handsome, a storybook figure, his voice a sensual baritone, his black eyes looking into my secrets. I'm not sure why, but I had the strangest feeling that he knew exactly what had happened to me on Saturday night in that hotel room in Kensington.

I worked extremely hard and by lunchtime I had done everything I had been expected to do and had some free time to start making my fortune. I registered my credit card with an online casino, clicked into the blackjack and bet £10 on the nine of clubs. I drew the Jack of Diamonds and the dealer drew two cards before going bust. I was already winning.

In an hour, I had accumulated a profit of £200 and called it a day. There was more work to do and I didn't want to make any mistakes.

That night, while Kate was lacing me into my corset, I saw in my reflection a different me. There was something about my expression: my eyes seemed brighter, more focused, my lips were fuller, redder, more pouty.

'Do I look different to you, Kate?'

'You look like a slapper. Did you get it off with that Ozzie?'

The colour crept over my neck. 'Absolutely not,' I said.

She grinned, then turned around so that I could lace her up. Kate had a narrow, V-shaped back with small breasts, but I pulled the corset strings so tight that what she had was all on display the way she liked it. She took a big breath and pushed them out a bit further.

'It's show time,' she said, and went trotting off to the main bar.

Men liked Kate. She was sassy with tomboy features, wide cheekbones and the most juicy pair of lips I had ever seen, like ripe cherries. Men seemed to want to protect her and through the course of the evening she tended to get fewer spanks on the bottom and more tips than me. I wasn't sure why, but it didn't matter. I knew the system. Kate didn't.

I paused and studied myself in the mirror. I did look different. Not *full of myself*, but more confident – less the schoolgirl, more the *femme fatale*. I hadn't eaten very much those last few days and it showed immediately. My waist had grown trimmer, my shoulder blades more defined and my boobs seemed to have become fuller, more rounded, more saucy, more tempting.

It dawned on me now, after lacing Kate into her corset, how incredibly important they are. Breasts, that is. I mean, your bust is everything, the shape, the weight, the form, the feel. The first thing a man looks at is your breasts. Then your waist. Then your bum. But it's your boobs that lead the way, the prow of the ship of which you are the master.

At school we were made to button our blouses up to our chins. The nuns were so obsessed with keeping our breasts hidden all the girls wanted to do was set them free. We wandered around the dorms topless in our navy-blue drawers, our breasts springing up and down like jolly toys. It didn't take much persuasion for you to allow the local grammar school boys to slide their hands up the back of your blouse and then you had to wait impatiently as they tried to unsnap your bra. You could spend an hour on the bottom field getting damp knickers waiting for them to find the combination and more often than not you'd have to do it yourself. Pop the buttons, disengage the bra, lie back and let those clumsy boys have a good feel. Girls really do love their breasts and they love having them on show. It's weird but true.

I leaned forward and planted a kiss on the mirror.

'You slapper,' I said in Kate's 'Sarf Lunnen' accent and slapped my bottom.

I carried my tray with a certain *je ne sais quoi* and endured more smacks than usual, though for some reason I minded less and collected more tips. It was, for a maths scholar, simple arithmetic: $2+2=4$. A teenaged girl dressed in corsets and skimpy black knickers draws men's hands to her bottom like iron filings to a magnet in the physics lab, like moths to the flame, like nuns to their knees. It was part of the job and seemed less demeaning that night, just a bit of fun. I was a gorgeous object and men for some cavemannish reason have a strange desire to venerate and despoil all that is beautiful.

People sipping cocktails were sliding their money across the blackjack and roulette tables. Men with plummy voices, Arabs in robes, soigné women with deep tans and chic dresses built columns of chips on the table before them and watched those chips sink like old tower blocks dynamited from their foundations. They hadn't studied the law of averages. They didn't know that games of chance ebbed and flowed, that through the power of mathematical probability the cunning player knows how to ebb in fractions and flow in primary numbers. I sucked in my waist, pulled back my shoulders and felt faintly light-headed as I toured the golden-lit room with my tray of complimentary poison.

I kept looking out for Sandy Cunningham and he finally turned up just after midnight in his crumpled suit. I dashed over with a Coke and it was sort of strange, because in the video film of our night together he was much taller than me, but in real life in my heels I was much taller than him. I told him I had won £200 online that day and he was really impressed.

'Better to be lucky than clever,' he said. 'Remember, ride your luck and cut your losses.'

'I will, I promise,' I said.

In the two or three minutes I was there he played three hands with £50 chips and pulled in £150.

I circled the casino. Jay Leonard, the soap star with the heavy hand, waved a £10 note in the air as I approached and I thought, ah well, in for a penny, put the tray down and presented my posterior for a moment's discipline.

SLAP.

'Ouch, that hurt. That really hurt,' I said. And it really did hurt.

'Best twenty quid I'll lose tonight,' he replied, and his mates laughed.

'That wasn't twenty, it was ten,' I said.

At that, like a magician, Jay pulled a rolled £10 note as if from behind my ear. 'One more for the road?' he suggested.

'Not so hard this time,' I said and bent forward.

He twirled his arm in circles like he was a propeller plane about to take off and the spank across my poor little bum was so hard tears jerked into my eyes.

'Ouch,' I cried, and all the soigné ladies gave me a dirty look as if I'd sworn in church. I suppose the casino is a sort of church, a place where the rich and famous go to worship money.

Jay Leonard rubbed my bottom with his palm. 'There, there,' he said. 'Don't tell me that little touch hurt?'

'Yes, it did.'

'Well, it's a good idea to get used to it.'

'What's that supposed to mean?'

'Your bum was made for spanking and I've got a feeling it's going to be getting more than its fair share in the future.'

'That's what you think,' I said.

'That's what a little bird told me.'

'Then my advice is don't listen to little birds.'

His mates all laughed – at him for a change, not me. Jay Leonard just grinned and looked pleased with himself. Television actors are always show-offs and, with as much dignity as I could manage, I retrieved my circular tray, tossed my head like a pony and went back to work.

I collected more drinks and, when I got back to the blackjack tables, Sandy was gathering his chips. He was having an early night and flying to Paris the next day.

'You are coming back?'

'I'm just doing the rounds. Can't stay too long in one place,' he said. 'The casinos don't like it.'

'I'll probably never see you again,' I said sadly.

'You'll be seeing me again, that I promise.'

Tuesday was a busy day at the office and it was late in the afternoon before I had a spare hour to log on to the online casino. By the time I was ready to leave at five, I'd won £50, acceptable but a little disappointing.

Wednesday and Thursday were a little better and, in all, I managed to bank over £300.

Thursday night at Rebels I was run off my feet. A party of Russian oil men drinking vodka tonics and shouting in agitated voices were losing their money as if there were no tomorrow, as if there were no longer hungry people in the world, and I couldn't help feeling special with my secret knowledge. Getting your bum tanned for the odd tenner is all very well, but you're going to be bruised the colour of an aubergine before you've got enough to buy a pair of Jimmy Choo shoes and, anyway, the Russians seem to think spanking the waitresses is all part of the service and save their tips for the dealers.

That night in my little bed, with the sound of the headboard in Melissa's room tapping against the wall, I came to what was probably the most important decision in my life. In a week, I had accumulated more than £500 and, with my savings, I had just enough to play the game with £50 chips: $1+2+4+8+16=31$ chips; $31 \times 50 = £1,550$. It was time to take Sandy Cunningham's advice and ride my luck.

There was very little to do that Friday morning and, when I finished, I should have gone and told the secretary that I was free. I didn't. I stared out at the spires and rooftops of East London. It was like taking a breath before diving from the high board. Everything was polished in the morning sun. The sky was blue and clear. I could see Tower Bridge and the London Eye. I was in the same pale-yellow suit and daring top that I had worn on my first day at Roche-Marshall; I thought of it as my lucky outfit. I closed the blinds, logged on and sat down to turn a few cards.

Ace of Spades, first card. I turned the Queen of Hearts and earned a bonus for the blackjack. Next hand: Queen of Diamonds and the eight of hearts. The dealer drew 17 and in two minutes I was more than £100 to the good.

I drew a six of clubs . . .

Time moves at a different speed when you're playing. It doesn't go faster or slower, it just vanishes like mist, like thoughts, like the past. You are living completely in the present, in a frozen moment, and that moment is pure and perfect. I lost a hand, I won a hand. I lost two in a row, doubled up twice and won it all back again.

I seemed to be winning more than I was losing and didn't feel the need to check. It didn't matter. The thing is, if you're feeling lucky good luck follows. When you draw 20 and lose to the banker's 21, you don't think about that; it's like a bump in the road. You click play, hit 2, and two chips light up on the screen for the next hand. I drew a terrible 13, twist and bust, and entered a stake of four chips. I was really unlucky with that one. I drew 19 to the banker's 20. I clicked on a stake of eight chips and didn't think of it as being £400, just eight chips. I lost again.

Did I have a moment's doubt? I think I probably did. But it was just a moment. I was playing the system and the only way to beat the system is to play it to the end. I hit play, hit 16, and had £800 riding on a red ten. I drew an eight and watched spellbound as the dealer turned two picture cards. I'd beaten the law of averages. I'd lost five

n a row. I sat motionless for several seconds before
ooking at my account. It was empty. I'd been wiped out.
'd lost everything. I sat there dumbfounded, staring at
he screen, unable to move, and at that terrible moment
Simon Roche appeared in the doorway.

'I just had some reports sent over for you to check. It's
rather urgent.'

I clicked out of the casino and stared back as if he were
a stranger. I wasn't flushed. The colour had drained from
my face. I was trembling, I realised, and took a grip on
the edge of the desk to steady myself.

'Are you all right, Magdalena?' he asked. His voice
seemed far away.

'Yes, yes I am,' I said in a tiny whisper.

'If you're sick, I can get someone else on it.'

'No, I am fine, really, I . . . I . . .'

'Look, it's nearly lunchtime, you should get something
o eat and see how you are after lunch.'

'Yes, I'll do that.'

He left the room and I continued to sit there. Just like
Daddy, I had lost everything. Like Mummy, I felt
suicidal. I left my office, rode down in the lift and walked
around London unable to eat, unable to think. I wouldn't
be able to go to the London School of Economics. I
wouldn't be able to pay my rent. I'd be punished like
some fallen heroine in Greek myth and be forced to wear
the corset and garter belt like a badge of shame. That
night and every night for the rest of my life I'd be
watching the gamblers at Rebels losing their money and
I'd be offering up my bottom to solicit their meagre tips.
I thought about fleeing abroad, to Spain or Italy. I
thought about jumping in the Thames from Tower
Bridge, and I thought I'd ask Simon Roche to give me a
full-time job. I didn't need a degree. I could do the job
already. I was working on important accounts. I had
access to all the files, all the software.

I was trusted.

35

4

Spanking

The reports were waiting in my inbox. I clicked open the first file and, as I did so, an odd idea entered my mind like a refrain and grew from idle thought to inspiration. I felt like Einstein confronting $E = mc^2$ on the blackboard inside my head.

I had obeyed the rules of the system. After losing five times in a row, I had stopped. That's what you are supposed to do. The next step was to start again. I thought, if I borrowed £310 from the Roche-Marshall sundries account, I could make a little money and put it back before anyone noticed. It was just a few clicks away.

The room was cool and quiet. My hands were clammy. There was sweat between my breasts. I hung my pink jacket on the back of the chair, sat very still, very upright, completely poised. This was a bad thing I was about to do, but it was the right thing. The only thing. There were butterflies in my tummy as I entered the Roche-Marshall account. I entered the account numbers, the secret code and keyed in £310. My finger hovered over the zero and, like an echo, I pushed the zero once more.

It would take weeks playing with £10 chips to get my money back. With £3,100, I could play £100 a time, and solve my problems before I went home at five o'clock. I'd lost once, it's true, but I had won every time before that. I was sure to win again.

36

I transferred the money from Roche-Marshall straight into the online casino. I drew a picture card first time out and won £100. The butterflies grew still. It felt good to be back on the tables again. Time went into that suspended-animation thing and I played the system, taking my winnings, doubling up when I lost, relying on the law of averages.

How did it go so terribly wrong? Why? I was playing the system taught to me by Sandy Cunningham. I'd seen him win over and over again. I was born under a lucky star. I was playing my luck. Better being lucky than clever.

It was nearly five. I had lost four in a row, but with 16 chips, £1,600, on the last card I would be able to put the money back in the Roche-Marshall account and still be up a modest £100.

I drew a nine, a four, the Ace of Clubs and then an eight.

I'd bust.

The cards disappeared. The money had gone. Computers don't pause for human grief.

I stared at the screen in disbelief. My heart was thumping. I could barely breathe. The flashing lights of the casino logo faded to black and I was gazing at the revolving shapes of the screen saver as if hypnotised when the door opened and Hannah, Simon's secretary, broke the spell. She was wearing a floral suit like curtains with white shoes and for some depressing reason I remembered Mother once saying that except at summer functions it was *déclassé* to wear white shoes.

'Mr Roche would like to see you before you go home, Magdalena.'

I didn't answer. I just nodded. My throat was constricted. A pain ran down my left arm. I thought I might be having a heart attack.

Hannah turned with a little skip on her white shoes and closed the door. I sat there, unable to move. If there had been a lock on the door, I would have shot the bolt and stayed there for ever. If only the windows had opened, I could have jumped seven storeys to oblivion. I could do nothing. Nothing. I sat like a prisoner in the dock waiting for the judge to don the black cap.

He appeared in the door, tall in his dark suit like a monster in a child's nightmare.

'Come through to my office, please,' he said.

I pulled my jacket on and followed.

He waited for me, closed the door and sat in his chair behind the wide desk. There was no chair in front of the desk and I stood before him as I had stood many times before Sister Benedict.

'Do you have anything to tell me, Magdalena?' he asked.

I lowered my head. 'Yes,' I replied.

'What is it? Speak clearly, please.'

I coughed and tried to look back at him. Tears had started to form in the corners of my eyes. 'I moved £3,100 from your account.'

'That's the first bit of honesty we've had from you.'

'I'm sorry, I'm so sorry. I was playing blackjack and I thought I was going to win. I lost all my savings, and then, then I just . . .'

I ran out of words. The tears were streaming down my face. On the desk was a parcel in a large plastic bag. He drummed his fingers on the surface, the sound for some reason reminding me of the headboard in Melissa's room tapping against the dividing wall.

'Now we know what you have done, what I want to know is what we are going to do to rectify the matter?'

'I'll do anything, anything.'

'Anything?' he said.

The words were like an echo from the past. I had a sense of *déjà vu*. I had a sense that my life, my destiny, was not in my own hands.

'Yes,' I said with a little more confidence. 'Yes, anything.'

38

'Magdalena, let us be very clear what you mean. Are you offering to repay your debt with sex?'

He made it sound so sordid. I took a deep breath. 'Yes,' I replied.

'You are absolutely sure?'

'Yes.'

This is what it had come to. I had slept with Sandy Cunningham to learn the system. Now I was offering my body to Simon Roche to pay off what I had embezzled. I was a slapper, a slut, a whore, a fallen woman. I was Mary Magdalene, unchaste, the *peccatrix*, the prostitute, the fallen woman. As if with some terrible inevitablity, I had become my namesake.

Simon was quiet for a moment and made a spire with his long fingers.

'You know, at any good hotel the concierge will arrange to have a whore sent to the room. Do you know how much that will cost?' he asked.

'No.'

'About £100,' he answered. 'I can go to Kings Cross and find a girl your age, even a good deal younger, and pay half that amount. There are a lot of girls like you, Magdalena.'

Girls like me? What did he mean? He made me feel small and dirty and insignificant.

'I am so, so sorry . . .'

'Now, Magdalena, when you say *anything*, do you actually mean *anything*?' he asked.

'Yes, yes, I do. I really do.'

'You must remember when you came here for the interview, I told you that I reward those who respect my trust, and those who betray it I punish with extreme severity?'

'Yes.'

'Taking money from my company accounts makes me feel as if I have been violated. I have been humiliated. I have been made a fool of,' he said. 'Do you appreciate that?'

'Yes, Mr Roche.'

'That is what I am offering you.'

What did he mean? Violated? Humiliated? What was the alternative? He must have been reading my mind.

'The alternative is that I call the police and let them deal with the matter.'

'No, no, I'll do it. I really, really will. I'll do anything.'

'Magdalena, take off your clothes and fold them here on the desk.'

'I beg your pardon?'

'Magdalena, did you hear what I said?'

'Yes.' My voice had become a whisper.

He sat back in his chair and I stood there before him, trembling slightly. I couldn't believe this was happening. It seemed unreal, like a dream. Like a nightmare. Men really are weird, I thought. I knew by the look in men's eyes as I passed that they fancied me. I'd known that since I was about fourteen, and there is power in the knowledge that you are desired. Simon Roche didn't merely want to have sex with me. He wanted to humiliate me, break me, remove any feelings of pride or power. No longer was I the desirable girl beyond reach, I was a thief being disciplined for what I had done.

'Miss Wallace,' he said in his dark voice and I awoke from my nightmare. This was real.

My fingers nervously undid the button of my jacket. I folded it as if to be packed in a suitcase and placed it on the desk where I had been told. What next, I thought? My top or my skirt? It didn't matter but I fooled myself into thinking that in having the choice I had some control. I lowered the zip at the back of my skirt, wriggled slightly and pushed the waistband over my hips. I stepped from the skirt, folded it along the seams and put it on top of the jacket. My lacy top had a row of six buttons and my fingers were all thumbs as I fumbled my way through them. I placed the top on my suit and, standing there in my little knickers and bra, I had never felt more exposed in my life.

I must have delayed a moment too long because he snapped his fingers and I hastily stretched my arms up my back to unhook my bra. I lowered the straps from my shoulders and, with false modesty, kept my breasts hidden until the last possible moment. I placed my bra on the pile and realised to my horror that my nipples had grown erect; gorged in raging blood, they were painful and pointing at him as if in accusation or alarm.

It was as if I'd just finished a gymnastics routine, a cartwheel, a handspring, a somersault. My body was clammy. My underarms were dripping. I was panting for breath. I couldn't control it. There was no air in the room. The shades were drawn and in the diffused light the feeling I'd had the first time I had been in that office came back to me, that sense that Simon Roche had been probing my hidden desires and secrets.

Did I want to be standing there taking my clothes off for him? Was that my secret desire? I thought I knew myself but standing there half-naked I realised I didn't know myself at all. A month ago I'd been playing hockey at school and talking about boys with their dirty minds and groping fingers.

So much had happened and so fast. I had taken a job as a casino waitress where my boobs and my bum were the only assets that mattered and had done so because it was daring, because I knew deep down that Melissa, for all her talk, would never have had the courage. I had slept with an older man – *and enjoyed every moment of it.* I had stolen £3,100 from the Roche-Marshall account and lost it playing online blackjack. Even Sister Benedict wouldn't have believed it.

Was this me? Was this the real me? In just four weeks I had gone from convent school to the edge of the abyss. A sigh left me and my shoulders sagged. I looked into Simon Roche's eyes and he just furrowed his brow and flicked his finger in a downward motion.

There was no escape. No way to double my bet. No way to put the stolen money back in the account. I hadn't beaten the system. The system had beaten me. I hooked my thumbs into the thin band of elastic, eased forward to lower the ivory silk over my bottom and, as elegantly as I could, I ran my knickers down my legs and over my shoes. As I was about to place them on the pile of clothes, he held out his hand and I felt utterly disgraced and wretched as I dropped my knickers in his palm. He studied the gusset and I'm sure it was stained and smelly.

'And your shoes, if you please.'

As I removed my shoes, he took a green and gold box from the plastic bag on his desk. He gave me the bag and told me to put my shoes and clothes inside. I did so and, the moment my clothes had gone, I felt bereft, as if with my clothes my very person had been folded away inside that bag.

He opened the green and gold box and removed a pair of black high-heel shoes which he stood on the desk.

He said nothing.

I stared at the shoes and back into his eyes. My lips began to tremble. My knees were giving away beneath me.

By the way, what size shoes do you take?

A narrow six.

That day at the first interview his probing eyes had looked into me and he must have foreseen the future. He had given me access to the passwords and codes. He had led me on to the path of temptation and I was standing at the end of the path barefoot, naked as a child, my breasts throbbing with the beat of my heart. Tears swam into my eyes and my hands were shaking as I reached for the shoes.

They were gorgeous shoes, shoes a girl covets, stylish but elegant. They fitted snugly and must have cost a fortune. The leather was so soft, the supports so solid, the heels so sleek and graceful. The moment I pushed my toes

42

into those shoes, my spine curved forward in a faint bow which made my sagging shoulders straighter, my breasts poised and, as I looked back at Simon Roche across the desk, he seemed to wear a look of approval and for that I was grateful.

In those high-heel shoes I was taller, my waist stretched and flat, my bottom clenched, my breasts tingling and alive, the black triangle of my pubic hair glossy and damp. I was at my physical prime, and in that situation it was some small solace and gave me confidence; stupidly, pathetically, at the far edge of my embarrassment was a touch of conceit. These two emotions had no place together except perhaps for a girl standing naked before a man who could do anything he wanted to her.

He stood. He walked around the desk, gazed down at the shoes, then approached the long leather sofa below the window. He didn't look at my naked body. He looked into my eyes.

'Magdalena, you are going to bend over this sofa, you are going to spread your legs, and I am going to spank you.'

He paused to let the words sink in. It seemed astonishing, unbelievable. He was going to spank me? Were people allowed to do such things? I'd read Anaïs Nin. I had read about girls being spanked. But wasn't that all fantasy? Did such things really happen?

'Do I make myself clear?' he added.

'I think so.'

'Have you been spanked before?'

'Just at school . . .'

'It hurts and it is humiliating. That is the point. I am going to spank you twelve times. You must not make a single sound except to count each stroke after you receive it. You can refuse to accept the beating and get dressed. If you do so, I shall put through a call to the police and report the theft of more than £3,000 from the company account.'

43

I took a deep breath. I was trembling. My breasts were still outrageously pert, betraying me. I could do this, I thought. To save myself I could take the pain and humiliation of being spanked. I'd stripped off my clothes without a murmur of resistance. What did a dozen smacks on my backside matter?

I gave a little shrug.

'That's not all, Magdalena. That is just the beginning,' he continued. 'I told you, I can have any whore in Soho for £100. Your debt is . . .' He paused, waiting for me to answer.

'£3,100,' I said.

'If you can accept the spanking, you will have earned the right to be taught the true meaning of the word discipline.'

His words hung in the air like black clouds on a sunny day. I swallowed. The feeling of fantasy was growing inside me. What could he possibly mean? What was he going to do? I really had no idea, no idea at all. Hadn't I been taken on a *trip around the world* with Sandy Cunningham? What more was there? I bit my lip, I shrugged, and I nodded.

'OK,' I said.

'I want you to be very sure of this.'

I swallowed again. 'I don't really have a choice.'

'Did I have a choice when you stole my money?'

I lowered my eyes and shook my head.

'You make your own decisions. That's the definition of being free.'

Free, I thought. I was stark naked and about to get a thrashing. How free is that? 'What will I have to do?' I asked.

He took a long breath through his nose. 'Anything. Isn't that the word you used?' he replied. 'A whore can be purchased for £100. Your debt is?' He was rubbing it in, making sure I understood the enormity of what I had done and the enormity of what I must do.

44

'£3,100,' I said meekly.

'So, Magdalena Wallace, beginning this weekend at my house in the country, you will spend the next thirty-one days at my disposal. You will do everything that is asked of you. You will be spanked and cropped, caned and humiliated, you will be penetrated and violated, as I have been violated.'

On more than one occasion I'd had my bottom caned at school and knew how much it hurt. 'Caned?' I said.

'Painfully so, Magdalena. That bottom you keep pushing out so arrogantly will be chastised by me and by others associated with me. You will be like a concubine in a harem. You will perform any service asked of you and you will perform that service immediately and without question. If you hesitate, you will be severely punished.'

There was a shooting pain in my stomach as if someone had taken my intestines in their fist and was squeezing tighter and tighter. *A concubine in a harem . . . perform any service . . . severely punished.* How did it all come to this?

'For thirty-one days?' I asked.

'Is the punishment out of balance with the crime?' he asked in return.

'Yes, I think,' I replied.

'That is the nature of discipline. When those thirty-one days have passed, you will be the most honest – and the most disciplined – girl in the country. You will be ready for that sparkling future you imagined you had.'

I nodded my head as I thought about that. Perhaps he was right. I had never done anything dishonest before and I certainly wouldn't again. I looked up as he continued.

'You will perform this task according to my will,' he said. 'How well you perform that task will be your choice.'

If I had a choice it was no choice at all. Did I really push my bottom out so arrogantly? I remembered that night studying my breasts at the casino and feeling so pleased they looked so pretty. I had brought this on myself. The alternative was to call the police. I'd have a record. My life would be in ruins.

I was pressing my nails into my palms, clenching my bottom. My breasts were prickling. I wanted to touch them. I wanted them to be touched. It was strange standing there stark naked, but not as strange as it would have been had I not allowed Sandy Cunningham to strip off my clothes and bore into the very heart of my being. I'd been compromised, embarrassed, and it was all my own fault. I deserved to be punished and, in some shocking and shameful way, there may even have been a small anonymous part of me that wanted to be a concubine in a harem. Had I not fought tooth and nail for the part of Sally Bowles in *Cabaret*? Did I not enjoy flaunting my body on the concourse at Rebels Casino? Simon Roche must have seen something in me that I didn't know was there and that was terrifying.

The sun must have come out from behind the clouds, lighting the room in golden bars, and again I had the feeling that I was a bird in a cage. I had been flying high and was about to have my wings clipped.

'Now, girl, bend over the sofa, spread your legs and don't make a sound.'

I did as I was told, leaning right over, my ribs cushioned on the thick arm of the sofa, my breasts hanging below me, my feet slightly splayed, my legs stretched to keep balance. I took a deep breath and waited.

When the first spank hit my bottom it wasn't like being spanked by the soap star at Rebels, or spanked playfully by Sandy Cunningham while I lay naked on top of him. Simon Roche's big hand caught the plump curve of my right cheek and a stab of fire shot through my body.

'I didn't hear you?' he said.

I had been trying so hard not to make a sound I hadn't said anything at all. 'One,' I whispered.

'Louder, please.'

'One,' I said.

Before the word left me, his big right hand had swatted my left cheek in the same position. I bit my tongue and gritted my teeth.

'Two,' I said.

The third stroke bridged the crack in my bottom and joined the other two, spreading the pain across the whole lower half of my poor bottom.

'Three.'

And again, his aim picking out a fresh spot to inflame and humiliate.

I spread my legs and braced my shoulders. 'Four,' I said, and waited for number five with equanimity.

I had stolen £3,100. It was a terrible thing to do. I deserved to be disciplined. I deserved a spanking. I was lucky not to be receiving a worse punishment and felt a certain comfort from the slow tide of pain spreading down my thighs and over the small of my back. He hit me again, much harder.

'Five,' I said, my voice stronger, more confident.

The thought of being spanked was far worse than the actual beating. I needed this. I would be all the better for it. Simon Roche was a scientist resetting my DNA, a novelist reshaping my character. I couldn't imagine what had been in my mind when I transferred the money from the company account to the online casino. I had been confused. I had tricked myself into thinking that I could beat the system. I had grown too full of myself.

The next spank took me to the halfway mark. 'Six,' I said, and the pain was intense but sustainable.

I wriggled my bottom to try to take the sting out of the burning flesh, and I'm sure all that wriggling must have made the target more appealing. I was provocative and arrogant, and I was lucky to get the chance to have that arrogance spanked out of me. I had been disobedient; worse, I had been dishonest, a wayward girl, an unruly child. I deserved to be punished and wanted to be punished so that Simon Roche would appreciate me again.

He paused for a few moments and out of the corner of my eye I noticed him swinging his arm, building himself up for the second half of the beating.

When his hand came down again the pain shot through me like a fire in the forest. Every inch of my soft flesh was aflame. My body was dripping wet, steaming like a pony after a hard ride. Tears flowed involuntarily down my cheeks, snot ran out of my nose. My throat was dry, but I didn't cry out. I clenched my fists and gritted my teeth.

'Seven.'

And then came number eight, harder still, the sound reverberating around the room and ringing in my ears. I had the same odd sensation that I'd had when I was playing blackjack. That time was suspended. There was no past. The future was unknown. There was just this moment. Me bent over the arm of a leather sofa, my dear little bottom raised to meet Mr Roche's big hand as it came down again, searing into my flesh, cleansing me of my debt, of my sins. When it was over, I would be a better person.

'Eight.'

I squirmed into a new position, pushed my head lower and pushed my bottom up further. It was strange but I felt comfortable like this, my body angled, my posterior perfectly poised as if in anticipation of pleasure rather than pain. When you force yourself to forget about the pain, there is a certain pleasure in being in someone else's hands, completely submissive, you don't have to make any decisions, you only have to remember to count the next spank.

'Nine.'

I pressed my eyes shut and the sting didn't seem quite so bad. It was like diving into cold water: the moment passes. Like anal sex, being spanked, I realised, could transform mysteriously from pain to an inexplicable feeling of contentment. The only obstruction to this rare state is in the mind, in the rules and conventions programmed into us at school, at home, by society, by forces outside ourselves. If we look deeper into the dark recesses of our minds we find new treasures, new pleasures, a hunger for new experiences. When you overcome a barrier in your mind like a hurdle on the athletics track it feels as if you are flying and the emotion is lit by an aura of excitement.

I tried to picture myself bent over in that shadowy office, stark naked, vulnerable, tall in black heels, my body long and slender and glistening with perspiration, my breasts hanging heavily and tingling with new sensations. I could smell sweat under my arms, feel the damp ooze between my thighs and the blaze sweeping down my legs to my toes and up my spine to my confused and feverish mind.

Down his hand came again.

'Ten,' I said.

I was almost there, almost eager for the next one. Something unexpected and terrible was happening to me. My sex was throbbing, pushing through my thighs. A sticky moistness was gathering about the inflamed lips. I could imagine nothing more shameful. I was finding perverse pleasure in my humiliation. I was panting for breath. The pain had stretched over my back, across my shoulders and down to the fiery tips of my tingling breasts, and with the pain was a warm, cosy, comforting feeling like taking a hot bath after a cold swim.

Down it came, harder than ever, his handprint branding my flesh, a shooting star of agony and ecstasy running up my spine and into my brain.

'Eleven.'

The dampness between my legs had grown into a steady flow. I could feel a hot trickle ooze down my inner thigh. My armpits were a lake. My hair was wet. Tears

49

had dried on my face. I sniffed hard and could smell my own arousal, the scent not of suffering but of nameless shameful desire. I pushed up on the balls of my feet and the tall heels of my shoes left the ground. I arched my back and pressed down with my hands and, as the twelfth great spank crossed my skin, something inexplicable happened: I started to come.

'Twelve,' I said. 'Twelve, twelve . . .'

I was gasping for air, wriggling like a fish on the end of a line, my body going into spasm as an orgasm, much bigger and more demanding than that time with Sandy Cunningham, ripped through me and I collapsed over the arm of the sofa, my bottom red hot and throbbing with pleasurable jolts of pain.

'It's nearly six, time to go,' he said.

I was unable to move. I just lay there, quivering and spent. He took my arm and somehow I eased myself unsteadily on to my feet. I thought I saw in his eyes an odd sort of pride, but that may just have been a reflection of my own feelings, and mingled with that pride was a sense of shame far greater than the pain of my burning bottom. I'd climaxed under his hand. I didn't know such a thing was possible. It wasn't something they wrote about in *Cosmo* and *Nuts*. This was a new world, and I felt privy to a marvellous secret more valuable than the system.

5

Journey to Black Spires

He took the bag with my clothes from the desk, lifted the telephone receiver and spoke to his secretary. 'I'll be at Black Spires for the weekend. I don't want to be disturbed unless it absolutely can't wait.'

There was a pause. I was panting for breath, my bottom like a burning brazier, ears honed trying to listen.

'I'm sure I will, Hannah,' he said. 'And you too.'

I'm sure I will what? I wondered.

It was time to go and the horror of what now faced me only entered my consciousness as he opened his office door.

'If you please,' he said.

'But . . .'

'Magdalena, this isn't a game. You understand our contract. You will do everything, and anything, and you will do so without question. Now, for the last time, is that clear to you?'

My head dropped. 'Yes, Mr Roche,' I mumbled.

'Now, head up and don't mumble.'

I made my way unsteadily like a sleepwalker across the pale wooden planks of the flooring, through the open door and listened as the lock clicked shut behind me. I was stark naked on the seventh floor of the Roche-Marshall building, my bottom scarlet, my thighs coated shamefully in my own discharge, my hair in tangles, my pubes sopping. There was sweat on my back, my body was taut and shapely in the magic black heels and it occurred to me as the lift opened that in high heels you feel less naked, you are poised rather than posed, and Simon Roche had been very clever acquiring them.

As we stood in the cool air of the descending lift I remembered rising in that mirrored amber-lit box at the hotel with Sandy Cunningham. That had been a week ago. I had done it all in seven days. Actually six! I had become a whore, a gambler and a thief. At least I wasn't an alcoholic, I mused, my lips creasing with the briefest smile as the thought flickered like a candle flame in the dark heart of my imagination.

I had been given a good spanking, something Sister Benedict had always said I needed. But the chill sense of foreboding before being spanked actually turned out to be far worse than the whiplash of Simon's hands on my bare bottom. I had a vague sense of satisfaction from having endured the beating. Knowing that I wasn't going to have a criminal record was an added comfort. My punishment was going to be less official, more traditional, more in-house, and a chill ran through me as I imagined spending the next thirty-one days as Simon Roche's slave.

The doors opened on the ground floor. I hung back peeking out through the open lift as if afraid of the light. I could see people moving about the front desk manned by Amanda, who looked like a man in drag and, for some reason, always seemed to give me a dirty look when I arrived for work each morning. She was signing a slip for a tall bicycle messenger, a Rastafarian wearing yellow lycra and a black helmet with flames down the sides.

Mr Singh, the uniformed porter, was standing beside the revolving doors, stern and stately with his mature beard and dark all-seeing eyes. When he saw us he came to attention like a toy soldier.

I stepped out into the main lobby as the doors were about to close. I felt small and hopeless, totally humiliated

What could I have been thinking? I had read articles in the *London Lite* and the *Evening Standard*. Gambling was an addiction. People were running up huge credit-card debts, they were losing their homes, throwing themselves under trains. Deep down, I had known all along that there is no system, there is no secret. Of course, you may have a lucky run and win. But luck runs out and, if you keep playing, you will always lose. Always.

'Are you ready?'

I had closed my eyes, blocked out the past. Blocked out the future. The lobby was brightly lit and the sun outside the glass building was still high in the sky. It was the end of July and it would be light until ten, and for some reason being naked in the daylight made me feel more exposed, like some nocturnal creature desperate to scurry back to its hole before the dawn predators came to gobble me up.

I nodded my head.

'After you,' he said. His voice came from another dimension, dark as night.

I took a deep breath, straightened my shoulders, sucked in my butterfly tummy and led the way, my black heels tapping out a drum roll as I crossed the concourse to the door that led down to the garage.

The bike messenger had removed his Ray-Bans and openly stared, enjoying the show – a nude girl parading through the glass beehive as if for a fashion shoot. The frankness of his gaze was humiliating but at least honest. Amanda wore a tight, condescending look about her lips, and I noticed that her scorn was lit, too, by the green-eyed monster. In every girl, I'm certain, there is an exhibitionist, a desire to expose herself, and I was aware that, except for my red bottom, I must have been an enviable sight in Amanda's eyes – an untamed, satiated young animal stepping from the wilds beside Simon Roche, the king of the jungle.

53

Mr Singh touched his fingers to his turban in a salute and glanced in my direction without actually looking at me. I was a naked Lady Godiva, Mr Singh one of those good citizens who lined the streets without taking so much as a peep.

Mr Roche opened the door and I felt proud that I had made it across the lobby without fainting or having hysterics. We descended the narrow flight of concrete stairs with their decaying smell of damp and ancient dust. Even in summer, history spirals up from beneath the pavements and foundations, the ghosts of Roman centurions, Viking warlords, slaughtered princes and barren queens. How could a girl in modern times be walking naked towards her own doom? A silver Range Rover beeped as the door locks were released and I climbed into the passenger seat as if this big shiny vehicle were a sarcophagus about to bear me down to the underworld.

He tossed the bag with my clothes into the back. 'You won't be needing those,' he said. I already knew that and considered it cruel of him to say so.

He turned the ignition key and the electronic doors across the front of the garage rose, letting in the sun. The car pushed out into the City traffic and I sat squirming on the black leather seat conscious that everyone in the world could peer through the polished windows and see me sitting there naked.

'Don't squirm down in the seat, Magdalena. It looks untidy,' he said.

I did as I was told.

I sat as if I were wearing clothes, the seatbelt emphasising the shape of my breasts, making them more prominent, my face half-hidden by my hair. It was embarrassing to be sitting there like that; actually, it was shameful, but I felt protected, as if in the hands of fate. I didn't have to make any choices or decisions. My credit cards, keys and mobile phone were in the plastic bag with my clothes in the back of the car. I was like a child in some ways, totally free, free of my clothes, free of responsibility. I just had to do *anything* demanded of me. In thirty-one days I would be free and, at that moment, it seemed an eternity away.

'Sit still,' he said. 'You're wriggling about.'

'That's because it hurts,' I replied.

'That's nothing, Magdalena. That was just a little bit of . . . foreplay.'

He saw my face screw up in trepidation and patted my knee.

'You can do this, Magdalena,' he added, his voice almost kindly. 'Like all things in life, if we accept new experiences with equanimity we learn and grow from them.'

'What do you learn from having your bottom spanked?' I asked petulantly.

'What do you think?'

I wasn't sure. It would never in a million years have crossed my mind that a man one day would smack my bottom – I mean, like that, naked over a sofa. I didn't know such things went on, even though Sandy Cunningham and Jay Leonard had both in their teasing way warned me that I was ready to have my bottom tanned and that with their preparatory slaps I was being primed for a proper spanking. The three men didn't know each other and yet they seemed like members of the same club, a secret league of gentlemen spankers. But that was just too silly, too paranoid. I put it out of my mind.

What had I learned from having my bottom spanked?

'Well?' he demanded.

'Not to take things that don't belong to me.'

'Isn't that rather obvious, Magdalena?' He sounded disappointed and angrily changed lanes, cutting in front of a black cab.

It *was* obvious. I sounded like a schoolgirl standing before Sister Benedict and I was anything but that. I was a woman with sticky thighs and a burning bottom sitting naked in a motor car. Perhaps there was some deeper meaning to my being punished in this way, some cryptic piece of wisdom I needed to learn and Simon Roche was about to teach me? I had wanted to believe he was just a pervert who had tricked me into stripping off my clothes, tricked me into taking twelve strokes from his leathery hand, tricked me into this journey to the evil-sounding Black Spires.

But no one had told me to take the money from the Roche-Marshall account.

I was the master of my own destiny and it seemed logical to be moving across London in a silver Range Rover ready to accept what was coming to me. Like fledgling birds being tipped from the nest for the first time, you only learn, I realised, by letting go, by letting go of everything you have ever thought or imagined or believed in, by letting go of all preconceived ideas and perceptions and flying on the wings of your intuition.

I had taken the beating and come through it, but it's not being spanked that transforms your thinking; it's the humiliation, the disgrace, the degradation, the feeling that now a barrier has been crossed it will be so much easier for the next barrier to come down. Each new ordeal prepares you for the next until who and what you are reshapes the helixes of your DNA and you become a different person.

... *You will be spanked and cropped, caned and humiliated, you will be penetrated and violated ... You will be a concubine in a harem.* His words ran through me like fear through startled birds. That's what I had been promised. That's what I had accepted.

'Well, Magdalena?'

I'd forgotten to answer his question. 'I've learned my lesson,' I said.

'You have learned a lesson. You told me at the interview that you believe in discipline. True discipline comes from total obedience. That, my dear, is what you are going to learn.'

'But what am I going to have to do?' I blurted out.

'You know the answer to that as well as I do.'

'Everything. Anything,' I said.

'Yes, Magdalena, anything and everything.'

His dark voice had grown still darker. A chill ran up my spine. To make it worse, he turned on the air conditioning and an icy draught rose up my legs and tickled my bottom. In the dead air of the car I could still smell the fruity seepage between my legs. Heady and intoxicating, it reminded me of the stables, pony riding, wearing shiny leather boots and riding tack. It seemed as if only yesterday I was a child and now I was sitting starkers beside a man who was all but a stranger, heading for the great unknown.

The cars moved like a steel snake along Commercial Road towards the Blackwall Tunnel. We stopped at traffic lights and a man in a white van did a double take as he saw me sitting there. His mate leaned over and coughed out a mouthful of smoke. They both had shaved heads and enormous eyes like some extinct variety of prehistoric insect, their features white and mobile like soft putty, shifting into a variety of expressions – shock, lust, a terrible envy. Girls like me travel naked in silver Range Rovers with men like Simon Roche, not insects in dirty white vans.

Girls like me?

These words flashed in my mind like a neon sign lighting up above the entrance to a nightclub. What sort of girl was I? A month ago, a week ago, I would have been able to answer that question. I was just like Melissa Maybury and Sarah Van Spall, a convent girl with good A levels and the future rolling out before me like the red carpet at the Oscars.

You make one wrong turn and the way ahead becomes misty and muddled. For some reason I remembered visiting the Mesquita in Cordoba the year I was fourteen and my younger brother Rafael was twelve. Before

Daddy lost his money, before I had to expose my charms at Rebels Casino, we had gone every year to Spain. Like Mummy, it was where I most felt at home, where in the primeval air I thought I might one day discover who I really was. In Cordoba I adored the whitewashed houses, the winding cobblestone streets and, most of all, the ancient mosque built more than a thousand years ago by the Moors, great astronomers and mathematicians who had kept the light of learning burning through the long night of the Dark Ages. The vast cupola above the mosque is supported by hundreds of tall, slender columns whose shadows make an intricate maze as the sun circles the building and lights the marble floor through the high-arched windows. I became lost in the crisscrossing layers of shadow and was surprised to come across the cathedral constructed within the building: a Christian place of worship in the heart of Islam. Even the zealots at the time of the Inquisition had been too moved by the beauty of the Mesquita to destroy it, and it had occurred to me that beauty was the only treasure worth seeking.

'Are you thinking about what I said?' he asked suddenly.

'No,' I said truthfully. 'I was thinking about the Mesquita in Cordoba.'

'Ah, yes, of course, you have something of the Andaluz gypsy about you, something quite wild and reckless.'

I had always thought of myself as being more cautious than reckless. Had I changed so much, died and been reborn? Cut flowers don't know they are already dead. 'My mother is Spanish,' I said. 'If she knew I was sitting here without any clothes on she would die of shame.'

'Are you dying of shame?' he asked. 'Or are you secretly enjoying yourself?' He waited for me to reply.

'I'm not enjoying myself, no,' I said.

'But you're not hating it either, are you, Magdalena?'

My cheeks burned with embarrassment. 'No,' I muttered.

'Did you ever imagine having an orgasm merely from being spanked?'

I didn't want to answer, but that was against the rules of the game: unspoken rules, to be sure, but I knew them nonetheless.

'No,' I said.

I sensed a faint smile about his lips, and Simon Roche never smiled. As he talked about my being spanked and having an orgasm, a strange charge went through my body. I became tense and was aware that a bead of juice was welling into my labia before leaking over the black leather seat. I could smell once more the faint aroma of arousal and wondered why sitting naked in the traffic surrounded by people dressed and stressed as they hurried home was a turn-on, that perhaps deep down I didn't know 'me' at all.

'Aren't you just a little intrigued to ponder what might happen in the next thirty-one days?' he continued.

'No, I'm terrified,' I told him.

'Really? That's marvellous. A touch of fear makes things much more exciting for everyone, even you,' he remarked.

'I'm not sure how fear is going to make anything exciting,' I said.

'You're not afraid of what's going to happen to you.'

'What?' I demanded. 'Of course I am.'

He smiled again. 'No, dear girl, you are afraid of what you might learn about yourself.'

He sighed as the traffic ground to a halt. We were next to the pavement outside a furniture showroom. I could see my reflection in the shiny glass, eyes bright, breasts firm, hair every which way. I tried to focus on what he had said, but it seemed totally unreal to be sitting there nude in black high heels, totally unreal that Magdalena Maria Manzano Wallace, the girl I thought I was, could have got herself into this disgraceful position.

The traffic started moving again.

'Magdalena, if you acquit yourself well,' he said, 'we will talk again about your future.'

I gasped. 'Really?'

'I always do what I say. Always.'

I had been so preoccupied thinking about the £3,100 I'd stolen I'd almost forgotten that I had lost all my savings. I didn't have a future.

'I'll do my best,' I said. 'But I don't know what I'm going to have to do.'

'Are you sure about that?'

'Yes, honestly,' I said, but, even if I didn't know exactly, I had a pretty good idea and the word *honestly* didn't exactly apply.

'Well, you'll just have to wait and see.' He sounded like Mother. 'Discipline is the path to happiness and freedom.'

It was a lifeline. I clenched my fists and resolved to try to do everything he wanted.

I glanced out of the window. Ten minutes in slow-moving traffic and already I was used to the blank stares of car drivers and van drivers, pedestrians on the sidewalk, men in kaftans with beards, women in long skirts, their heads and faces covered except for their shiny expressive eyes. In a multicultural society, I was the fallen woman, Jezebel, Mary Magdalene. I had, as Sister Benedict was wont to say, got too full of myself.

I couldn't help feeling sorry for myself sitting there with my red bottom and yet, perversely, at the same time, I felt vibrant, alive, my fingers and toes tingling with pins and needles, my body vibrating with new sensations that zinged through my nervous system. My breasts seemed fuller, firmer. My nipples were fizzing fireworks about to explode, and it took all my willpower not to reach for them, caress them, roll the soft pink buds between my fingers as I had done so often in the shower after hockey and at night in the dorm surrounded by sleeping girls. I sat with my shoulders back, knees together, hands over my pussy, the scent of my juices hanging in the air. I was leaking still and was sure when I got out of the car there would be a puddle on the black leather seat.

Two girls my age in short skirts and off-the-shoulder tops stared into the car as we ground to a halt. They waved their hands like I was a celebrity and I couldn't stop myself smiling. My mood had lifted. I was on a roller-coaster – terrified one moment, excited the next, apprehensive of where we were going and anxious to get there.

When I saw the money belonging to Roche-Marshall disappear from the computer screen I'd felt suicidal. There appeared to be absolutely no escape. I had been ensnared by my own greed, trapped in my own labyrinth. When I got the opportunity to save myself by bending over to display my white bottom I had done so really without a second thought. I had stepped from my clothes and slipped with a sense of relief into the shoes Simon Roche removed from that green and gold box.

Those shoes were another mystery I didn't think about at the time, but now, looking down at my feet in the car's footwell, those courtly heels that made my spine arc in a bow and pulled back my shoulders so that my breasts were pushed forward seemed oddly perfidious, a Trojan horse in a game of wits.

'Why did you buy these shoes?' I asked.

'Don't you like them?'

'Yes, yes, of course, but I mean, why?'

'They fit all right?'

'Yes . . .'

'I thought you'd like them.'

'I do, but how did you . . . how did you know?'

'You know the answer to that question as well as me.'

'I don't.'

'You will,' he said with a tone of finality and I let it drop.

He had asked my shoe size before I stole the money and, if he knew I was going to rob his company before I knew myself, he was even smarter than I thought. Was I so transparent? Did he know that when temptation was put in my way I would seize it? It didn't make sense. He didn't know I worked at Rebels Casino. He didn't know I would meet Sandy Cunningham and take up a life of gambling and theft. He can't have done.

It seemed as if from the very first moment when I went for the interview at Roche-Marshall circumstances had contrived to give Simon Roche power over me, the power to do anything he wanted. I had taken off my clothes. I had given him my damp knickers to inspect. I had slipped into those beautiful black shoes, stretched naked over the arm of the sofa and allowed him to spank me. It had been painful, but pain, I realised, could mutate from base metal to gold, from agony to a strange inexplicable ecstasy.

Perhaps that was the great secret the alchemists had been seeking. It wasn't spiritual rebirth, it was corporeal. I wasn't connected to some higher spirit, but something deep and earthy. Like my ancestors who worshipped pagan gods before the Christian missionaries arrived from the Holy Lands, I belonged to the soil, to everything ripe, fecund, pubescent, and Simon Roche seemed to have unmasked my true nature.

Under Simon's hand, the tectonic plates had shifted on a fault line running through me and, as his last and hardest spank crossed my inflamed bottom, I had erupted in a vast embarrassing orgasm that sent a tidal wave of magma gushing over my thighs. It is hard to believe that such a thing is possible and I certainly wouldn't have believed it had Melissa or Sarah told me.

'Ah, about time,' he said, changing lanes again and accelerating.

The car plunged into the dark tunnel, deep into the earth, deep below the river, and as we rose into the light on the far side it felt as if on one side of the tunnel I was one person and now I was another.

The steel snake broke up into hundreds of parts, shiny as fish, as the car raced towards the M2. I enjoyed the speed and wanted to go faster. We turned off towards Faversham. It was getting on for eight, the sun high still, the sky, after the haze across London, pastel like a sheet of pale-blue silk. I knew the names of the villages; I had gone to school not far away, on the coast.

We passed oast houses and windmills, orchards laden with fruit, fields of strawberries and yellow rape seed, everything healthy and fresh and growing. He turned on to a lane that ran between mature oaks and, rounding a bend, I saw two black spires rising above the tree line. A three-storey house with many windows enlarged on my retina like a photograph in developing fluid, then vanished again as the lane dipped and ran along the side of a tall fence overgrown with ivy. Beside an arched gate there was a painted sign with the words 'Black Spires – Private'. The gates opened the moment they recognised the silver Range Rover and we crunched over a long drive arcaded by trees, the house coming into view again.

On each side of the house stood round towers supporting the spires, and below the slate roof the cream stucco walls were pierced by arched windows and decorated with a loop of fleur-de-lys in black iron that ran across the façade between the ground and first floor. Black Spires looked like a dwelling transported across the sea from Normandy, out of place on the English coastline, but when you are naked in a new place everything is strange and nothing is strange.

The car circled the drive and came to a halt at the bottom of a flight of six stone steps. An Oriental man in baggy black trousers and a collarless shirt emerged with a smile and automatically took my bag of clothes from the back of the car.

'Here we are,' Simon said.

I stepped nervously on to the drive and at that same moment two giant poodles ran down the steps from the open door, circled me and began licking my knees and nipping at my ankles. My nakedness and my ripe smell seemed to be driving them crazy; one jumped up my back, and the other would have sniffed and licked those parts of me that were more moist and intimate had I not stopped the animal with a few sharp taps across the nose. 'No, down. Down,' I said, and the beast barked and nuzzled its wet nose against my thighs. I brushed it away. The other poodle pushed me from behind, and I swatted it with a swift backhander.

I glanced at Simon, expecting to be scolded, but he just seemed vaguely amused and continued watching as the two beasts tried to ravage me. I realised in that instant that Simon Roche was something of a sadist, and I assumed that in me, being there naked fending off his lecherous dogs, there was something of the masochist.

'No. No. No,' I shouted. I hit one of the poodles really quite hard and they both ran back up the steps.

'Lee-Sun, this is Magdalena,' Simon now said as if nothing had happened and the man named Lee-Sun bowed ever so slightly.

He hurried up the steps with my bag and entered the house. We followed behind him. Simon stopped on the top step and I remained beside him, unsure what I was expected to do, as he turned to enjoy the landscape I assumed belonged to him.

Trees stretched densely in both directions. I could see a tower at the top of a low hill in the distance, and I could hear the sea pounding the shore on the far side of the house. The air had the same briny smell I knew from the convent built on the Westgate cliffs and looking out over the same stretch of coastline, so awfully close and yet it could have been on another planet, from another lifetime. A month ago I'd been wearing a tartan skirt and a straw boater. Now I wasn't wearing anything at all.

64

6

The Mystery of Nudity

The moment had arrived. I had bathed, washed my hair and anointed my skin with creams and perfume. Lee-Sun dressed me in all that I was to wear, leather straps that circled my wrists and ankles, a leather choker and a wide leather belt that sat above my protruding hipbones.

As he buckled up the bracelets and belt, he ran the tips of his fingers between my skin and the leather to make sure each item fitted snugly. It tickled, a shiver ran through me and, as I giggled, I recalled Sister Benedict once telling me that grown women laugh, only girls giggle.

I tried to control my nerves as Lee-Sun bent and attached the anklets, his round face filled with concentration. The straps and belt were ornamented with silver rings, the purpose of which I didn't know, which was probably just as well.

I stepped into those treacherous high heels and again got that sense that my body was being pulled upwards as if by an invisible thread connected to the sky, stretching my legs and spine, straightening my shoulders, placing emphasis on my breasts, which seemed to have grown fuller, more prominent since I'd had my bottom spanked, the chemical reaction from that painful pleasure maturing me into a ripened fruit like the apples turning red on the trees we'd passed on our way to Black Spires.

Lee-Sun stood back to study his work, as a painter stands back to get a fresh perspective on a portrait. There was nothing louche in his gaze, and his expression didn't change. I wanted him to say something, to compliment me, perhaps, to say good luck, as someone always does before a hockey match or a race. But he said nothing. He nodded sharply, then turned his eyes towards the closed door. I was ready.

There was a tall mirror behind me and when I turned and saw my reflection it looked like somebody else, a girl like me, but not me. It seemed so strange to be standing there naked except for the black leather straps cutting the line of my white body into segments. Lee-Sun had combed my hair and attached those straps as if I were a pony being groomed for a gymkhana. Like a pony, I had allowed him to go about his ministrations with a docility that produced in me a vague loss of identity. The girl in the mirror was me, but a new version, a new incarnation. I was no longer Magdalena Wallace, schoolgirl, casino hostess, accounts clerk. I was a marvellous object, a healthy young animal to be licked and nipped and toyed with, just as the twin poodles had come at me with their hot wet tongues ready to play.

My dark hair hung heavily about my shoulders. I had run a razor under my arms and down my legs. My pubes, a shade darker than my hair, were curly and perfumed, an untidy nest Lee-Sun had trimmed patiently with a tiny pair of scissors. The leather belt gave my slender waist added definition and my breasts had never looked perkier. A month ago at school I still had puppy fat and puffy cheeks. It is astonishing how a few weeks skipping meals and working nights can make such a difference: my shape, the delicate shadows below my cheekbones, and most of all the look in my dark eyes, a look that was both anxious and determined, apprehensive, even a little excited.

'If you please,' Lee-Sun said.

66

I turned away from the mirror. I was hanging back like an actress afraid to go out and play her part on stage. I had no idea of the time, but through the window from the third floor the sky was ribboned in orange, the day fading to night, the sea clawing at the beach. I had travelled twenty miles up the coast and gone in three weeks from being a schoolgirl in a convent to a concubine in a harem. Sister Benedict had predicted that something unconscionable was going to happen to me but she would never in a month of fasting and prayer have divined the speed and depth of my fall from grace. It was biblical.

There was a single star in the sky. That's me, I thought, alone in the vast dark universe. Why did Daddy go and lose all his money? Why did I take the job in the casino? To show off because Melissa would never have done so, because Melissa didn't have the figure or the *je ne sais quoi* to dress in that little basque and fishnets.

I had been carried along by a sense of daring and adventure. I suppose I liked being on show, and the fetish clothes I changed into each night I thought of as a costume you would wear on stage. I was flaunting my breasts and my bottom to best effect, but that was just to earn the tips that would help pay my way through uni. The real me was the girl who had won the maths prize at school and went to work each day as an intern at Roche-Marshall. I had been balancing on the high wire. I was Icarus with wings of wax, naked in leather straps and ready to fly again.

I turned away from the window.

'It is time,' said Lee-Sun.

'Will I be all right?' I asked, knowing I shouldn't.

He nodded his head very slowly as if considering my silly question. His expression remained impenetrable.

'Yes,' he then said.

I looked into his eyes and he bowed from the waist. I crossed the boudoir to the door. I turned the handle, closed my eyes, took a deep breath and stepped out into the third-floor corridor.

I could hear voices rising up from below, men talking, laughing, the sound of music, Bach, I thought. I made my way down the stairs, tummy jangling with nerves, back straight, cautious in the high-heel shoes. I turned into a small hallway with dark-wood walls and a table with flowers standing on an Oriental rug. The arched windows were polished by the last rays of the sun and I could just make out my shadow as I paused at the bottom of the stairs.

The voices had grown louder. I had reached the halfway stage. I was an adventurer crossing the desert. There was still the opportunity to turn back, though not in my case, not unless I wanted Simon Roche to return my clothes and call the cops.

The next step would take me beyond safety, beyond sight of the known into the unknown and unexplored. One more step and I would be in the hands of providence. I gave a little cough. My throat was dry. I could barely breathe. The smell of anxious perspiration wafted up from under my freshly shaved arms, and there was a certain dampness in the crack of my bottom I was tempted to wipe away but didn't.

I took a good grip on the pineapple carving at the top of the second flight of stairs and ran the palm of my hand down the polished banister, drawn by the siren call of voices. Step by step I approached a large baronial hall where the drapes had been closed and flickering candles gave the scene an ambience that was dreamlike, decadent but not uninviting. There was a high vaulted ceiling supported by broad columns decorated with sculptures of nymphs. The dim light, the high ceiling, the columns and those celestial creatures gave me the feeling that I was entering an ancient temple.

There were perhaps fifteen or twenty people, mostly men, mostly wearing dinner suits and bow ties. I saw three girls dressed identically to me in nothing but leather straps and realising that I wasn't alone gave me some hope that I would survive this terrifying ordeal. I had allowed Sandy Cunningham to remove my clothes. I had stripped before Simon Roche in his office. But I had never been naked in a room full of strangers and, entering among those suited men, I felt like a human sacrifice prepared for some primitive ritual, one of those nymphs from the supporting columns, only made from flesh and blood.

The voices stilled as I crossed the threshold and the moment of silence made me feel more vulnerable, more exposed. The men assessed my body like farmers considering dogs and horses, their eyes running over my breasts, my nipped-in waist and long legs, the directness of their appraisal reminding me of the bicycle messenger polishing his Ray-Bans as he watched me cross the glass lobby at Roche-Marshall. Could it only have been a few hours ago? It felt like an eternity, as if time had become formless and I was a space traveller moving at light speed between different dimensions, from the known world to all that is perilous and alien.

I came to a halt just inside the doorway. I took a breath and tried to look nonchalant as I gazed about the room. Two of the girls were in the far corner beside a tall man wearing a loosely knotted tie and a belt with a big turquoise buckle. The girls turned with blank expressions and I wondered if like me they were concealing their fear behind a cloak of cool detachment. The third girl was sitting on a long, low sofa peeling back the lips of her vagina to reveal the metal stud buried in the pink flesh.

Simon Roche was standing behind the sofa talking to a dark-haired man of about thirty, perhaps a little more, with broad shoulders and an intense expression. Simon nodded in my direction and the man immediately made his way towards me.

This was it. This was what I had been prepared for, and I was glad he wasn't old, and glad he wasn't English, or least he didn't appear to be. He studied me for several moments, my breasts, my lips, my eyes. He didn't speak, but in his expression I sensed approval, although that could just have been me projecting my need for approval. The man took my hand and led me out of the main hall through one of the two sets of double doors on our right into another room with recessed windows such as you might find in a restaurant or hotel.

The room was dimly lit but I could clearly see a girl dressed like me suspended by the rings in her bracelets from hooks on one of the columns that supported the arch over the windows. The girl's toes barely touched the ground, and a man who had loosened his bow tie was holding the cheeks of her bottom and driving his tongue between her legs. The lapping sound, like a dog at its water bowl, was loud in the confined space of the window nook, and the pungent perfume of lust was hypnotic like the whiff of marijuana.

When the girl had reached the level of moistness the man desired, he released her from the hooks and, without a word passing between them, she stretched out on the wide banquette before the windows. The man removed his clothes without so much as a glance in our direction and proceeded to feed his erection into her wet bottom.

I remained rooted to the spot. The man with me supported my elbow. I covered my mouth with my palm and watched the naked girl rolling her hips, drawing the man deeper inside her, and I felt ashamed being there, a voyeur at what in that first moment I considered a squalid, distasteful affair, a scene from some late-night film on cable television.

I imagined the girl was reluctant to be there in that window nook, that like me she had been forced to perform this service. I wanted to turn away but my feet were glued to the floor, my gaze following the line of the girl's back, the slow cadenced motion of her bottom. I could hear the even beat of her breath, and slowly, like

70

the sun coming up over the sea, it dawned on me that, on the contrary, the girl was not unhappy to be there, that this was an exchange, a contract, perhaps, as with Simon Roche I had a contract to be here, erasing my debt as well as my wicked crime.

As this realisation passed through me, I removed the hand covering my mouth with a hint of embarrassment that I had made such an immature schoolgirl response, that my reaction had been so typical, so clichéd. I took a deep breath and, as I watched the girl on the banquette through fresh eyes, without preconceived notions of right and wrong, good and bad, in the light of the special world that existed within the walls of Black Spires, I began to find a certain beauty in her movements, an aesthetic quality that provoked in me a sense of calm anticipation. The fiery tips of my breasts were prickling and I watched now with a feeling of wonder and unexpected exhilaration.

The girl, as if aware of the tableau vivant they were creating, manoeuvred herself into a shape that was strangely, artistically pleasing, pushing down on her spread palms, her slim arms straight, her back curved in a taut bow, her bottom rounded into a perfect circle like a target broken by the arrow of the man on his knees behind her. There was something animal and yet completely natural about this pose, the girl surrendering her body in a way that would bring her partner ultimate pleasure and, in doing so, pleasuring herself.

It occurred to me for the first time that sex in this way, with strangers, was more sensual, more fervent, more passionate. Sex for schoolgirls is just clumsy groping, a finger in your pussy, a little wet cock that flies briefly and flops like a shot bird. In the long hall behind me there were men, not boys – men, I assumed, who knew exactly what they wanted, what they expected, and the girls, brought there for whatever reason, determined to fulfil those expectations and, in so doing, fulfil their own.

It was strangely empowering as it dawned on me why the men were dressed and the girls were naked. There is something logical about it. Nudity *is* erotic and eroticism, it seemed to me, can reach the very core of our being and take us into that sacred place where you find your true self, the place that school, the church and society conspire to conceal. When you are naked, all barriers are down. There is no pretence. You are just you. A girl is a sexual being. We dress and act out our sexual role at all times, subliminally and yet intuitively.

For a girl, being naked is just a continuation of what's normal, at what's hinted at in the clothes we wear - skinny tops, short skirts, each item carefully chosen to expose sections of our body like slices of ripe fruit. Our clothes are less for protection than for insinuating all that lies beneath. Clothes are not worn to hide our nudity, they are worn to emphasise it and, artfully attired, a girl can appear more than naked.

Every time you pump up your breasts and go out with an inch of lace framing your cleavage you are inviting every man in the street to gaze with longing and desire at your breasts, to imagine the touch of your skin, the moistness of your pink secluded parts. You tell yourself that you are dressing for you, but you're not. You're dressing to be ogled at and lusted after. You dress for men, so being undressed for men was consistent with what you are, what I was at that moment watching: that awe-inspiring girl with her perfect bottom spread for a man I'm sure she didn't know, his cock a lance buried brutally in her pretty bum.

It was a marvellous and unnerving revelation. So many things that had always been unclear and ambiguous suddenly made sense. The girls at school were constantly unbuttoning their blouses and the nuns never seemed to tire of telling them to button themselves up. The girls were desperate to have their cleavage on show and made up for it on Saturday afternoons when we were allowed to go into town. We wore cardigans over our T-shirts and took them off to show our breasts to the sun the moment we left the school gate.

The town girls all looked like little prostitutes with their cheap clothes and kohl-blacked eyes; they had angry expressions and I always wondered what they were so angry about and assumed it was because the town boys deserted them to pursue the convent girls like hungry jackals the moment we threw off our cardies and snaked our way into town.

We were playing the game of sex, the oldest game in the world, the one invented by Eve in the Garden of Eden. We wanted to go to the best universities and become high flyers in the City or read the evening news on the BBC. But what we wanted most of all was to be admired as gorgeous sexual beings.

My heart had been pounding since I'd left Lee-Sun in the room at the top of the house. Suddenly it was still. I continued to be afraid, but the iron fist gripping my tangled entrails had loosened its grip. It was velvet now. I knew that anything and everything that can be done to a girl was to be done to me, but the sense of shame and humiliation lessened as it occurred to me that the prime reason why we do not give in to our natural instincts is because it makes a mockery of the rules and hypocrisy of so-called decent society: blessing the planes before dropping the bombs, the politician leaving office for untold fortunes in foreign places, moving the pederast priest from one parish so he can sin again in another.

I didn't follow all that. I didn't care about all that. I felt free of all that. There was just this moment. I had always wanted to fly, to be bold and daring; that's why I had felt instantly at ease wearing that defiant little costume at Rebels Casino. Progressing from the corset and shiny black knickers to nudity hadn't turned out to be such a big step after all.

The hand that had been holding my arm moved to m
backside. I was startled at first, but controlled myself a
my companion fondled me as you would a prized anima
a unicorn, perhaps, his caress following the curve of m
bottom, his long fingers moving slowly, continuously, th
movement hypnotic and lending the scene in the windo
nook before us the serene formality of a painting by or
of the old masters.

The man on the banquette eased himself out of th
girl and she remained on her hands and knees, he
breasts full like tolling bells beneath her, waiting for th
next instruction. The man sat back on the cushion
pulled at her leg, and, as she turned, I saw her clearl
for the first time. She had the most striking face I ha
ever seen, small neat features, dark-green eyes tha
seemed to gleam with an inner light, pink petal lips an
a thick swatch of dark-red hair that tumbled like fi
about her white shoulders.

In the crepuscular light with the leaded glass behin
them, she took the man's erection into her mouth. He
movements were slow and steady as she eased her lip
down over the trunk of his quivering penis, pausing an
coming back up again, slowly at first, then faster like
machine gathering speed, on and on, thighs tremblin
her bottom pulsating, the cheeks like bellows opening an
closing. I understood spontaneously and intuitively wh
men were obsessed with girl's bottoms, why they wante
to kiss them, beat them, nurture them with creams an
beat them again.

Sandy Cunningham had spanked my bottom. Ja
Leonard had spanked my bottom. Simon Roche ha
spanked my bottom. Strangers without number at Rebe
Casino had spanked my bottom. The moment a girl i
exposed and defenceless, men want to bring their bi
hand down on her bottom. They want to insert them
selves in her bottom. They are fixated on bottoms. Gir
think about their breasts and men think about thei

74

ottoms. It was useful to have this knowledge, although
hat I was going to do with it I didn't know.

I carried on watching the girl, her lips pulled back over
er gums as she took the length of the man's cock deep
nto the soft pink heart of her mouth. I remembered
andy Cunningham introducing me to his strong Austra-
an erection, how my instictive aversion to fellatio
nstantly transformed with my greed to learn the system,
ow the pain and humiliation of being buggered for the
rst time lifted so quickly and I started to roll my hips,
ush my toes into the bed and rock my bottom urgently
p and down the shaft of his steely penis. The spread
heeks of my bottom were greased with the discharge
ooding from my pussy. I had bitten into the bed cover,
ushed up on to my knees, and it had felt as if I were
eing carried along on a wave of intoxicating pleasure.

Sandy Cunningham had discovered the secret me
aiting to be found. He must have known that I was
eady to leave childish pleasures behind me and enter this
trange land where being unclothed seemed natural and
he private exertions of sex in all its stripes and colours
as an open and public event. Not for the first time I felt
hankful for that night in the hotel in Kensington.
Vithout it I would not have had the confidence to be
tanding in the twilit room, harnessed in black leather
ondage straps, a stranger stroking my naked bottom.

The girl was massaging the man's balls, squeezing
hem gently, pausing for breath, her tongue flicking
bout the head of his penis before taking it again into
he depths of her throat, up and down, on and on, the
ulse of her breath rapid but even, the lapping sound of
er wet lips reminding me of Simon's poodles, the slap
f her breasts like the hands of a child clapping from
heer joy. Just ten minutes earlier, with my mechanical,
reset notions, the scene before me had appeared base
nd vaguely squalid. Now it seemed normal, natural,
un.

The man groaned. His body stiffened. His face clenched in spasm. He pulled the girl away, clutching the back of her hair, and with his free hand he aimed his semen over her face, across her forehead, into her eyes, over her nose, the goo slipping over her cheeks and back into her mouth. A trickle of sperm ran down her chin and with a fingertip she delicately drew the stuff back between her lips. I had never seen two people having sex before. had never seen a girl sucking off a man, and the way he unloaded his essence over her face seemed shocking, fascinating and completely mesmerising.

How quickly the perverse appears pleasurable, the immoral innocent, the vulgar aesthetically pleasing. In just a few minutes an encyclopaedia of new thoughts had flooded my mind. Things I knew nothing about seemed suddenly clear.

The girl with the flaming hair was beautiful, the girls in the grand hall were beautiful, and it seemed to me that beauty has to be punished. Sister Benedict never exactly said as much, but at school the plain and plump girls were prefects and house captains, while the pretty girls cleaned the blackboards, we carried the litter to the boiler room and we were castigated for breaking even the most petty rules. Beauty is desired and beauty has to be profaned, sullied and sacrificed.

The man at my side had not asked my name. I had not been introduced to him. Like the girl with green eyes and the girls in the hall, I was not a person, I was an object there at Black Spires to perform a service, and knowing that made it easier not harder to accept. With acceptance the fear lifts and other emotions filter into your consciousness.

Now the performance was over, the man looked spent, his face drawn, his eyes listless after the *petit mort* of his orgasm. But the girl with sperm drying on her face looked refreshed, more alive, a goddess dressed in her nudity. She took the man's limp cock into her palm and gave it a lick. It quivered briefly again with new life and she lowered her mouth over its length and sucked it clean.

The girl had been bending over and now stretched her back, swung her legs round and placed her feet on the floor. The man fluttered his fingers, dismissing her as you would dismiss a concubine in a harem, and I recalled Simon Roche's words.

The girl stepped into her black high heels and strode, spine straight and with utter elegance, out of the room. We followed, the intense man with his hand about my waist, his fingers tucked into the leather belt. As the red-haired girl exited into the hallway, we made our way towards the corner of the living room where several men were watching the two girls I had seen earlier with the tall man with the turquoise belt. The girls were stretched out on a long wooden table, head to toe like the sign of Pisces, their tongues like keys each picking at the other's lock, their heads bobbing up and down as they sucked the juices from their partner.

The girl on top had dark hair pulled back in a band and all I could see of her from my position close to the head of the table was her long narrow back, her head bent at an angle, her crown rising and falling above a statuesque blonde with corkscrews of bubbly hair and a thin unblemished body. The blonde girl's pussy had been shaved, giving her a childlike look, innocent and debauched like a figure in the background of a painting by Breughel. The puffy lips of her vulva were pulled back to allow her companion's tongue to worm its way around the swollen nub of her clitoris. Both girls were moaning, groaning, humming, the onomatopoeia of their song magnified in the quiet room where the sound of Bach seemed far away as if in another building.

The girls were immediately below a chandelier that illuminated their ivory flesh and made the men in their black suits seem like spectres drawn to the feast. The blonde girl moved faster and faster, her bottom rising and falling with a little slap back upon the table. She drew back her legs and arched her spine in a contortionist display of muscle control and rocked her shaved mound up and down in orgasm, her song losing its tune and growing in pitch.

The tall man with the jewelled belt appeared to be the conductor of this dissonant duo and, while the girl on top was still reaching for her climax, he brought his hand down on her backside, beating the plump round mounds over and over again, the white flesh turning pink. The blonde on the bottom returned her tongue to her friend's gaping vagina until the dark-haired girl achieved what she was so urgently seeking and let go with a piercing scream, her vast roaring orgasm creating a cacophony of broken music.

'Just look at that, they can't get enough,' said the tall man with what I thought was probably a Texan accent. He pulled the little blonde by her ankles, separating the girls, and lifted her legs in such a way that she was hooked on to his shoulders. He lapped at her oily orgasm, his meaty tongue reaching deep inside her gaping parts, the juices flooding from her, coating the Texan's chin and spreading over her soft thighs.

Another man slipped his cock from his trousers and buried its length in the mouth of the dark-haired girl. She went up on her hands and knees, making the same tableau as the flame-haired girl when she was being anally pierced in the other room, an arrangement that arches the back, pulls in your tummy, shows the weight and shape of your breasts, a position that changes the definition of what it is to be merely human and shows a potential for being fully physical, part human, part animal.

I was spellbound watching this intricate scene, the dinner-suited men in bow ties, the naked girls with black straps about their ankles and wrists, the chandelier above painting fields of light and shadow on their delicate curves, their long limbs and fine bones, the depth of their poise, their composure, their ability to be living in the moment as only pure creatures in nature ever really do.

Those two girls, the one on her hands and knees, the other with her back on the table, her pussy locked into the mouth of the Texan, were denied all rights, any sense of self-determination, but this, I thought, is what being truly erotic is. Choice removes the potential to reach beyond yourself, to seek and find that certain indescribable something that poets and drug addicts try to reach and try to explain and never can. The scene was charged with vibrancy and drama. Anything could have happened. Like Caligula ripping into the stomach of his wife and dragging out his own unborn child with his teeth, the Texan might at any moment have stopped lapping at the blonde and eaten her. The man at the other end of the table could so easily have throttled the dark-haired girl and ejaculated into her dead mouth.

This didn't happen, but the fact that the mental image ran through my mind was at once both horrifying and electrifying. It was a relief to know that deep in the dark, untamed parts of myself I possessed such an imagination. In the past I had glimpsed briefly – in distant villages across the Iberian peninsula, with the sound of flamenco echoing over the sea and the smell of olive trees and baked stone permeating the air – the spectre of my twin self, my avatar, but I had always been too young to understand my strange desire to swim naked at night beneath the canopy of stars, to run naked through the hills, and had suppressed these pagan inclinations.

I was suddenly aware that there is only this second, that life is fraught and fragile and often pointless, that to be truly alive is to consent to life *in extremis*, to consent to life to the point of death. I had been in danger when I left school of going to university, getting a degree in economics and making my way like a drone among drones, of existing in the world like a wave lost among other waves. Instead I was standing naked in a room full of dark-suited men, a man clutching the leather belt about me, that belt and those bracelets highlighting my nakedness. I wasn't free, I was in bonds, and those bonds were liberating.

Some of the men gathered about the table had stopped watching the girls and I became aware that they were watching me, watching my reaction. Was I appalled or stimulated? They would have had no way of knowing. I was lost in my own thoughts. The past seemed to be vanishing like the ice caps, the future was uncertain, nonexistent. I felt like a fully formed foetus floating in the amniotic soup waiting to be born, to be reborn, and, as that image nursed me in its fleeting embrace, the past and the future came flooding towards me in a great icy cold wave that almost knocked me off my feet.

Sandy Cunningham was standing on the other side of the table.

7

Betrayal

He was standing at the back of the crowd of men watching the two girls, his saucy blue eyes bright as chips of sky, a smile on his rugged features. He nodded at the man still clinging to my belt and my companion led me away from the table towards him.

'Hello, Sergio, how are you?' he asked.

'Ah, so you are here,' the man with me answered.

'Where else am I going to be?'

Sergio nodded in acknowledgement of the obvious and the two men shook hands before edging away from the crowd. My throat had gone dry. My knees were shaky. I was in shock. I mean, what was Sandy Cunningham doing here?

The two men spoke for a few minutes, business, numbers, stock-market prices, a world that was familiar to me yet alien in this vaulted temple with the plaster nymphs on the columns supporting the roof, the flesh nymphs performing in the candlelight, a complex symmetry.

For the first time since descending the stairs from the third floor I felt the full impact of what it means to be undressed, naked in a room full of men in suits. Even Sandy looked smart in his dinner jacket, his bow tie neatly arrayed in two sensuous wings, the elegance of his black attire in counterpoint to my white unclothed body, the contrast magnifying the sense of my nakedness, intensifying the erotic tension – and that, I recognised, was the purpose of the *mise-en-scène*, each minute detail arranged as if by a film director to create an air of sublime decadence and pleasure.

I had a feeling that the level of pleasure and decadence had yet to rise, that all that I had witnessed until now was merely a dress rehearsal for the atavistic orgy that would surely take place and would surely sweep me along to places I wasn't sure I wanted to go – and yet, deep down, deep in the primitive depths of my being, it was the place where my intuition seemed to be telling me I truly belonged. I could only assume I had been named Magdalena for some good reason.

One imagines such scenes taking place in brothels in Asia and South America, in Washington, in the Mayfair homes of Russian oligarchs. But to be here on the Kent coast, in the Garden of England, to be a part of it, suddenly felt unreal and extraordinary. I had been justifying my presence in the pragmatic terms of the mathematician, that clearing my debt of £3,100, as well as avoiding the risk of a criminal record, wasn't merely practical, it was wise and essential. But seeing Sandy Cunningham at Black Spires shook the frail house of cards I had erected in my subconscious. There was a part of me that took pleasure in being naked in that room among the plaster nymphs, ready even for what might transpire. But on another level I was a schoolgirl still, an inexperienced teenager who belonged back along the coast at the convent I had left a short time ago, a silly girl playing at being a grown-up in a world where I didn't belong, even if my toned, mature body clearly revealed quite a different story.

Do I sound confused?

I was. I had never been so confused in my life. It seemed as if I had been offered an impossible choice at Rebels Casino: offer up *anything* in exchange for knowledge of the system, a multi-entry visa to the world of independence and freedom. Now my choice was to play my namesake, Mary Magdalene, the harlot, the sinner, or get turned in to the cops. The choice was no choice at all. Was that life in the real world? Is all choice a question of compromise?

I had been holding at the same time two finely calibrated and opposing opinions. On one side I believed that the activities at Black Spires were just fun, daring, a secret and unique experience. But across the scale, I regarded it all as shameful and humiliating, an amusement perfectly normal for some, I'm sure, but one hardly pursued by girls like me. There was that phrase again. What kind of girl am I? What kind of a girl was I to become? Parents, school, life. Nothing prepares you for all these opposing choices.

Standing there urbanely in his dinner suit in that room of strangers, Sandy had shifted the finely weighted balance. My confidence had gone and a million doubts and fears held me in their terrible grip. The man I now knew as Sergio left and made his way across the room to Lee-Sun, who was pouring flutes of champagne.

The girl whom I had seen earlier showing off the stud in her vagina was being hoisted up on a wire connected to the two rings at the back of her belt. She spread her arms like the wings of a bird and I watched as she swung like a pendulum to and fro, an older man with snowy white hair pushing her gently as if playing with his grandchild in the park.

The two girls on the table had come to the end of their double act, and another girl I hadn't seen before, a tall, striking black girl with hennaed hair and silver bracelets around her ankles, strode barefoot through the crowd like a Maasai across the Serengeti, the silver bracelets tinkling like tiny bells as she went.

Everything that had started to seem normal to me suddenly felt weird, as if two worlds had collided, and, even if I bridged those two worlds, I couldn't understand how Sandy Cunningham belonged in them both as well.

Sergio had collected a tray with three glasses of champagne and paused to watch the activity around the girl suspended from the ceiling. The swinging had stopped. Another man had appeared with a small metal box from which he took a pinch of white powder that he sprinkled over the pink inner walls of the girl's vagina. The older man with snowy hair sniffed and licked and sucked off the powder before setting the pendulum back in motion, the girl flying back and forth like a mechanical bird.

I looked back at Sandy.

'What are you doing here?' I said.

His leathery features opened in a broad grin. 'I could ask you the same question,' he replied.

I shook my head. I'm not sure why, but I hadn't been quite so discomfited being naked among strangers, but with Sandy it was different. I felt a blush move over my neck and cheeks.

'But how do you know Simon?' I muttered

'Simon's an old mate of mine.'

'But . . .'

He smiled again and I noticed how white his teeth were. 'I'm not sure if I should let you in on the secret,' he said.

He was teasing me. He knew what I was thinking, and he knew I knew. I had been absolutely certain there was no link between me stealing the money from Simon's company and my lesson in learning how to beat the system from Sandy.

There was a link. There had to be.

'He knew I worked at Rebels?' I asked softly, my shoulders sagging.

'Course he did. He had you figured out right from the start.'

'What's that supposed to mean?'

'Well, from what I hear, you turn up to an interview at an accountancy office wearing a sexy little skirt and your tits hanging out.'

'That's not true,' I said.

But it was true. That's what Melissa had advised me to do, flaunt myself, and I didn't need to be told twice.

Was I so obvious?

That's what Sister Benedict was always saying, and I was growing tired of her creeping into my mind, now, of all times. She was like an avenging angel, like the ghost of conscience past. We are taught in schools like mine that we can have it all, be it all, that we can go anywhere, do anything. But it's not true. There's a glass ceiling an inch above girls' heads. If we try to rise up through the ceiling, we come crashing back down again, and it occurred to me that perhaps it's best not to try to break the glass, but to follow our instincts and find a way like Alice to pass through the glass. That's where I had gone so dreadfully wrong.

'I didn't tell Simon I worked at the casino, though,' I now said.

'So, he checked you out. That's how business works,' Sandy enlightened me, knitting the fingers of his hands together. 'Knowledge is power.'

I shook my head. It still didn't make sense.

'He probably got that Indian fella to follow you.'

'Mr Singh?'

'Yeah, that's the one. There's a lot more to Mr Singh than meets the eye,' he remarked. 'But then, that's true of all of us.'

He gazed down at my pert nipples. They were throbbing and erect like two missiles pointing at him. I had a terrible temptation to touch myself, an anxiety to be touched, and had to fight the impulse.

'So,' Sandy continued, 'once Simon knew you were parading around in a casino with hardly a stitch on, he gave me a call.'

'So it wasn't just chance that I met you?' I said.

'Almost nothing is chance, and nothing that succeeds is left to chance,' he said philosophically, and I stood there, naked except for the straps about my neck, ankles and wrists, trying to work out what he meant. A smile puckered the corners of his lips. 'I like a flutter and I like the fillies,' he added. 'All in all, it worked out all right.'

'All right for you,' I said hopelessly.

'And you, as well.'

'That's not true.'

'Isn't it?' he said. He glanced about the long baronial hall. 'Did you ever imagine you'd come to a place like this?'

'No,' I replied. 'Not without any clothes on.'

'You'll get used to it,' he said coldly, and I felt even more confused.

The thing is, I didn't object to being unclothed, not really. When Sandy had taught me his so-called system I had sat happily naked on the hotel bed, my pussy leaking discharge into my pubic hair, the warm animal smell rising to my nostrils and making me feel quite giddy. I'd just been done anally for the first time and I wasn't feeling ashamed or horrified. I was buzzing, glowing, vibrant. My *karma* had been reset. I had become in that instant a different person.

My eyes dropped and I looked down at myself. My breasts were full to bursting, pushing out with primal eagerness. My ribcage was well defined like a suit of armour, my tummy concave between my extruding hip-bones, the butterflies flapping their wings again. I was looking better than I had ever looked before, like the models posing on the pages of *Nuts*, like the pierced and tattooed girls on the porn sites we had bookmarked on the computer at school, Bangbus and Far East Media, astonishing scenes of girls climbing into vans with strangers, stripping off for a few dollars and offering up

86

their pussies to the camera. Oral sex, anal sex – it seemed like the girls wandering the streets of America would do anything to be on camera.

Even more enthralling was watching the girls lining up at Far East Media to have their bottoms spanked by callused hands, with hairbrushes and leather belts. I watched those scenes and must admit I was curious to know how it felt to be spanked and never imagined I was so soon to find out.

Visiting those websites was an obsession throughout the sixth form and continued to be so even after the nuns discovered the history function on Vista and made the offence of entering those sites punishable by death – or, worse, being sent down. The girls of the upper sixth had become addicted to internet porn and paraded naked in the dorm after lights out, walking on the balls of their feet, pulling in their waists, pushing out their breasts. Girls adore their own breasts. We want them to be seen and admired.

We were sheathed by day in calf-length tartan skirts, blouses with high collars buttoned to the throat, wool blazers with a badge showing Saint Sebastian pinned through with Roman arrows. At night, with the milky glow of the moon slipping through the leaded windows, we shed these uniforms, tossed off our long nightdresses and enjoyed our primordial nudity – me more than most, I'm sure, the cold Kent air making the invisible hairs on my arms and legs bristle. My pubic hair fleecy and damp with arousal, I'd crawl under someone's sheets and in the pale-green light of an Apple Mac defy the rules and watch scenes from Bangbus and Far East Media depicting girls in acts of fellatio and cunnilingus.

Once entering these sites was prohibited, girls who had never logged on to them before began to do so. It is the human predicament. We are drawn to the illegal, the illicit, the hidden, the unknown. After seven years behind the walls of a convent, girls want to shake off their old identity and reinvent themselves. We want to take off our dull sexless uniforms and run into the future, preferably naked.

Sandy Cunningham must have read my mind because, as I looked up, he took a grip on my belt with one hand and, with the other, slipped a finger between my legs, ran it in a sawing motion through the lips of my vagina, and held his hand up like a piece of incriminating evidence, his finger slicked with juice and shiny in the shadowy light.

My mouth fell open. I was so embarrassed and watched speechless as he rubbed the gummy excretion between his thumb and finger before tasting my essence on his tongue.

'You're ripe and ready, girl,' he said. 'Simon knew that the moment he laid eyes on you.'

I was mortified. I had allowed this man to take me in all my openings, but the way he was treating me at that moment was insensitive and humiliating. I had assumed as I watched the other girls that I was ready to go through with whatever was demanded of me. Now, I was beginning to wonder. So far I had merely been a voyeur. I still didn't know if I could actually perform erotic acts with strangers watched by other strangers. I felt bitter, used, at a loss.

'Yes, but your system doesn't work,' I said with irritation.

He just smiled. 'It's all down to the law of averages. It's bloody hard to lose five times in a row. I win all the time.'

'I didn't . . .'

'I'll tell you why, Magdalena. If you try too hard, if you want to win too much, the law of averages will be out to get you.'

'That's not true . . .'

'What you put out into the universe comes back tenfold. If you're greedy, you get nothing. If you're grateful, if you're submissive to the law, it makes sure you come out all right.'

I shook my head. 'That's just silly,' I said. 'You set me up.'

'You set yourself up.'

'Oh, no, I didn't.'

'Oh, yes, you did.'

He was grinning. I burned pink with shame. I was standing there naked, breasts full as two ripe melons, pubic hair smelling of my own seepage, and talking like a child.

He hooked his fingers over my belt and pulled me close again. 'You must cultivate what I call an attitude of gratitude,' he said. 'You had a chance to make a name for yourself working for Roche-Marshall. That wasn't enough for you. You wanted more. You didn't want to learn the system, you wanted to beat the system. If you train yourself to take what comes and accept it with gratitude, it'll all work out.'

'I only wanted to pay my own way through university,' I said.

'You do that, Magdalena, by working your way, by being yourself,' he said. 'I play the system and win because I can afford to lose. I'm grateful when I do win. I don't complain when I lose. I don't complain and I don't go dipping my hands into other people's wallets.'

The red flame of my embarrassment burned even brighter. Not only did Sandy Cunningham know Simon Roche, he already knew what had led me to be standing there in Black Spires in the altogether. I went to speak, but at that moment Sergio reappeared with the tray and I unconsciously took one of the flutes of champagne. The men did the same and joined the rims of their glasses. Sandy looked at me.

'To you,' he said.

'I didn't know you drank,' I responded, remembering all those glasses of cola I had delivered to him at the casino.

'Here's a word of advice,' he responded. 'Champagne is one of life's small pleasures. Never say no to champagne, and never say no to life's pleasures, small or big.'

He clinked my glass with his. It sounded like a bell ringing at the entrance to a lift and I went into robot mode. I raised the champagne to my lips. The bubbles went up my nose and made me quiver, the coldness of the drink and the warmth of the room making my head spin. I hadn't eaten all day, my tummy was empty, the effervescent rush of alcohol seemed to burn the back of my eyes and I felt a trickle of perspiration run down my back.

Sandy tugged again at my belt and a slurp of champagne spilled over my chest. It seemed careless, heartless, as if I didn't matter. As if I was nothing. I was angry with Sandy Cunningham. And I was angry with Simon Roche. He must have known I wouldn't be able to resist temptation, that I would lose all my money and, in desperation, turn to the only source available to me: the Roche-Marshall sundries account.

That's why he had given me the computer codes.

On the Monday of my second week at the office, after that disgraceful night in the hotel with Sandy, he had asked my shoe size. He had known. He had always known. My being here at Black Spires wasn't chance. It wasn't destiny. I had been duped and lured here and the thought made tears well up in my eyes.

'You tricked me,' I said to Sandy and he just grinned.

'When you're a thief you take your chances,' he replied, and the tears spilled down my cheeks in a spluttering shower.

'I'm not a thief,' I cried.

'No,' he said. 'You're a girl who can resist anything except temptation.'

I stamped my foot, spilling more champagne over my breasts. I placed the glass back on the tray on the table at our side and, with as much dignity as I could muster,

I stormed out of the room, back across the hall and up the two flights of stairs to the boudoir where I had been clipped and creamed and clad in black leather straps. I slammed the door behind me.

With nervous fingers straining over the buckles, I undid the straps and threw them across the room. I searched through the drawers and could hardly believe my eyes as they alighted on a torture garden of whips and canes, a cat-o'-nine-tails, a glass phallus, a plastic cock attached to a pink leather harness, clips and clamps for purposes I couldn't imagine.

The drawers boomed like cannon as I rammed them shut. I turned away and was shocked when I saw my reflection in the mirror. I looked like a wild beast, my hair styled as if by a windstorm, black smears war-painted across my cheeks. There was the sweat-sticky residue of champagne between my breasts; my nipples were so painfully erect I squeezed them as hard as I could and suddenly knew exactly what the clips and clamps in the chest of drawers were for.

I was almost tempted to go and try for myself, but that would have been giving in to an instinct too far. I could smell the pungent musk of my own arousal infusing that small room with the scent of lust. It was shameful and confusing. I didn't want to be a disciplined drone in the City, but I didn't want to be a submissive drone in the living room at Black Spires either. I didn't know what I wanted.

In the bathroom I washed the smears from my face, I douched the wet discharge from between my legs and found in the cupboard the bag with my own clothes. I pulled back my hair and felt like the old me as I dressed and stepped into my shoes. It was a relief to find my mobile phone and turned it on.

There were two texts, one from Melissa: *Where the hell RU?*

I texted back: *Youll nvr blv me.*

The other was from Sarah. *Going to Ministry of Sound. Coming?*

I texted Sarah. *Cant. Wish I cld*, and the messages reminded me of who I once was.

'I want my life back.' I said the words, whispering to my reflection, but caught a curious look in my eyes, a sense that I was watching myself from beyond myself, that the girl standing there in a pale-yellow suit was an image of how I used to be, a photograph from a sixth-form trip to the Louvre when I had worn the suit for the first time, the mischievous display of cleavage swelling over my buttoned blouse and sending Sister Benedict into a paroxysm of holy fury.

She had pointed at the sky. *He's* always watching, she'd said, and shamefully I had thought that if that were true *He* would have adored His creation, my hair shining like a raven's wing, my long limbs sculpted by years of gymnastics, the prettiest girls in the upper sixth clustering about me like moons drawn to the pull of a celestial being. Pretty girls like to be with the prettiest girls to show how pretty they are.

Summer was coming. The end of term was coming. I would soon wriggle free of my schoolgirl skin and be released from the cloistering angst of Sister Benedict, her whiplash tongue the symbol of the whiplash cane she kept mounted on her office wall, the mute reminder of her capacity for cruelty, her abhorrence of beauty, that inaccessible quality that exasperated her more and more as it blossomed on me like a rare orchid.

Of course I knew I was attractive. Pretty girls always do. You can't help but compare yourself with other girls; girls in the street, in the newspapers, on the sides of buses, on advertising hoardings. You know from the look in men's eyes when you board the bus or the tube and they either look away to avoid seeing that which they can never have, or they press closer than they should to feel for just a moment the warmth of your flesh through their clothes. They want to get close to you, smell you, take you in on their senses and imagine in their dirty minds all the things they want to do to you.

By the time you are sixteen and have tuned into Youporn and Bangbus, you know what it is men want to do and you know if you are the kind of girl men want to eat and bite and spank and lick and pierce. You are afraid and intrigued by this knowledge, attracted and repulsed; you want to remain a virgin and you want to be a whore. Sex makes you think about sex. It makes you grow moist between your legs with that sticky wetness you scoop up with the tip of your finger and savour on your tongue, the bittersweet taste of being a grown-up.

You know when you are in a café or bar with your girlfriends and the men at the next table are watching if it is you they are watching. And why. It gives you self-confidence. Poise. A feeling of power. It is as if you are a gift to the world and you can bestow that gift on anyone of your choosing. And it is you who has the choice. There is the person you see in the mirror, the person you present to the world, and as you are growing up you become aware that inside there is another you, the real you, bursting like a baby bird to come out of the shell.

Was my choice of mathematics at the London School of Economics just a ridiculous whim? Was I going against my true character? People told me to go to drama school, become a model, get on a media training course and read the news. I had the 'televisual' look, they said: trustworthy and intelligent, sexy yet serious. I was, they said, a girl with it all, and now I was a girl with nothing, nothing but the prospect of a criminal record.

Sister Benedict had called me conceited, vain, narcissistic and shallow. She accused me of seeking mirrors to assess my reflection. It was true: when I got back to the dorm I would strip off my uniform and check my reflection, a self-fulfilling prophecy, a hand on my flat tummy, my fingers gently squeezing the buds of my pink nipples, stroking the lush tuft of my velvet pubes, turning to examine the neat sphere of my bottom, a mathematician with dividers calculating the perfect geometry of the arc. I would slap my backside as you slap a pony to make it gallop, quaking as the delightful warmth burned my skin. I dreamed of being spanked before I actually imagined being spanked, and being spanked seemed to have awoken me to my true potential.

It occurred to me that Sister Benedict had had more of an influence on my life than Mother, who was always busy doing something, although what I was never quite sure. Father, poor man, had invested everything on that one big deal with the Chinese man and watched every penny he had slip from his grasp as, in an unbearable parallel image, I had watched my savings cleared from the computer screen in Simon's office.

The Sister with her voodoo inclinations had predicted that I would come to no good, that I would come to some place like Black Spires. Everything I had done since walking from the gates of the convent in Westgate a month before had conspired to bring me here to this small room in my pale-yellow suit wanting to leave and wanting to stay and not being sure what I wanted at all.

I sat on the narrow bed and looked around the room – the long mirror, the flowers carefully arranged on a shelf, the leather bonds scattered across the floor, the arched window with its view of the black night. Now I was ready to go I remembered that I had stolen £3,100. I was certain if I got the train back to Victoria Simon wouldn't go to the police. I would tell them everything, how I had been tricked into parading about naked against my will – how I had been tricked into offering up my bottom to a man in a Kensington hotel room.

I was angry with Simon Roche, and I was even angrier with myself because I knew in the heart of my subconscious self it hadn't been against my will. Not entirely. I had enjoyed the attention in my fetish clothes at Rebels, and it was irritating to acknowledge that I liked being naked. I adored being naked. It had given me a thrill to enter the living room and see all eyes turning in my direction. Being naked suited some perverse thing inside me that I had been coming to accept before Sandy Cunningham turned up with his self-assured smile and bow tie.

My heart was pounding. I was breathless. I crossed the room and gazed out at the sky. It was pierced by a billion stars. I thought about classics at school, how the gods when they die don't disappear but transform into animals and mortals and constellations. I wanted to be up there with them, a star in the sky, a god of the night.

I thought about everything that had happened since I started work at Roche-Marshall. In truth it had been fun. I had been balancing on the high wire. I had felt completely alive, free after years with Sister Benedict watching my every move, her grey eyes like an x-ray machine seeing through my uniform and finding shapes and forms to criticise.

The Sister had made it clear that she didn't like me and I knew deep down that it was only because by the time I turned seventeen I was taller than her, the school's Madonna and Mary Magdalene, the virgin and the whore. I was all those duplicitous things that had driven Sister Benedict behind the cloistered walls of the nunnery, where she could look with envy and despair on girls like me – and on me in particular. I had hated her and now I felt sorry for her. It had been a mistake to take the money from Simon's account, the mistake she had predicted and longed for. I would make up for it. Somehow, I would pay him back.

I huffed on the glass and wrote the figure £3,100, then rubbed it out again.

What if he did go to the police?

He could prove I was a thief and I am sure they wouldn't believe me if I said he had spanked my bottom, driven me across London without any clothes on and then had me dressed in leather straps, soft creams rubbed into my skin, my pubes trimmed. My mother, if I were to be charged as a criminal, would finally make good her threat and commit suicide. Spanish women are hysterical and dramatic. She would do it to prove a point. Daddy would be so ashamed, and poor Rafael, when he started in some state sixth-form college with the chavs, would be devastated. I wouldn't only be ruining my life, I'd be ruining theirs too.

A shooting star crossed the sky and vanished. Life's like that – a shooting star. A moment of brilliance and it's gone for ever. If only Sandy Cunningham hadn't turned up. I would be down there still ready to confront my fate. It was hard for me to face up to it, but I had been manoeuvred in a certain direction and, once on that course, I had hurtled off as if on a helter-skelter recklessly spiralling down, down to the mess I'd made of things.

I had been given a chance to pay for my mistake, and now I'd gone and blown it. I checked the time on my mobile, grabbed my bag, took one last look about the room and, at that moment, there was a soft tap on the door.

8

The Gift

The door slowly opened and standing there was the girl with flaming-red hair. She entered, closing the door behind her.

'I thought you might need some moral support,' she said.

'I was just about to go home,' I told her.

'I wish you wouldn't.'

I was surprised by this remark. What did she mean? 'But why?' I asked.

She didn't answer. She just shrugged and asked, 'Is it your first time?'

'Yes.'

'I remember mine. I was terrified,' she recalled and smiled. 'What's your name?'

'Magdalena.'

'We're both Ms,' she said brightly. 'I'm Milly.'

She smiled as if there was something extraordinary in this coincidence. She then crossed the room and stood just a few inches from me. This was a little unnerving, and more so when she leaned forward to press her lips to mine. I wasn't expecting this, although having seen the girls downstairs on the table supping from each other's wet parts it shouldn't have surprised me.

The taste of her lips was sweet but hard to describe, the taste of dew to a robin, perhaps, or honey to a bee. Those lips were, as I had observed in the window nook below, the most marvellous lips imaginable, soft yet firm, pliant yet tender, pink as the inner lips of her pussy, I'm sure, and, as that thought went through my mind, I wondered where it had come from.

What was happening to me? Could I have changed so much? And so quickly?

When I was dressed in the livery of black leather straps, had I taken on a different personality? Or had I become who I really am, who I was meant to be? It should have been strange and abhorrent arriving naked at Black Spires and being prepared as a fetish object by Lee-Sun. But it wasn't. I felt like an actress about to go on stage, Sally Bowles in fishnets and a bowler hat, or rather leather bands and trimmed pubes: not me exactly, but one of the characters within me, a character capable of any role, any form of perversion.

I had experimented with girls at school but, like those occasional rolls on the bottom field with the local grammar boys, it was all clumsy and fumbling, an awkward kiss, a grope, a feeling of something lost rather than gained. With Milly it was different. This wasn't playing. She was a reminder of who I was, of what I could become, a mirror image of me in the uniform of black straps that I had cast off and thrown angrily about the room.

She ran her arms under my yellow jacket and over my shoulders, peeling the garment from me then tossing it on to a chair. Patiently and without haste she undid the buttons on my blouse and I watched as if I were not a party to this, as if this were a scene from one of those girl-on-girl internet sites we had discovered with unadulterated relish at school. Did the nuns look at those sites in secret? I'm sure they did.

Milly eased the blouse from my waistband and it slid from my shoulders to the floor. Her arms went round my waist, dextrous fingers unclasped the button at the back of my skirt and she lowered the zip. She pulled, I wriggled my hips and sighed as my skirt fell about my feet.

'Mmm. That's better,' she said.

I nodded again, dipped my toe into my skirt and kicked it away from me. My knickers were drenched. I could smell sex in the air. I had been lifted on the wings of those erotic activities in that high vaulted hall among those men in black suits, lifted and lowered and lifted again. Watching sex is wanting sex.

Milly unsnapped my bra, the cups fell away and she balanced my breasts in her white hands as if taking a cake from an oven, or holding a tray with treats, or an offering at an altar, and that's how I felt, that I was an offering being offered a second chance.

She was staring into my eyes and I realised suddenly that Milly's eyes were my own eyes, the same colour, the same shape, the same intensity; our eyes were dark mirrors that held each other. As I looked into her eyes I was seeing inside myself. I was meant to be here. Milly was meant to be here. The stars were in alignment. I had been so confused, so filled with doubt, but as I looked into her eyes it was like the sun burning away the morning mist and revealing a golden landscape.

Her palms left my breasts, moved to my ribcage and down over the curve of my sides to my knickers. She nipped the elastic between her thumbs and forefingers and pulled my knickers down to the floor. I stepped away from that sopping little triangle of ivory silk and sighed once more. I was naked again and a tremor of relief ran through me as she rubbed her pubic bone against mine, as she circled my shoulders with her arms and kissed me again.

That kiss was long and breathless, as if each of us was transferring the breath of life to the other. I had been one person a few minutes ago. Now I was another. I had been full of anxiety and doubt. Now I was brimming with desire and passion.

As we broke away, I stood back and gazed at Milly, her long body with the straps about her neck and wrist and ankles, the wide leather belt with its pattern of rings, the light tracing shadows over her curving thighs, over the ripples of her ribcage, over her vermilion-flamed nipples. I touched my own breasts instinctively and the hard little buds darkened with blood between my curious fingers. I looked up.

She stood back, taking my hands, and we looked into each other's eyes as if in them we would find clues to our own destiny. Milly's breasts were pulsing and I had an urge to reach for them. As that urge passed through me, she took my hand, placed my palm on the firm swell of her flesh and I could feel the blood racing through her veins. She let out a low moan, as if the air had been pressed from her lungs. My mouth was dry. could hear the motions of the sea pounding outside, the wind rattling the glass in its frame. I could smell something sweet and delicious, a tropical flower like frangipani.

Milly bridged the distance between us and kissed me again, her lips alive with unfamiliar sensations. My lips opened and, as Milly's tongue slipped into my mouth, a bead of sweat ran down my back into the crack of my bottom. Between my legs I grew sticky and the lips of my vagina opened as the wings of a butterfly open when it is released from the cocoon. Milly drew back. Our lips parted, and parting was such sweet sorrow.

She led me across the room and I lay back on the small bed and opened my legs. She gazed down at the sweet sticky goo leaking over my thighs. She kissed my forehead in the centre, in the place of the all-seeing eye, then ran her tongue over my face, my chin, down between my breasts. She paused, popped one erect nipple in her mouth and bit gently down until I squealed with pleasure. She tasted my other breast before continuing her journey, her tongue painting a shiny wet stripe over my tummy through the dark forest of my pubic hair and into my wet throbbing sex.

At that moment, I seemed to rise off the bed and float away, my body light as a feather, reborn with new sensations. I understood at that second, really for the first time, that I was born to give and receive pleasure, that it was the multifaceted geometry of entwined limbs that I was born for, not the cold arithmetic of accountancy.

Milly buried her head between my legs and made herself comfortable, sliding her body across the bed and spreading her thighs over my head until I was gazing at the most gorgeous sight I had ever seen, all the coils and spirals leading to a neat, pulsing bud I wanted to caress with my tongue. As I did so, somewhere far away at the other end of my damp body Milly made the connection complete.

We were joined, tiny tongue to pulsing rosebud, pulsing rosebud to tiny tongue, and we rocked like some wondrous machine, tasting and savouring each other's juice, and I discovered that the smell of frangipani was the smell of Milly, the perfume of her deliciously oiled labia. We drank our fill from the chalice of each other as if supping the stuff of life, changing positions, me on top, Milly below, side by side, each drinking from the holy orifice, the silky liquids flowing over our soft white thighs and coating our bottoms.

I understood now the value of the belt Milly was wearing and regretted that I wasn't wearing my own. With that belt there is something to cling to, and I pulled at the leather strap, the purchase making it easier to reach the soft membranes in the depths of her vagina, her thighs bucking and thrusting greedily as the vibrations rocked and quaked her eager body.

The constellations beyond the windows shattered and re-formed. Shooting stars appeared and disappeared. Others came. The planets circled. My senses were more alive than they had ever been. I could feel a tingling sensation like sparklers or tiny fireworks fizzing at my nerve endings. It was like being fully awake after a long sleep and seeing some undiscovered place. I was Magellan or Simon Bolivar striking out across a new unexplored continent of eroticism and lust. Milly was my guide and I wanted to see and feel and touch everything.

When Milly climaxed a sprinkling of warm nectar, like some elixir sprayed from an atomiser, touched my taste buds and I realised there is nothing like the taste of girls, a taste that is salty like seawater, but as sweet as ripe figs, sticky as peach juice, yet smooth as satin, fragrant like saffron, like a tropical night, as soft as baby's breath. The taste and smell and feel of Milly in my mouth sent messages whispering down through my inner core and I jolted as a vast rolling orgasm made my body burn and break into sweat.

We were gripped by this miracle of total connection, this photo-finish, this cosmic explosion. There is something marvellously gratuitous and invigorating tonguing another girl and being tongued, in this mutual act of autoeroticism. I had often wondered if I were a lesbian and I realised at that moment that I wasn't, that the concept meant nothing. I was a sexual being and sex, like the rainbow, comes in many colours and shades.

From the drawer, Milly removed the phallus on the pink leather harness and fixed it into place. She slid two straps between the cheeks of her bottom and buckled them at the back. There were two short straps on the harness which she connected to two of the rings on her belt and, again, I marvelled at how practical the black leather bands were, how a girl dressed in anklets and bracelets, a choker and a belt was dressed for anything.

The phallus bobbed up and down above her belly as if with some intent of its own. Milly smiled. 'It looks so silly,' she said. I smiled too.

I was about to get done by a dildo and the very thought was terrifying but thrilling, too. It was something

I would never in a million years have imagined doing and now it seemed the most natural thing in the world. Once you divest yourself of clothes and walk naked among those who are dressed, there is no telling where it might lead. Once you break this taboo, is there any taboo that might hold you back?

I don't think so. It seemed to me that, where there's a taboo, it's perfectly normal to go right out and break it. The big no-no at school was opening the buttons on your blouse to allow your cleavage a glimpse of daylight and, of course, that's what we all did the instant we got the chance. By going naked in the grand hall at Black Spires, I had reached the logical last step on the path of disobedience, I had unclasped all my buttons and done away with my clothes.

Girls fantasise about sweeping away taboos and living the dream of posing naked for the newspapers, stripping off for television soaps, having sex on *Big Brother*, albeit surreptitiously, and being seen in the homes of millions. Up to a certain point, transgression in public is possible, the barriers keep getting pushed back, but there is always an invisible point which is not crossed. That point, it occurred to me as Milly placed her hands on my knees and opened my legs, did not exist at Black Spires.

The creature bounced before her, thick and erect. I am not sure why, but I wanted to kiss it, to kiss this inanimate thing because it was joined to Milly. It was a part of her, and I drew it towards my lips and took the round head into my mouth. I licked the sides, up and down, then lay back, knees spread wide, and invited the pink dildo into my body. It was long, hard, inflexible. It reached deep into my womb, touching the edge of my soul, and withdrew, in and out, in and out. Milly's breasts slapped gently against my own making my nipples tingle and buzz like points of an electric circuit.

Deep inside me there was a reservoir of oily juices. The

103

pink phallus burst the banks and, as the floodtide of warm oil gushed from me, all my tension and doubt came flooding out in a warm syrupy deluge. If I had been betrayed by Simon and Sandy, it was only because I had willingly played the role they had created for me. They saw in me the wanton girl easily aroused, a girl ready for their erotic and esoteric world. Like Milly, I belonged at Black Spires.

She went up on her knees. The pink prick slipped from me with a slurping noise and hovered in the air. A teardrop of discharge clung to the tip and I licked it off.

'Wow,' I said.

'Turn over,' Milly whispered, her eyes mesmerising and bright.

I did so obediently, willingly, pushing my bottom up and my knees down into the thin mattress, arching my back. Milly rested her left hand on my side and, with her right, guided the penis into the small winking eye of my bottom. It seemed so big, so hard, so demanding. The muscles at the entrance to my anus grew tense and pushed back, rejecting the beast's admission. She pushed harder and I grew tense.

'Milly, please . . .'

She ignored my pleas and quietened me with a slap on my bottom with her left hand. Milly was just as patient as she had been undoing the buttons of my blouse. She pressed in and released, pressed in and released, until with a popping noise like you make by putting your finger in your cheek and pulling it out quickly, the bulging head of the phallus slipped between the slippery walls of my ass.

Ass. Ass. Ass.

I loved that word. It was so American, so graphic, and I whispered it to myself as slowly but surely she forced the long pink dildo down, down into the heart of my being, in and out, in and out, ass, ass, ass, deeper and deeper until she reached the end of her journey and it was like a pin bursting a balloon as all the air escaped from my body in one long rush. My moment of doubt had gone.

'Yes. Yes. Yes,' I cried.

She was clutching my thighs and drilling into me, the motion opening my body, but opening my mind, too. When Sandy Cunningham that night in the hotel pierced my bum the experience had seemed shocking, painful, vaguely awkward. Milly driving the phallus into my bottom felt natural, elegant and suddenly painless. I had been imprisoned by a morality imposed on me by school, by convention, by my mother. With each thrust of that artificial cock strapped about her waist, Milly was hammering down the walls of that prison to set me free.

I could hear the flamenco clap of flesh on flesh, but beyond that rhythmic beat there was no sound but the ghostly silence one imagines existing in deep space. We were alone in our own universe, two girls encountering the gift of sex, the gift of girls, I thought briefly, a thought I was sure would come back into my mind again and again during the thirty-one days of my ascent on Sodom.

I had been fighting my natural instincts, my feminine intuition, that innate desire at eighteen to know everything I could possibly know about myself, my hidden self. I had not been born with this ripe rounded body for it to languish unseen and unappreciated in dreary clothes in dreary offices, in the lacklustre light of a computer screen pulsing out numbers and statistics.

Like a stripper on stage, I had been revealing my body in enticing parts – my legs in short skirts; the ripples of my spine in backless blouses; hipbones and bellybutton in low-slung jeans; neck and breasts in skinny tops, and no top at all last summer when Daddy rented a house at Puente Romano in Marbella, before the Chinese man disappeared and the money ran out.

Just as we open the windows of an Advent calendar in the days leading up to Christmas, I had been uncovering my body a piece at a time, preparing myself for the ambiguous pleasure of going naked. Stripping for Simon Roche in the diffused light of his office seemed merely inevitable, the next step on the stairway in Marcel Duchamp's *Nude Descending the Staircase* – the nude's journey, like all journeys, not taken in bounding leaps but one step at a time, as the Buddha did, we're told, on the road to Nirvana.

Duchamp's painting features on the cover of a book of nudes Melissa had given me on my eighteenth birthday, an encyclopaedia of girls in drawings and photographs from Helen of Troy to Marilyn Monroe, all revealed in nothing but their silky flesh. Girls want to be naked, 'girls like me' want to be naked, and no matter how much we fight it, circumstances will conspire to tear off our clothes. It seems ingrained in us to want to overstep the limits, to find our regressive, ancient self, the shaggy avatar within, that triangle of matted hair on our lower belly the last vestiges of the animal self straining constantly to break through the thin veneer of society's conventions and domestication.

Some of the girls at school had started shaving their pussies so that they looked like children, but I had a sense that men were drawn to the enigma of our pubic hair, our creamy, uncontrollable discharge producing the faint whiff of the stable; that bare hairless flesh is more desirable with the token of our prehistoric self, a re- minder of the animal we once were and can be again if the man knows which buttons to push.

For some reason, I felt at peace, eyes closed, head buried, my back arched, the globe of my backside neatly divided, Milly riding up and down on the phallus, drilling inside me as if within my hidden passageways she might find some marvellous secret. Time had lost formality and shape, the awareness of yesterday and tomorrow, of things to be done and things achieved, of hurry and waste. Time was never wasted, for time not doing one thing was spent on another, and doing nothing at all was of itself doing something.

It occurred to me, too, that I lived each moment with an imperceptible tension, an anxiety, a need for continuous pretending, sudden improvisations, quick justifications of who I am and what I am doing. In sex, as in pain, you are in the present moment, and it is only in the present that we are truly and completely alive.

One night on that holiday in Marbella, I wandered through the gardens of Puente Romano to the bay. A hot wind was blowing across the Mediterranean with the scent of the red sands of Africa, the fragrance of pleasure and lust. I was embraced by the night, by the heat, by the moon and stars. I slid from my pink bikini and swam naked. I swam for a long time and, when I left the sea, I reached for my swimwear and, instead of dressing, I walked through the gardens among the courting couples and families making their way home from the restaurants and bars, those two scraps of pink material in my hand, my body free in the hot Andalusian night.

It was the first time I had done something quite so brazen, walked naked in a public place, and the feeling was exhilarating, enriching, empowering. I had felt completely, utterly, thoroughly alive. I was living in the present, as I was that moment on the narrow bed on the top floor at Black Spires.

My breath grew faster, my heart beating in my chest. I could hear Milly, too, panting for air, and suddenly, as the piston beat of the phallus moved up a gear, we both gasped in climax, her girl-juices and the jism of my inner being erupting in a liquid gush so warm and heady I felt for a moment as if we were melting, molten essence to be reshaped for whatever the future had in store.

We collapsed in a tangle of limbs and giggles. Milly's petal lips found my mouth and we kissed again. The phallus was bouncing about between us, wet and silly, strapped in a harness about her. She rolled over.

'Undo it, Magdalena,' she said, and I slipped the strap from the buckles.

She took the dildo from me, passed the straps between my legs, through the crease in my bottom, and tightened the buckles about my waist. I was kneeling on the bed, the pink cock jumping up and down like a small excited boy. What a wondrous thing it was, this male appendage with the smooth sides and bulbous head. Milly leaned forward, licked the shaft, then took the head into her mouth. She looked up into my eyes as she sucked that cock, and I felt the pressure of her tongue pass through the plastic like an electric current and ignite the star of my swollen clitoris. It's weird, but it doesn't seem to matter how big your orgasm, or how many you have, there is always more juice up there waiting to come flooding out.

Milly lay back, spread her legs and I fell on her like a satyr in a mediaeval painting, pushing up into her wet places and driving the dildo deep into her throbbing pussy. She closed her eyes and threw back her head to reveal her long throat. I was tempted to bite that white throat, I felt so aroused raising and thrusting my hips, the pink thing impaling her like the arrows on the school badge piercing Saint Sebastian. Milly moaned and cried, thrusting her pelvis and drawing the beast in still deeper, her total abandon revealing to me that to submit to the will of another provides its own unique pleasures, that there is power in submission as well as domination.

It also occurred to me, at that moment, pushing this hard pink cock up inside this slender girl, this mirror image of myself, that sex with someone you barely know, with a stranger, has its own special allure. Sex with Milly was a form of masturbation. The base of the phallus fitted snugly within the oval of my moist labia and nursed my clitoris like a fingertip.

Milly pushed down from the pit of her back and wrapped her long legs around me, locked at the ankles. I thrust harder and she let go with a scream that must have frightened the seagulls nesting under the eaves, a scream that made the room tremble and shake out the dust lodged in lost forgotten corners. We collapsed, wet and spent, her hot discharge coating my thighs, mixing with my own.

The dildo slipped from her drenched pussy and I lay on my back, the shaft of plastic slicked and erect above my belly. She rolled against me and pushed the tip of her tongue into my ear, nibbled on my ear lobe, licked my cheek.

'I can hear your heart racing,' she whispered.

I smiled. I stroked her red hair, her shoulder, so pale in the moonlight. I felt happy, satisfied, like a greedy cat, in touch with the moment. I could see the moon through the leaded windows.

'I'd been about to go,' I said.

'Are you glad you didn't?'

'What do you think?'

'You are going to be happy with your new life, Magdalena.'

I wasn't sure what she meant. *My new life?* 'I don't understand . . .'

'Once you become a slave of your senses, there is no way back,' she said. 'Once you submit to the gift of pleasure, you want to give and receive the gift again and again, in different ways and the same way, for ever and ever.'

I lifted myself up on my elbow to look at her. The shadows made by the moon's glow give Milly's features the look of a costume mask, carved and perfect, too perfect to be fully human, her blaze of red hair like a beacon in the misty white light. She was extraordinarily beautiful, too beautiful for a normal life.

'Stay there,' she said, and slid from the narrow bed.

She filled a bowl with warm water and returned with a cloth and some soap. She washed the gooey stuff from

109

between my legs, the cheeks of my bottom, my thighs, the champagne stickiness from my breasts. She then went and found my belt, the straps that fitted around my neck, my ankles and wrists. As she buckled them in place, I felt as if I had come home after a long journey, that I was me again, and all my worries over whether or not I had been tricked by Simon Roche and Sandy Cunningham didn't really matter. If I had been deceived, it was by my own greed, by the allure of the blackjack table, that sensual click of chips moving across the green baize. If I had in any sense been betrayed, I had betrayed myself.

When Simon asked me at the interview whether I looked 'fetching in a leotard', I should have guessed that there was more to Mr Roche than the dull accountant he was pretending to be. Numbers, he remarked, demand the subjugation to discipline. 'That's something I like in a girl!'

All the clues were there. He had measured my legs in cherry-red heels, he had taken a long look at my breasts peeking outrageously over the top of my blouse, and had set about finding out exactly who I was and what he must have assumed I subliminally desired. He had given me access to the Roche-Marshall codes, to all that money lying unused in the sundries account. He had placed temptation before my eyes, but it was I, not Simon Roche, who had given in to that temptation. I was sure he had discovered that Daddy had lost his money and I was obliged to work in Rebels, dressed as if for a night at a fetish club.

Sister Benedict like the Ghost of Christmas Past slipped once more into my mind. *If you dress like a harlot, you become a harlot. It's the law of cause and effect.* That's what she said to me that day we visited the the Musée du Louvre in Paris, and those words for some reason had stuck in my mind like a jingle you keep humming even after you've grown sick of it. We had entered the museum as a group and I went straight to the one painting I was dying to see. I had queued for ages and was suddenly standing alone before Leonardo da Vinci's masterpiece, the *Portrait of Lisa Gherardini* – the *Mona Lisa*.

Everything that has been said and everything you imagine about the *Mona Lisa* is true. *La Gioconda*, as she is called, really is enigmatic, and what you can see in her brown eyes and cheeky smile is the look of a woman who has just got out of bed and can't wait to climb back between the sheets. I recognised that look, not as a girl with heapings of sexual experience, but a girl anxious to leave the confines of Saint Sebastian and begin my experience.

It had been at that moment that Sister Benedict made her appearance. She scrutinised me as I was scrutinising the portrait and transferred the sexual subtext from Leonardo da Vinci's painting to me in my pale-yellow suit.

'If you dress like a harlot, you become a harlot. It's the law of cause and effect.'

'Thank you, Sister, I will bear that in mind,' I said, and she swept off in her long black habit to ruin some other girl's visit to the museum.

Do parents not know when they send their daughters to convent school they run the risk that their little sweetheart, while confined behind the ivy-clad walls, will turn into either the virgin or the whore, that the nature of this old-fashioned education draws you to one extreme or the other? I looked like the Madonna but I thought like Mary Magdalene, the fun girl, the risk taker.

I had my mother's features, but my father's sense that life was meant to be spent on the high wire. I had been treading slowly, a step at a time, over the abyss and it had taken so little for me to go plunging into the void . . . my shoe size, the system, the hypnotic turn of the cards, Sandy Cunningham in his creased suit scooping in blue £50 chips. All the clues were there and only now, with

Milly carefully fixing the buckle that held the choker tight to my neck, did I see the pieces of the puzzle slot together and form a picture in my mind.

Simon Roche must have known I was going to get into financial trouble and plunder the accounts. But how did he know I was the sort of girl who would with little persuasion strip and bend over the arm of his black leather sofa to be spanked – spanked to the state of that shameful orgasm? Most girls would have wept and waited for the police to come. Not me. I opened my buttons and, like Saint Sebastian, I bared my breast to take the martyr's punishment.

Was that flash of cleavage at the interview enough to tell Simon Roche everything he needed to know about me? Was I that obvious? While Simon played the Devil placing temptation in my way, I so easily stepped into the persona of Faust. I craved carnal, not spiritual, knowledge and the moment I entered the secret code into the Roche-Marshall computer I was irrevocably damned.

'What are you thinking about?' Milly asked me.

I smiled. 'Oh, God, I'm not sure. The Devil tempting Faust.'

'You never quite leave the convent behind. Not ever,' she said.

'But how did you know?'

'I know lots of things, Magdalena. All in good time . . .'

She sat cross-legged on the bed and stroked my leg; it felt nice. 'There is no greater gift than the gift of pleasure,' she said, continuing her theme. 'And of all the gifts, none is so great as erotic pleasure.'

'You mean fucking?' I said, but she didn't laugh.

Milly was deadly serious as she explained what she meant by the gift, and it was strange because I had already been thinking of sex as a gift. But there was more to it than that. The erotic, truly pursued, she said, is an art form that can inspire us, lift our hearts, revive the soul – just like the *Mona Lisa*, I thought. People speak of

112

talent as being a gift, and being a master of erotic love is a true talent.

'A gift, a personal gift, not like a present, can never be owned or bartered or sold,' she said. 'To be alive is a gift and, if your body is your gift, you must accept that with gratitude and dispense the gift.'

I recalled Sandy Cunningham speaking of gratitude. 'You must cultivate an attitude of gratitude,' he had said. 'You didn't want to learn the system, you wanted to beat the system.'

'Dispense it to, like, anyone?' I asked breathlessly.

'Oh, no, Magdalena, you have to be discerning,' she answered. 'The gift is eternal and grows upon being given. Once given, the receiver is obliged to reciprocate and pass on the gift. Only those who understand the nature of the erotic as art are worthy of receiving the gift.'

It all seemed so complex. 'How do you know who's worthy?'

'You just get a feeling for it,' Milly said, her pink lips turning into a smile. 'When you give yourself completely, to a man or a woman, when you submit to their will, you create a psychic bond with that person, a trust, and that trust turns on the light of your inner being. We are only alive to the degree that we can allow ourselves to be moved. Your role, my role, is to be a vector of pleasure.'

'A vector of pleasure,' I repeated. It sounded so amazing.

Milly stepped from the bed, her back faintly curved from the perfect turn of her round bottom, and stroked her fingers through the flames of her fiery hair. She reached out and pulled me gently from the bed. We held hands and looked into each other's eyes, our own eyes, the tips of our breasts just touching and sending shivers of pins and needles through my body.

'Are you ready?'

'I am now,' I replied.

'It's show time,' she added, and opened the door.

113

9

Nude Descending a Staircase

There are flowers in Spain called *Las Señoras de la Noche* with blooms that open only at night. They enjoy the warmth without the sun and glow a pale-ivory colour in the light of the moon. I had always admired those flowers and realised that I was one of them, a Lady of the Night, my skin radiant as I descended the stairs with Milly, our black heels tapping out a drum roll to mark our entrance.

Heads turned, eyes watched, conversations paused and continued. There was no haste at Black Spires. Time was suspended.

There were more people in the hall now, twenty or so men in dinner suits and about ten girls dressed like Milly and me in the livery of the erotic. Most of the girls were my age, maybe a couple of years older, but there was one among us who I guessed was close to thirty, a striking woman wearing an elaborate turquoise and amber necklace with a long pigtail down the middle of her back. She was unclothed, the female uniform, it seemed, but without the bindings about her wrists, ankles and neck. She stood tall and proud in her nakedness telling a story while a group of four men listened intrigued.

Had she been sharing the gift since she was eighteen? I wondered. Once you embark on this life, does it become eternal, as the gift, Milly had said, was eternal? Everything was new, a little daunting, but exhilarating too.

114

With my breasts firm and tingling, with a faint dampness on my back and around the puffy pink lips of my vagina, I could no longer imagine a life in the merciless domain of numbers, a career juggling figures in the Roche-Marshall office. In this erotic sanctuary with the wooden beams and vaulted ceiling, I felt as if I was back on the high wire. *Anything* might happen. We talked at school about *tantra*, about the 365 ways to have sex, a different position for every day of the year, and I couldn't wait to try them all.

Lee-Sun was still dispensing flutes of champagne and a girl with red and green dreadlocks, her body embroidered with tattoos, was passing blini, little pancakes heaped with caviar and sour cream. Jazz was playing. I had thought at first it was canned, but I was wrong. As I moved deeper into the hall I was surprised to see in a recessed alcove a quintet – a piano, saxophone, clarinet, double bass and drums, the drummer hunched over with eyes closed as he tapped wire brushes over the snare at his side.

We dipped into the canapés and I could barely tear my eyes away from the girl in dreadlocks, her breasts a portrait gallery behind the blini arranged on her tray. Now that I was closer, I could see the tattoos crowding for space over every inch of her body. Over her breasts, down her arms and legs, her hips and ribcage, her back and her bottom were likenesses of men, young and old, men with piercing eyes and narrow lips, men with generous smiles and strong jaws, men with a look of angst and men with gritty determination, the faces drawn on her flesh about twice the size of a passport photo, their expressions changing with her movements and the pulse of her breath.

'Amazing,' I gasped.

'It was everyone I'd ever slept with,' she said with an air of retelling a familiar joke. 'Then I ran out of space.'

I smiled.

She smiled and the faces nestling about her cleavage seemed to smile too. I felt drawn to this girl who had created this souvenir of her lovers and resisted the temptation of counting them. I took another blini, popped it in my mouth, and the caviar and cream slipped down my throat like ambrosia. Milly had collected some champagne and the bubbles tickled my nose as I sipped from the tall glass she gave me. I was learning to appreciate life's small pleasures and, as I gazed about the room, it occurred to me that I didn't want to be anywhere else in the world.

Before I'd gone rushing off in a huff, I seemed to recall the drapes in the hall being closed, perhaps to deny the last remnants of daylight. But they were open now and through the tall arched windows the ghostly light of the moon added a counterpoint to the warm glow of the candles suspended in candelabra from the ceiling and standing here and there in tridents. Their light was reflected in the suits of armour, shields, the display of swords, and picked out details on seascapes of sailing ships and portraits of country squires with the same dark countenance as Simon Roche.

Along each side of the hall were alcoves with upholstered benches and dark corners from which squeals of pain and pleasure added a choral accompaniment to the jazz. The nymphs carved on the columns had come to life, their cherubic faces saucy yet omniscient in the dancing shadows made by the candles. As we threaded our way among the columns, the perspective changed at each twist and turn, the effect reminding me suddenly of the Mesquita in Cordoba.

Everything, it seems, is linked. Just as Duchamp's nude on the staircase, the figure cut into slithers to show a sense of movement, descends unavoidably from one step to the next, life is a series of inevitable steps. The moment Daddy shook hands with the Chinese man in a hotel room in Penang, the echo resonated across the seas and

116

continents to that hotel room in Kensington where a man peeled off my clothes, enlightened my every orifice and set me in motion, one step at a time from Rebels Casino to Black Spires and down the staircase at Milly's side into the heart of the drama.

I had never before seen a room like this, or people like this; the girls self-assured with their bodies unashamedly displayed, the men all with a certain ill-defined similarity, a certain mien which I could only describe as the look of power, the look Daddy had before he lost his money. Like Daddy, these men would never find pleasure in the same way as other men. They seek out the edges of things, the dark extremes where only the brave and reckless dare to go. Their brains are always ticking. They rarely sleep and they rarely smile; Simon Roche was a good example. In his glass temple in the City of London, Simon didn't have friends. He had employees, secretaries, lackeys. It was in situations like this, I realised, in this ambience of domination and submission, among the swords and shields, where he was truly himself.

Normal desires would never satisfy Simon Roche and Sandy Cunningham, nor any of these men. I was sure they all had wives, one wife after another, trading in the old for the new with hosts of children to carry their names and genes into the future. They are individuals, I thought, men who don't make connections in the normal way.

That night in the hotel room in Kensington, when Sandy calmly removed my clothes and proceeded to do me in every way, it was his air of confidence that persuaded me to let go of all uncertainty and let it happen. Boys just want a quick feel, a quick poke, a quick hand job. Men like Sandy, like all the men in the grand hall, had deeper needs. They were in no hurry to satisfy those needs and, when they did satisfy them, it would be in ways I could only begin to imagine.

117

My imagination was set alight as we joined a grou
gathered about an alcove where two men were playin
chess across an enlarged board. Two girls dressed like m
with the addition of masks, one red, the other black, knel
on the side of the table like acolytes learning esoteri
moves from grandmasters.

The chess pieces were red and black ivory, long
vaguely phallic with oversized heads. The two mer
playing were the Texan I'd seen earlier and an Arab in ,
long white jalabah, his distinctive sunglasses, moustach
and goatee familiar, perhaps from the newspapers.

As their turn came, the men didn't move the chess
men, but pointed to the piece they wished to move and
to the square they wished to move it to. The girl a
their side, the red mask working the red pieces, th
black moving the black, had to bestride the tabl
without upsetting the pieces and lower her cleft over th
bulbous head of the chosen piece, the motion causin;
them to wriggle in such a way that it made thei
bottoms and breasts tremble and vibrate, to the deligh
of the audience, me included.

Lifting the chessman didn't appear to be as difficult a
lowering the piece on to the chosen position, and it too
all the force of their vaginal muscles to complete th
move. The rounded heads of the pawns, the castl
battlements, the queen's crown and bishop's mitre glis
tened with streaks of discharge, and the chessboard wa
dotted with dewdrops of girl-juice.

Chess has never been much of a spectator sport, bu
played in this way there is all the tension of motorcycl
racing, a sense of imminent catastrophe and disaster. Th
people in the audience were holding their breath as the
watched the girl in the red mask move crablike, her whit
toes with pearl varnish on the nails manoeuvring to ge
purchase on the marble tabletop.

She lowered her bottom as if to pee, squatted over th
bishop nominated by the sheikh, her flared labia lik

some exotic sea creature dropping over the pointed headwear and conveying the piece at an angle across the board as it slipped and slurped from her wet pussy. Gravity was pulling the bishop down the greasy channel, while sheer pussy power sucked it back up and finally plopped it out on the desired square to a thumping round of applause.

The old Texan adjusted his bootlace tie as he leaned forward and studied the move. He drummed the table with his fingertips, the audience went silent, and finally he pointed at the black queen on her home square and across the board to the pawn left unprotected by the bishop's precipitous advance.

The girl in the black mask was Oriental, small and lithe with no body hair, a neatly depilated pussy and powerful calves. She stood and stretched one leg across the board to make an arch. With her hands on her waist, she lowered herself over the unsuspecting pawn, sucked it up with one fierce snatch of her snatch, and held the piece as if gripped by an invisible fist. She stepped back across the table and thrust her prominent mound at the Texan. Taking the base of the pawn, he ran the domed head around the creamy curve of her labia before placing it in his mouth.

'Texas tea,' he said.

He put the piece to one side while the Oriental girl went through the same performance, straddling the table, seizing the queen before, with perfect vaginal control, positioning it in the centre of the square formerly occupied by the captured pawn.

The men clapped and I was sure they must have been thinking, if she can do that with those chessmen, what's she going to do with the swollen king bulging at the front of my trousers.

I gazed at Milly. I gazed at the faces of the men around the table, and it occurred to me that it is in the small things in life that people find happiness; that the rather solemn, arrogant game of chess can be enlivened with such a simple, inoffensive innovation, that winning and losing is less important than the pleasure of taking part.

Four weeks earlier and about a dozen miles from Black Spires, I had been a schoolgirl at a convent, bursting from my uniform. My skirt had grown too short for my long legs. The buttons of my blouse could barely contain my impertinent breasts. I was unusually fit from the vaulting horse and parallel bars, but too rounded and luxuriant to pursue gymnastics. I was made for a different path and I got a sense of what that path might be the moment I slipped into fishnets at Rebels and Kate pulled the laces tight on my Lycra basque. I stepped into high heels and realised instantly that a naked girl would always feel dressed in heels, that heels shape you and make you.

It was in black heels and nothing else that I had set off on my journey from Simon's office back along the familiar roads going south into the Kent countryside. I had found myself. I belonged here. I had been drawn here by something more than mere chance. The imps of destiny are always shuffling the cards and dealing the hands you play. I was meant to apply to Roche-Marshall to be an intern, to work at Rebels, to gamble my way into debt and duplicity.

How else would I have found my true vocation?

I was overcome suddenly with a feeling of liberation and contentment. I could feel the hand of fate squeezing my hard nipples, stirring the warm oils in my throbbing sex, in the sense of arousal piqued by my own nudity.

The past and the future had become remote, abstract, mere concepts. In the dancing shadows made by the candlelight, with the hallucinogenic jazz haunting the high ceiling, I was in a present that was dreamlike, a fantasy, a fleeting, harmless decadence one imagines, as you may imagine being a princess or winning the lottery, but never really believes is going to come true.

It had taken time and imagination to create this scene at Black Spires. In the house of fate, this mansion with many rooms, nothing had been left to chance. Just as the men wore the look of power, the girls wore their beauty unashamedly but without arrogance or hubris. With tattoos, studs, shaved mounds or ample hair, with ivory-white skin like Milly or the ebony shine of the Maasai, the girls seemed special, each in her own way, and I wondered if there was anything special about me beyond being eighteen and eager to learn.

I could see more clearly now what Milly had meant by the gift: that sex, erotic sex, imbues the participants with an unimaginable power, a power that grows as it passes among those who understand and are humble to it. Milly with that plastic dildo had reached new places hidden inside me and unlocked a desire for more, more extremes, more innovations. She had taught me by actions rather than words that, of all the gifts a girl has, nothing is more precious than the gift to give and receive the ecstasy of orgasm, that pure moment when the body dissolves into its own essence and reaches perfection, a moment of satisfaction for people who can never be satisfied.

Wasn't this the meaning of life, alchemist's gold, the philosopher's stone? Those last months at the convent I lay awake night after night thinking about my future. After five years behind those high ivy-covered walls, I had learned that the only truth, as the philosopher Wittgenstein had said, was in numbers, that words were the invention of man, the device of the devil. Like molten steel, words can be moulded into anything from prison bars to an extension bridge to be thrown over a river that may or may not exist.

People were so good at spinning those words and throwing out advice – jugglers with sharp knives – take a gap year, be an accountant, go to the LSE, have a career, so many words I didn't really know where I was going or what I wanted. Numbers were truth and I was a perfect

34-24-34. I was five feet and ten inches in bare feet, 70
inches in primes, 10 times lucky 7. And it's as rare as
ambergris to lose five times in a row at blackjack.

What did it mean? Was it just words? That clever little
Hungarian Ludwig Wittgenstein adored the axiomatic
certainties of numbers and said philosophy consists of no
more than this analysis: whereof one cannot speak,
thereof one must be silent.

Wow!

It was good advice. Daddy had lost his money.
Mummy was suicidal. I was flat broke. What was there
to talk about? After leaving Saint Sebastian, I lay in my
bed in the flat I shared with Sarah and Melissa wondering
what the hell Wittgenstein meant. I had been accepted as
an intern, but I was bursting for adventure, desperate for
adventure. After those nights at Rebels I came home and
didn't sleep because I didn't want to sleep. Every time
you go to bed you wake another day older.

A smile came to my lips, not the sort of smile that comes
when something is passingly amusing. This was a smile
that comes from deep down in your gut. For some
reason, I was so happy I slapped Milly's bottom as hard
as I could.

'Ouch,' she said. 'You are such a bitch.'

She was grinning. She understood. We were sisters-in-
arms.

We moved further through the hall. I noticed Simon
talking to the Spanish man – 'Sergio Buenavista,' Milly
whispered, as if I should know who he was, but didn't.
The two men were watching a display by twins, gamine
girls with short boyish haircuts and green bindings rather
than black, the colour matching their emerald eyes.

I knew men were fascinated by twins and to accentuate
the fixation the rings on their leather bracelets and
anklets had been clamped together like the links of
handcuffs, hand to hand, foot to foot in pretty green

heels. They were facing each other as two other men spanked their bottoms with their bare hands, first one, then the other, and with each blow the twin receiving the smack was thrust into the other. They were dripping in sweat, their heads thrust back with looks of rapture, and, after being ravaged so thoroughly by the pink plastic cock in the room above, I could see how this playful spanking was amusing for those watching and a pleasure for those taking part.

The men gathered about the older woman were laughing uproariously, her story ended.

'I find it hard to imagine her taking a beating,' I whispered to Milly.

'I have a feeling her gift is giving beatings,' she replied, and I realised I had a lot to learn.

At that very moment, Simon hooked his fingers over the side of my belt and pulled me towards him. His eyes were black orbs that danced with reflected flames of the candlelight; he was devilishly handsome, authoritative, intimidating. Sweat prickled my underarms.

'You're over your little spat?' he asked.

I flushed. 'Yes,' I said. 'I'm sorry . . .'

'Try not to let it happen again, Magdalena.'

'I won't, I promise.'

He stood back and took a closer look at me, at my perky breasts, which I knew he admired, but then at *me*, into my eyes, into my being.

'You seem different,' he said.

'Do I?' I replied saucily, with more confidence.

He glanced from me to Milly and back again. 'She is quite something,' he remarked.

'A gift,' I responded, and he flashed one of those occasional smiles.

'As are you,' he said, and I felt inordinately proud.

He took my champagne glass and gave it to Milly before leading me into an alcove containing a *prie dieu* of the sort Sister Benedict kept in the window nook in her room in the high tower at the convent. I had assumed it was positioned for her private prayers until, alone one day in that room waiting to be reprimanded, I knelt on the chair and realised it had a perfect view across the courtyard into the uncurtained dorm of the upper-sixth girls.

Did Sister Benedict watch us parading about in the nude showing off our burgeoning young breasts? I thought she probably did and I'd probably find the bird-watching binoculars she carried on field trips, if there was time to rifle her drawers. There was no time. She entered and caught me kneeling on her sacred chair. She looked into my eyes, just as Simon Roche had done, and I looked back with defiance and knowing.

She knew I knew, and that created a sexual frisson as she told me to stand, lift my skirt and bend over the desk. What had I done wrong? I can't remember and it doesn't matter.

It was to be the last time that Sister Benedict tucked the hem of my skirt neatly in the waistband and pulled my knickers down to my knees. She took the cane with the shepherd's crook handle from the wall and I listened to the whoosh as she brought it down through the air testing the spring, the angle, the significance of the 'follow through', as the coach had told us in tennis.

Caning girls may have come to an end in state schools, even most private schools, but my Spanish mother had signed an agreement of acceptance that corporal punishment at the Convent of Saint Sebastian was an obligatory form of chastisement for errant pupils, of which the Sister had clearly decided I was one.

'I am going to give you six of the best, Magdalena. What do you say?'

'Thank you, Sister.'

I squirmed in embarrassment. I had been disciplined like this before, but still it was humiliating, a teenaged girl made to bare her bottom and accept a thrashing from this

124

aging voyeur, this degenerate Peeping Tom, this woman in charge of my pastoral care.

She sliced the air once more, bringing the cane down through the empty space beside the desk. She placed her leathery hand on the small of my back and whipped that instrument of torture across the neat little white hills of my perky young bottom that Simon had accused me of pushing out so arrogantly as I paraded through his office. The cane bit into my flesh like a line of fire and the pain was immediate, agonising, yet unfathomably tolerable.

The second strike came, landing with a crackle like lightning a few inches below the first, closer to the curve of my bottom, closer to my moist pudenda pushing through my slender thighs, and for some reason I remembered once shuffling through the dictionary during a Latin class and discovering pudenda came from *pudere*, to be ashamed, and thought it silly. How could something so pretty and so normal be shameful, even displayed so candidly for Mother Superior?

I clenched my tummy, gritted my teeth, held my breath and waited for the third.

It came down like the strike from a sword, cutting diagonally across the first two and searing into the soft flesh, the points where the raised weals intersected sharp stabs of agony on a field of pain. Sister Benedict expected me to cry out. I had heard other girls howling like wolves from the tower, but I had no intention of giving her that satisfaction. Snot ran from my nose and tears welled in my eyes, but I gritted my teeth and my voice lay locked in my dry throat. I had been caned before. I could take it.

'Halfway there, Magdalena,' the nun said smugly, and I wondered why beating my bottom gave her such pleasure and could only conclude that my bottom was unusually appealing and there is something about beauty that bullies and tyrants want to despoil.

'Thank you, Sister, I said, and found it hard to keep the tone of irony out of my voice.

I paid for that tone. You always do. The fourth strike from the cane was much harder than the other three. Just as in tennis, the Sister had found her pitch, her angle, the cane sizzling as it raced through the air and cracking like a whip across the top of my thighs, missing my sex by a fraction, the heat and its proximity to the lips of my flower making me writhe and leak over her desk. With all my wriggling, my underwear slipped down my legs to my feet. The nun unceremoniously grabbed my ankles, slipped my knickers over my shoes and dropped them a moment later on the desk, a moment in which I was sure she had examined the gusset for evidence of my wanton arousal.

'Keep still, girl,' she said.

I tried but it wasn't easy. I was panting, trembling.

What is it about pain that it can be moulded perversely into a strange and violent pleasure? The heat from the fourth blow had shot like an arrow between my legs, through the channel of my vagina and burst like champagne bubbles against my throbbing clitoris. The pain was excruciating across my thighs, yet the delight about that hidden little nub of mystery was beyond belief. It was like putting one hand in fire and the other in arctic waters, the combination exciting conflicting emotions.

My eyes flickered open and I was shocked to notice a small portrait of the Madonna on the wall above the bookshelves, a painting I had never seen in the Sister's office before. That painting could have been a portrait of me, the same waves of night-dark hair, the same full, plump, rather impudent lips, the same large soulful eyes, the same look of agony and confusion that I at that moment must surely have worn. As the Sister was beating my backside, she was gazing across her desk at that portrait. She was chastising me, but this was also an act of self-flagellation. Inside Sister Benedict there was a void and she was beating her way through the empty space in

126

search of herself, in search of the Madonna she dearly wanted to be.

The conflicting sensations continued with the fifth strike that she placed across the very top of my taut buttocks, just below what I'd learned was the sciatic nerve, the vibration through that nerve, up my spine and into my brain like an electric pulse that made my whole body break into a sweat. I wriggled like a fish; I couldn't stop myself.

'One more,' the Sister said, and I noted now a faint tinge of admiration, even compassion.

Sister Benedict made a soft sawing motion across my bottom, choosing her spot. I held my breath. She drew back and I listened as the cane cut an arc through the dry air and licked across my backside like a dragon's tongue, like the blade of the guillotine. The strike crossed the other five swelling rails, completing a pattern of cruel graffiti and sending that electric pulse from my brain straight to my bladder. I had drunk two glasses of orange juice and a cup of tea at breakfast. I had nervously swallowed a bottle of Evian before climbing the steps of the tower. There had been no time to go to the lavatory.

'Now, on your feet,' she said, and I pushed up with my hands and slid unsteadily from the desk.

The hem of my skirt was still tucked in the waistband. The jerking motion, coupled with the feel of the cool air on the pulsating lines across my bottom, added to the mounting pressure inside me. I thought for one terrible second I was going to climax standing there in front of Sister Benedict, that the spasm around my swollen clitoris was going to erupt in that elusive phenomenon, an orgasm, something we talked about at school but never expected to come true.

But it wasn't to be my first orgasm. That would come a month later under oddly similar circumstances.

No, it was worse than that. Much, much worse.

127

A stream of urine gushed from between my open legs, splashing noisily on the stone floor, not a trickle but a powerful hissing jet that just kept coming. I stood there petrified in disgrace and humiliation. And Sister Benedict stood there spellbound by this unexpected turn of events.

Was this my fault? Was it her fault? Was it providence? She didn't know. I didn't know.

The golden shower like a rising tide spread in a lake about my shoes and meandered slowly with the room's faint slope towards the door. As the force of my pee died down, dribbles still dropped with a splash in the puddle below me and we remained motionless like people in bed at night waiting to see if a dripping tap is ever going to stop.

The Sister's mouth had dropped open. Her eyes were shiny. We looked at each other and in that look was an alarming complicity. My face was streaked with snot and tears, my hair wild like a tropical storm. I was naked from the waist down. What Sister Benedict had seen was the Madonna taking a leak.

She was shaky on her small feet, her shoes engulfed in urine, her heart racing, eyes wide and staring. Nothing had ever given her more pleasure and she would remember this scene for the rest of her life, this dark-haired girl with her soggy pussy and blazing bottom and long white legs standing there before her with golden liquids gushing from her young body. She would take this memory with her when she knelt on the *prie dieu* in the window nook at night and stared through binoculars at the girls in the upper sixth parading naked across the dorm.

So much had happened since I had left Saint Sebastian that this scene in the tower, shocking though it had been, had fallen to the back of my memory. It was the last time the Sister had beaten me and, from that day on, she appeared to have a faint flush about her cheeks when I sat in her Latin class or our eyes met across the chapel.

Her final report when I left school painted me in the sympathetic lines of the Madonna on her office wall and, to my complete surprise, I got an A in classics.

That day in the Sister's office came back into my mind as I followed Simon into the alcove at Black Spires. I knew what was expected of me and knelt as if in prayer, my tummy and ribcage against the back of the chair, my full breasts nestled on the low padded rail at the top.

My mouth fell open as Sergio Buenavista produced his conquistador cock and slid it between my pouting lips. I closed my eyes. I could smell olive oil, crispy pan, the silky touch of the Mediterranean, and remembered swimming naked at Puente Romano.

Not counting the dildo, only one penis had been in my mouth before and that belonged to Sandy Cunningham. I had anticipated hating the experience, but it had turned out to be rather enjoyable, as it was now, wrapping my tongue around the throbbing extension of this handsome Spaniard. I sucked for all I was worth, up and down, in one cheek then the other, biting and nipping the smooth stretched skin, flicking the tip of my tongue into the groove around the head of his cock and running it back down the shaft again.

Sergio gasped and groaned, pushed deeper into my throat, then gripped the back of my head so that he could release a great spurt of hot semen that filled my mouth and pressed out of my lips. I kept going, the milky stuff oiling the shaft as it softened and he withdrew.

'*Muy bien. Qué boca tienes!*'

He whispered the words, and of course he didn't know that I spoke Spanish.

He had loved it. I loved it. I loved the feel of his frothy warm come seeping through my teeth, over my lips, across my cheeks and chin, dripping on to my breasts, my nipples puckering in pleasure and surprise. And as I knelt in the *prie dieu*, my spine was curved and my long white

129

neck was drawn back to take another hard cock in the space vacated by Sergio.

My next conquest filled my throat and I performed the same surgery, nursing the hard thing, teasing and tormenting the pulsating head with its unseeing eye, taking it down deeper into my throat and sucking hard until, like a geyser erupting, another floodtide of hot stuff filled my mouth with that lemony, cheesy, subtle, unnameable tang I remembered from that first time with Sandy Cunningham.

His sperm was still dripping over my face when a third man unbuttoned his flies and presented his skeleton key to unpick the lock to my puffy full lips. As he pressed his penis into the soft tissue of my throat, I wondered if this was my gift, that with consummate skill I could nurse these throbbing pieces of the male and receive their essence in exchange for the gift of relieving all tension and anxiety.

'*Muy bien. Qué boca tienes!*'

What a great mouth, Sergio had said, and I revelled in the compliment.

I licked and sucked, I nipped and tacked, and this man whose face I hadn't seen withdrew his cock, held the moist shaft in his clenched palm and, like a fire-fighter with a hose, put out the flames of my burning cheeks by spraying my face with his sperm. It went up my nose, over my chin, over my forehead, into my eyes and he pushed the hosepipe back into my mouth for me to suck out the last hesitant drop.

There was a muted round of applause which I heard but didn't see. I was unable to open my eyes as they were thick with spunk, but I imagined a group must have gathered about our alcove, and a fourth man presented his gift, slipped it into the wash of semen coating my throat and drilled inside the soft membranes as if in search of something small and lost. He reached his climax deep in my gullet and I was still gagging his sperm down when he withdrew and another cock pressed into my cheek.

My neck and throat were getting sore with all this activity but I thought this was a small price to pay for the service I was performing and, anyway, I knew from gymnastics that muscle burn heals by working through the pain. I was giving and receiving the gift. The universe was in order.

I reset my jaw and another muscle-hard piece of meat pressed down my throat and tickled my windpipe. It was bigger than the rest, I thought, the enormous head clanging my tonsils like church bells. I had self-learned the technique of swallowing, drawing air from deep in my lungs and breathing through the narrow passage encircling this monster that pushed deeper and deeper down and down as if into the core of my being.

My eyes were closed, but I pressed them more tightly shut and tried to visualise myself kneeling in the *prie dieu*, my face and dark hair coated with semen, my breasts pushed out, tingling with pins and needles, gummy with layer after layer of fresh essence. What I could see was something aesthetically pleasing, completely natural, a perfect young girl with gymnast poise nurturing her gift, a girl who had found in life the very thing she was born to do.

My eyes flickered open and I caught a glimpse of the Arab's sunglasses, his thick moustache and goatee, his head thrown back, his jalabah pulled open. He withdrew the monster and added another coat of jism to my sticky features, the stuff pouring out of him in vast spurts like milk from the udders of a cow, enough, I was sure, to fill a bucket, and all of it drenched my face, my chin, my breasts. When he had finished, he pushed his cock back into my gaping mouth and his taste, I realised, was rare and exotic. I recalled walking through the Grand Socco, the market in the old town in Tangier, the aroma of spices, roasting lamb, mint tea and hashish smouldering in brass hookahs.

There were more, five, six, seven, I lost count and what did it matter? I did what was expected of me, I received and I shared the gift. I sucked those hard cocks until they were soft and satisfied. I lubricated my skin with enough semen to give an elderly woman a facelift and, when it was over, I went upstairs with Milly where I showered and rubbed my body with precious oils.

The night wasn't over. It had barely begun.

10

The King Makers

The staircase descended before me once again and, when I entered the grand hall, the lights appeared to be darker and the activity more intense. Several of those men in dinner suits were now dressed in their birthday suits. They were on chairs, on the floor, in corners and alcoves, their bodies decorated with the limbs and mouths of heavenly girls.

I stood and watched one of the men I had seen spanking the twins. One of those gamine girls was now sitting astride his hips seesawing up and down the mast of his stiff cock while the other squatted on his face, her wet gash over his mouth. The girls were facing each other and, while their pussies like pistons pulsed rhythmically up and down, their lips were pressed together in a continual kiss.

In the next alcove, I watched a reverse mirror image. The Maasai was on her back taking one man between her legs and sucking off a second balanced precariously on the edge of a table. The two men, like the twins, were facing each other, not kissing, but negotiating a contract. I heard them tossing out numbers, percentages, production schedules, penalty clauses, and it made perfect sense that business should be conducted in this way, not in the stale air of board rooms, but in casual summits of extreme intimacy, in the midst of an orgy.

An orgy!

The very word sent a shimmer of excitement up my spine. It's something a girl always imagines in her secret dreams, but to actually be there, to be a part of it, was so amazing I had to pinch my pulsing nipples to make sure I didn't wake up to the chime of the chapel bell and realise I was late again. I wasn't late. I wasn't dreaming. I was wandering without haste through the grand hall stark naked, the leitmotiv of my new life. Far from being ashamed of the way I am, I was at peace with myself, knowing that it would have been impossible to be any other way. We become what we are.

I looked round for Simon Roche but couldn't see him. I recalled for some reason that day at my interview, how Heathcliff from *Wuthering Heights* had pressed into my imagination as Simon swept back his hair and fixed me with his penetrating eyes. It was at that moment that he peered into my schoolgirl mind and read my unknown desires.

Would he penetrate other parts of me that night at Black Spires? I really had no idea. Simon's desires seemed governed by his faith in discipline. He had stripped and spanked me in his office. He had taken me through the pain barrier to the heights of that embarrassing orgasm. He had guided me to the alcove containing the *prie dieu*. But it was Sergio Buenavista who had led the file of men who left on my flesh the gift of their warm semen.

I was certain Simon had not been among them. He appeared and disappeared like a shadow in the flickering glow of the candles, a good host ensuring his guests were accommodated. He was both present and absent, and when I joined the revelry, as I surely would, in my fantasy Cathy would finally know the touch of her Heathcliff.

Another chess game was in progress and two different girls in masks were leaking over the board as they conveyed the pieces in their fit young pussies. The girl in

134

the red mask had shaved her pubes to devil horns, which I thought totally brilliant, not that the devil's clasp prevented her dropping the red queen and scattering the opposing pawns.

We remained watching for a few moments, but the game after the brief upset grew monotonous and the erotic, I realised, needs constant change and variety; repetition is the death of desire.

It was so easy to wander blindly into the world of cliché. Most people do. They don't choose their lives. They follow the well-beaten path into the abyss of tedium and obscurity. I had been until this day, this night, nothing more than a reflection of society's rules and codes, its prescriptions and formulas. Girls from council estates get their lips pierced and a tramp stamp across their lower back; they dream of being a Page 3 girl and end up working in supermarkets. Girls from boarding school go to uni, dream of being TV presenters and marry men who work as bankers. The girls, rich and poor, have babies, the dreams perish and they stare into the mirror as lines carve disappointment into their faces. They grow old. They grow old quickly.

Simplistic? Of course. But no less true.

From Saint Sebastian, I had gone straight into an accountancy office to beef up my CV before starting at the London School of Economics. I was on that well-beaten path until temptation flashed across the computer screen and I was enticed by the deadly sin of greed, mesmerised by the unknown, lured to the high wire. The high wire is life, they say. Everything else is just waiting.

A faint smile pressed into my lips and the shiver of excitement running up my spine was replaced with the tang of want.

I wanted *everything*. I rolled my shoulders and stretched like a cat. I had guzzled the life-giving force from a dozen men and transformed their essence into raw energy, a new identity. I was a rare exotic bird from an endangered species. I had broken the shell of the cliché and was reborn as the girl I was supposed to be – not a girl, a woman, a slave to my senses.

Simon knew me better than I knew myself. He had divined my potential. I was there at that country house to receive and exchange and to pass on the gift. Didn't Sister Benedict always say, quoting You Know Who, that you reap what you sow. What you put out comes back in giddy unfathomable pleasures Simon Roche understood implicitly and I could only begin to imagine.

After half an hour upstairs with Milly, I had come to see that, when you submit, the potency of pleasure is that much greater. Just as the moon's light is a reflection of the sun, submission is a mirror image of domination, the yin to the yang, the perfect interplay of opposites.

Milly's fingers linked my own. The red queen had lost confidence after her spill and was under threat from an upstart black pawn.

'Mate in three,' she predicted.

She was right.

We journeyed on.

The girl illustrated with her lovers was suspended with arms outstretched between two columns, her bare feet spread and resting on the heads of two stone nymphs. The lips of her vagina were ornamented with two golden rings and the pink folds of her sex were dangling from the vine of her pubic hair like forbidden fruit on a tree in the Garden of Eden – not an apple, according to Sister Benedict, that was the wrong translation, but guava, the dark exotic fruit native to the Caribbean and South America, a detail, if true, which threw into question the veracity of the entire Old Testament.

This thought flitted through my mind as we passed under the arch of the girl's legs and I stretched up to drink from this upturned chalice.

'You're incorrigible,' Milly said.

'Thank you,' I replied.

The Arab and the Texan were talking quietly together.

'Oil prices,' Milly whispered. 'They decide.'

'Decide what?' I asked.

'How much oil costs per barrel.'

'But it's a market, surely, it fluctuates depending on supply and demand,' I said.

'That's what they want people to think. It's not like that. Nothing,' she emphasised, 'is ever as it seems.'

'It would be dull if it was,' I responded, something I'd read once, and it drew a smile from Milly.

I looked back at the two men totally oblivious to the sexual acrobatics being performed about the room.

'And they decide?' I repeated.

'The men here are the most powerful men in the world. Didn't you know that?'

No, I didn't know that, not that it came as a complete surprise. I glanced across the hall at Sandy Cunningham and Sergio Buenavista. They were sitting together in an alcove, Sandy with his trousers about his ankles, the Oriental girl on her knees sucking him off while he chatted with the Spaniard, and I couldn't help feeling a little rush of pride that Sergio at this moment did not appear to require the same service. I had sucked him dry.

'Sandy Cunningham?' I asked

'He owns CunniLingus.'

I was shocked. I used the cut-price airline every time I went to Spain. I remember the controversy over the name when the company was launched, but that had been calculated, it was all free publicity, and in less than two years CunniLingus was on everyone's tongue and the airline had become the biggest carrier in Europe. I knew. I had read the *Financial Times* every day while we were studying economics with Sister Agnes.

'Amazing,' I said, and glanced at Sergio.

'Wine,' she said. 'He owns half of Cataluña.'

'Simon?'

'You don't know?'

I shook my head. 'No, I don't know anything,' I admitted.

The men gathered at Black Spires were the men who made the decisions, Milly explained. *The* decisions. They were entrepreneurs, oil men, diplomats, media moguls, landowners and aristocrats – Sergio was the Duc de Peralada; they were financiers, bankers, the heads of international institutions, a cabal that stretches around the globe and promotes the careers of politicians whose views serve the interests of free trade and the multinational corporations.

'They are the king makers,' she continued. 'It is within their power to pick who governs.'

'What about democracy?' I said. 'Don't the people decide, one man, one vote?'

She smiled, those lovely lips like a rare bloom, one of *Las Señoras de la Noche.*

'No, Magdalena, it's not like that. The king makers choose. They know when it is a good time to have a war or a recession, when the war should end, and when optimism should replace fear and doubt. Chaos doesn't just happen, it is created – it keeps people in their place. And when chaos does happen naturally, in some disaster, they rebuild the stricken area in their own image – or, like in New Orleans after the hurricane, they leave it to rot. When people give money in those big charity appeals, they decide how and where that money is to be spent.'

I looked back at Milly aghast. 'But it can't be true,' I said.

'Remember the tsunami in Asia a couple of years ago?' she asked and I nodded. 'The aid money went to help international companies build tourist resorts in the places where the coast was cluttered with fishing villages and native communities. Tourists bring wealth and fishermen don't need pristine beaches to ply their trade.'

'But that's terrible . . .'

She shrugged. 'That's the way it is.'

'That doesn't mean it's right,' I returned.

'It doesn't mean it's wrong either.'

I thought about that and something else struck me. 'Why isn't there anything in the newspapers, on television?'

'There is, sometimes, little snippets. But they own the newspapers, they are the media. The *club*,' she said, stressing the word, 'began in the 1950s to counter what they saw as the threat of global communism. Now they shape the world to suit free enterprise – and the communists have joined the club.'

The Oriental girl had concluded her ministrations with Sandy and he was buttoning his flies before shaking hands with Sergio. Had a business deal been concluded? Would CunniLingus now be carrying Sergio's wine? Or was that too simple, too obvious? As Sister Agnes always said, you have to look below the surface of things, in the space between the numbers, in the subtext underpinning the words. I glanced around at the men, naked, dressed, half-dressed, the most beautiful girls you would ever see catering to their every whim and desire.

'The men here? In this hall?' I asked.

'They're not all here, Magdalena,' Milly said, as if answering a child. 'There are thousands across the world. They all know each other and they work together to make the world the way they think it ought to be.'

'At the expense of everyone else,' I said impatiently.

'They believe it is to the benefit of everyone. They are creating what they call the New World Order. War and famine are purely economic,' she said, and of course I understood that.

'I learned that at school,' I put in.

'They are working to make a world where free trade will finally do away with the need for war and famine.'

She gave another little shrug, as if this was a theory she neither believed nor disbelieved would work in practice. I gazed at her perfect lips, her perky breasts, her carved hipbones and taut tummy. It seemed weird to be standing there naked except for the bondage straps with this gorgeous creature discussing the intricacies of power politics, weird and yet, suddenly, not so weird.

What Milly had said made sense. It was something I had come to feel intuitively studying economics with Sister Agnes. She had left her job as a high-flyer on Wall Street to take holy orders; she was a dedicated teacher and I learned a lot from her, although the principles of economics are something you just know, as baby birds know how to fly. I had never bothered to think about the ramifications that deeply; at school, you want to get As, not change the world, and if you do want to change the world, then you'd better get those As first.

I stared into Milly's eyes. They were wise, knowing, composed, bright like chips of glass in a stained-glass window. Her voice reminded me of a wind-chime, delicate, at perfect pitch, those cupid lips turned in such a way that you could never imagine a lie passing through them. From the moment she had entered the room upstairs after my tantrum, I'd been certain I'd seen her before, that I knew her from somewhere.

'Who are you, Milly?' I asked.

She smiled. 'I was waiting for you to guess,' she answered and took my two hands. 'I'm an Old Basher.'

'What?' I almost fell over.

'Camilla Petacci. I left Saint Sebastian's when you were about fourteen,' she explained. 'I remember seeing you like a young pony hurrying through the corridors with your hair flying like a mane.'

'You must have been one of the older girls we were so envious of.'

'I suppose,' she said. 'I went to Cambridge and now . . .' She shrugged and glanced about the room. 'Now this is me.'

'That's, like, amazing . . .'

'Not really. If you think about it, we can do whatever we want. We are the lucky ones.' She glanced down at our naked bodies and gave her little shrug. 'We were born like this.'

'And you never wanted to do anything else?'

'I did think of becoming an actress,' she replied. 'I did a film that won a prize at Cannes. I was slated to do another with Tyler Copic . . .'

'Tyler Copic?' I was flabbergasted.

Milly nodded. Everyone knew Tyler Copic, not that I was interested in his movies; they were for me just propaganda, simplistic yarns about good and evil, with America the guys in the white hats, the emblem of all that is Good, the evil menace threatening the New World Order portrayed by terrorists or Russians or the Arabs.

'He's here somewhere,' Milly added, and glanced over my shoulder.

Tyler Copic was here. The Texan and the sheik were deciding world oil prices. Sergio owned Cataluña. It was incredible.

'Why didn't you make the film?' I asked.

'I got bored. I don't like being paraded around in public,' she replied with a smile. 'Not dressed, anyway.'

I sighed and all the air gushed from my body. I then remembered that Milly hadn't told me about Simon Roche.

'Simon?' I asked.

'It's like a mediaeval court. Simon's the chancellor,' she answered. 'If there is going to be a war or a famine, a billion dollars spent on aid in Africa, or a merger between two foreign banks, Roche-Marshall crunch the numbers.'

Everything had been worked out, planned, organised. War, famine, chaos and disaster were just strategies in the global game of chess. I went quiet as I let this sink in. Was this the adult world? The real world? Most people didn't know these things; they didn't even suspect these things. I was privy to the greatest secret of our times, a

conspiracy. The world of business, the media, of compe
tition was not how it seems. Nothing is how it seems, as
Milly had said.

'And us? Me and you, the others?' I asked her.

'You have to answer that question on your own.'

'What's your answer, Milly?' I said. 'What's you
future?'

'The future normally looks after itself,' she replied with
that characteristic shrug she had. 'I suppose I'll marry a
cabinet minister or a congressman – someone who need
a companion with a head on her shoulders. Women have
a more important role to play than you may think
especially educated women.'

'Join *them*?' I said, indicating the men in the hall with
my chin.

'Haven't you noticed? Even Arab monarchs have
pretty foreign wives and most of them have probably
passed through Black Spires.'

'Really!'

'Really.'

It was a lot to take in. I felt chosen and cheated, both
at the same time. I was here to give the gift of myself, and
would receive in exchange the gift of knowledge, of
touching and being touched by power: the ultimate
aphrodisiac, I'd heard it said.

'The members of the *club* are special and you are
special, Magdalena, or you wouldn't be here,' Milly
chimed in her melodious voice.

I felt lines furrow my smooth brow. Was I special? Or
was I just another shapely naked girl, here to serve the
fantasies of the most powerful men in the world?

We were facing each other, our breasts almost touching, and it occurred to me that it didn't matter. Nothing
matters except the present moment. The nude doesn't
have to see the entire staircase. Just the next step. I was
here now. In thirty-one days my debt would be paid. I
would be free and there would be another new day,

another beginning. I was, for this brief time, a part of the New World Order. A tiny part, an associate member, but it was an exciting time to be alive and I felt a faint spasm deep in my damp vagina. I was eighteen. Milly was twenty-two. I had plenty of time before I made any giant decisions.

She was standing motionless while my heart beat furiously in my chest. I admired Milly's stillness, just as I admired the way she moved like a bird on unseen waves of air, with unpretentious elegance. She wore her nakedness like an invisible suit of clothes. I had never seen her dressed, but it appeared that in rejecting clothes she was also rejecting the complex condition of womanhood in order to be a complete human being.

Milly had had the chance to become famous playing a role in a Tyler Copic film. But she didn't want to be famous. The famous give themselves to the great unknown public, to the fans and feature writers. They become icons and icons are in some peculiar way already dead. At Black Spires the girls in their nudity were the embodiment of life.

If Milly had been dressed, if all the girls had been dressed, the party at Black Spires would merely have been following the conventions of standard social gatherings, powerful men, pretty girls, bonking behind closed doors. By stripping away our clothes and dressing us identically in strategically placed black straps, the erotic quality of our true nature had emerged automatically, naturally. The girls had been turned into beautiful objects without challenging opinions and identities. The men of the New World Order were men who got straight to the heart of male desire and, I was beginning to suspect, female desire, too.

I gazed again at Milly, Camilla Petacci, a Cambridge graduate, an actress, an Old Basher, the most beautiful girl I had ever seen. I stared again into her widely spaced eyes and what I saw was a look of equanimity. She understood the quintessence of the gift and it seemed suddenly that, once you embrace this universal concept, everything falls into place; it is the key piece in the Chinese puzzle that makes all the other pieces fit together.

Once more I had that sense that I was in the right place at the right time. We were living in the new millennium, the age of freedom, of female self-determination and empowerment. My being there at that country house was an opportunity, not a punishment, the chance to mould myself into the epitome of grace and fleshly perfection. I wanted to realise my own slowly forming desires and exude the miraculous arousal of a woman desired before all men's eyes.

Knowing what you want is a long step towards getting what you want. My body was trembling with mysterious yearnings and nervous perspiration rose in a sheen over my skin. I felt tingles like cold fingers stroking the chords of my back bone. I was a Stradivarius waiting to be played.

Milly leaned forward, our breasts touched and I felt a burning sizzle in my nipples as she pressed her perfect lips to mine.

As we parted, I half turned and Sergio took my hand. '*Ven guapa,*' he said in Spanish.

And I was whisked through the hall, past the musicians playing something familiar, a movie theme from a Tyler Copic film, most probably. We passed below a wooden arch and reached another flight of stairs that I hadn't seen before. The Duc continued to hold my hand as we climbed the staircase to a passage lined on each side with closed doors.

We walked the length of the passage and entered a large, circular room, the tall, phallic-shaped space occupying one of the Norman towers at the far ends of the building. The curving walls were a continuous mirror such as you see in a ballet school, the arched windows above like blades of moonlight. The walls supported a dome made of countless mirror tiles, a mosaic where I could see myself cut and sliced and reflected in a million different ways.

The room was bare except for the black carpet on the floor and the round bed like a giant white lozenge below the dome. It was a room designed for one thing only.

Sergio closed the door behind me and watched as I strode on black heels around the perimeter of the room: Magdalena, the wayward girl from Saint Sebastian's endlessly repeated, stark naked in this sumptuous boudoir, her hair like black fire in the subdued lighting, the mirrors around me and above me allowing Sergio Buenavista to study my every curve and coil, my long legs climbing to that arrogant bottom, the slope of my V-shaped back reaching wide shoulders with well-defined shoulder blades, the source of angel wings waiting to grow, the swell of my breasts that had grown fuller since I entered the dark portals of Black Spires.

I could see myself, too, from every angle. Without clothes, except for the straps accentuating my sexuality, there is no fumbling, no foreplay, no doubt as to why I was there in this temple of mirrors. I felt neither vanity nor self-possession, but a sense of freedom, that air of equanimity I had seen about Milly.

The abstract perception of myself as a new school leaver stumbling into adult life had transformed into the solid reality of me as a marvellous gift of pure animal sexuality. I had always thought of myself, the inner me, and my simmering, unripe passions as two separate things, two concepts at odds with each other. Now, at that moment, in the infinity of reflections, I could only imagine my existence in terms of my passions. It was me in those mirrors, the real me. This is who I am, I thought. This is what I want.

Sister Benedict, like Simon Roche, had known that

right from the start. The Sister had tried to beat it out of me, and Simon over the arm of his sofa had beaten it into me.

I approached my prey and he drew me below one of the three chandeliers hanging on long chains from the dome. He took a grip on the heavy flesh of my lower lip and pinched down until my lip must have been as red as a rose in full bloom. He pulled me closer, a hand on the small of my back, and transferred my stinging lip into his mouth, biting down gently and sending quivers through my entire body.

He ran his hands over my shoulders, down my arms, over the line of my waist. He stroked my prominent hip-bones, my fluttering tummy. I was ready for anything, but anxious nonetheless. I wanted to be my best. My breasts were throbbing, jutting from me like the prows of pirate ships, the Jolly Roger flags of my flaming nipples demanding attention. I thought he would reach for them, squeeze them, bite me hard. But he didn't. He turned me round, unbuckled my belt, and dropped it on the floor at our feet. In the soft light of the chandelier he spent a long time studying my bottom. It was pink still from the beating and he prodded me with his fingertips to see, I suppose, how tender it was.

When I had first arrived at the house, after fending off Simon's lecherous poodles, Lee-Sun had led me upstairs to the dressing room and produced a bottle of ointment he said was arnica. I bent over the end of the narrow bed and, swallowing my pride, allowed him to rub the pale creamy liquid into my inflamed bottom. My first instinct had been one of acute embarrassment, the hub of my sex appearing through my burning thighs, the winking diamond of my bottom thrust in the air. But Lee-Sun's attention was solely therapeutic and I got the feeling that he had performed this task with spanked girls many times before. The fire in my bottom dampened down and the pain soon went away.

146

As Sergio began to caress the plumpness of my rounded cheeks, there was no pain, but I felt mortified as I started to leak, the oily juice gurgling from my pussy and coating my thighs. I was like a faulty tap that needed a new washer. And he was like a child with a toy, or a sculptor who had just finished carving a human figure and was admiring his masterpiece.

He stroked my back and my bottom as you would stroke a horse, in long, sensitive caresses, from the scruff of my neck, over the sloping curve of my prickling spine and down to the sopping place between my legs, each stroke drawing more creamy liquid from that never-ending well somewhere inside me. He eased my legs apart. He ran the flat of his hand between my cheeks and I was so wet there I heard sucking and slurping noises as the side of his hand sawed slowly back and forth. For some reason I visualised a knife cutting a birthday cake covered in whipped cream.

I would have been happy if this had gone on into eternity, just standing there below the shower of the chandelier's light gazing at myself replicated over and over again in the curving looking glass, while the Duc de Peralada, the man who owned half of Cataluña, plumbed the warm waters of my erotic nature.

Any lingering doubts I may have had about my role at Black Spires, and perhaps I had none, had faded like mist in sunshine. I was born to give and receive the gift of pleasure. I would never have been satisfied with one man, with groping hands, with clumsy boys. I wasn't built for it. I bored easily, I knew that. The sisters at the convent said that. I needed continual change and surprise, new demands and challenges. I had always considered myself special – most people do, I suppose – but now I knew in which way I was special. Just as Milly, that paragon of female perfection, recognised in Cannes that she was not born to be an actress, I knew, as I had always suspected, that the cold certainties of numbers would tire as I embraced the warm uncertainties of the flesh. I was naked, as a girl like me should be. I had found myself. This was my gift.

Of course I knew there were girls who reluctantly worked as prostitutes to feed drug habits or luxury lifestyles. Those girls hated what they were doing. It was a chore, a bore, a disgrace. They hadn't grasped that paid sex, vanilla sex, repetitive sex is not the same as the gift of sex, that the erotic is always consensual, that the pain of being bound and spanked must be measured against the pleasure. I may have been tricked into coming to Black Spires, I may have tricked myself, but I knew the moment I descended the sweeping staircase beside Milly, an Old Basher of all things, that I was where destiny in her modest way had always been leading me.

The Duc had fallen in love with my ass. He wanted to take that precious little plaything and place it like a Teddy bear on the pillows piled like a snow drift on his four-poster bed in his castle in Spain, a place I imagined with ivy climbing the walls and white swans on a silvery lake.

Juice was running in a stream down my legs and tickling my ankles. If he kept on caressing my backside, his warm hand stirring my reservoir of sticky liquids, I would leak over the floor and flood the carpet in a scene that could have been envisioned by Isabel Allende, that syrupy substance climbing the walls, coating the mirrors, consuming us in a human sacrifice, that macabre, primitive, oddly exciting ceremony we had touched on once at school with daring Sister Nuria.

It is always the most beautiful girl in the tribe who is chosen to pacify the Gods. She is stripped of her garments and I recall the Sister saying that being naked while others are dressed is in itself a form of sacrifice, a reminder of a long-forgotten ritual, a practice remembered and acknowledged in that house of fun and commerce by those men who ruled the world.

I had always wondered why they choose only the most desirable girls as offerings, and it was suddenly clear to me: ugliness would be an affront to the Gods. Ugliness is a compromise, a stingy gift. Ugliness cannot be spoiled and to despoil as well as to caress is the interplay at the heart of eroticism. The sacrifice of beauty gives meaning to beauty as well as mortality, and I understood something I had read once in a book that I wasn't supposed to read: that assenting to erotic pleasure is assenting to pleasure to the point of death.

My mind was turning, churning, spinning, chattering to itself, zooming off every which way. My body was electric and my head was exploding with new ideas and sensations. Sweat beads formed pearl necklaces over my back and juice dripped down my legs and slipped inside my high-heel shoes. I had come a long way since climbing into the silver Range Rover in the garage in London to set off on this miraculous journey. I had learned more about love, sex, the erotic, the gift of being a girl and the gift of giving myself as a girl in two hours than I'm sure most girls learn in a lifetime.

When Sergio ceased his caresses and slapped my bum with the flat of his hand, it woke me from my trance. For a moment, I wasn't sure where I was and only remembered when I saw a ring of Magdalenas stretching around the walls of the room.

'Ouch,' I screamed.

'This is nothing, *cariña*,' he said, his perfect English slipping. 'Now, you can bend over.'

I paused for a fraction of a second, then did as I was told. He picked up my leather belt, doubled it over, and brought it down across the curve of my protruding bottom, first one cheek, then the other, the crack ringing out and echoing over the mirrored dome.

It was painful, but not as painful as Sister Benedict's cane, and, as the belt came down for another taste of my sweet flesh, it struck me like a revelation that the Sister had beaten me in her office with a sense of cruelty, but Sergio was thrashing me in a mood of fiery passion, that an object of beauty, like my bottom, I assumed, must first be spanked and sullied in order to be cherished and worshipped. It was another enduring symbol of the sacrifice; it was the reversal of normal conventions and the erotic, I decided, entails the breaking down of those conventions, of established patterns, of preconceived ideas.

My desires had been immature to the point of naiveté. I wanted sex, lots of sex. I was a hot, healthy young girl of eighteen with an eternal if shameful leak between my legs and breasts bursting to break through my clothes when I was wearing them. I was constantly in rut. But that thirst for knowledge that strikes girls of my age is often disappointing.

Sex in the standard legs up, cock in, spunk over your belly sort of way leaves you wondering what all the fuss is about. Sex without orgasm is like champagne without the bubbles. I'd sneaked down to the bottom field to meet the local grammar school boys at sunset enough times to know how frustrating the experience can be, their fingers like grappling irons clawing at your knickers, the way they slip in and slip out like a thief in the night leaving little more than an empty space and a sense of inertia. Sex has to be full on, overpowering, all-absorbing and the sex that follows acts of sadomasochism had to be most gratifying. Being spanked stirs your passions, it makes your nerve endings vibrate, it releases all those boiling juices bubbling inside you.

It was good to have these thoughts passing through my mind as Sergio Buenavista dealt with the other end of my body and brought that leather strap down for another lash, much harder this time.

'Ouch,' I cried again.

It stung like hell and drew a surging gout of juice from my sopping pussy. It's an odd sensation, the vinegary

150

stripe of fire across the lower cheeks of your cute little ass, then this urgent spasm that runs parallel with the sting up your spine into that crucible in your brain where pleasure and pain are mixed into the alchemical potion I presumed was ecstasy. The body builds a tolerance for all sensation, even pain, particularly pain, and you start to need more. Sergio was burning up his energy, and I found myself relaxing, accepting the pain and drawing that energy into myself.

He kept this up, thrashing my backside with the same rhythm as the drummer beating his snare in the hall downstairs, the pace slowly gaining momentum, and it suddenly occurred to me that this was a flamenco beat. The Duc de Peralada was a matador and I was a bull being prepared for his sword.

With the next thrash across my rosy cheeks, I turned and reared up at him. I roared from deep in my throat and moved back to the curved edge of the room. I kicked off my teetering heels, scraped my toes through the black sand of that shaggy carpet and charged, head down, my forefingers making horns. He managed to pull off his jacket with the red silk lining and turn it into a cape. He was quick, but not quick enough. I caught him a glancing blow as he executed a two-handed pass they call a veronica.

'Bravo! Bravissimo!' he roared.

The bull in the bullring always returns to the same spot, the place where it feels safest. I did the same. I caught my breath as he pulled off his bow tie and shirt. His muscles rippled on his broad chest. His dark eyes were lit with glints of light from the chandelier. I charged again. I thought I was ready for his trick with the cape, but, as I was about to make contact, he pirouetted in an elegant swirl and I stumbled across the circular bed, the moonlight like silver daggers spearing the windows.

He jumped on top of me. 'Now I've got you, my little *toro*,' he said.

I wriggled to get free, but he was strong. He enjoyed the struggle and so did I. He pinned me down with his knees and took a grip on my arms. Captured game tastes sweetest and he licked my wet underarms, my chin, my cheeks. He tasted my inflamed lips, his tongue caressing my teeth, my throat as if in search of the semen he'd left there earlier in the evening.

As he kissed me, he stretched my arms back and hooked the straps on my wrists to two of the rings set conveniently and evenly spaced around the entire edge of the bed. I was netted, bagged. I was his. He stood away from the bed and as he dropped his clothes on the floor I watched his movements repeated endlessly in the circle of mirrors.

He looked into my eyes as he jerked his cock very slowly up and down. My lips were ablaze and my mouth had dropped open.

'*Qué boca*,' he said – what a mouth.

He climbed on the bed and as he slipped his cock down my gaping gullet I had a body memory of this warm, olive-scented piece of the Spanish aristocracy conquering the soft tissues and delicate membranes of my mouth. Just as I had walked the perimeter of the room, I rimmed the outer edges of the eye of his cock with the tip of my tongue and felt him judder in spasm as he withdrew.

He was in no hurry. He left my throat to run his tongue into the dripping gash between my arched legs. I opened for him like a flower and like a little bee he buzzed around the enlarged nub of my pulsing clitoris, poking, licking, caressing, each manoeuvre taking me higher into the thin air of places where I had never been before.

And a silly thought slipped through my mind. I thought one day I would write this memoir of being eighteen so that grammar school boys would know that when girls tiptoe from the convent to find them at sunset they should seal their lips and eyes with tender kisses, gently draw down their panties and slip that talkative tongue into the honey pot of their sopping eager pussies. If only you knew, that's what girls dream of.

I pushed my shoulders back, I spread my legs, I lifted my bottom from the round bed and wanted to draw that tongue, that head, that man inside me. I wanted to hold on to his shoulders and had to make do with pulling against the rings binding my wrists. I could receive pleasure but only in ways Sergio dictated. I could see that, once a man grants rights to a woman and removes her restraints, he imposes limits on himself.

Sergio had complete power over my pussy and took that insatiable little beast to places I never imagined existed. His tongue was a conquistador and my clitoris was an unexplored continent dreaming of being subdued, crushed, dominated. I had stopped thinking, counting, calculating and was overcome with pure sensation. There was no past, no future, just this smooth, constant motion, this perfect dance. I could feel contractions, and clenched his tongue with my powerful vaginal muscles, the action making him gag as he reached still deeper down the channel of my screaming vagina. I was going to come, and already the moment of *petit mort* was chasing behind my orgasm.

As the contractions grew in pace, he withdrew his tongue from my pussy and my body deflated like a Christmas balloon as he rolled me back in such a way that my toes were touching my secured wrists. He now slowly, forcefully eased that lively lingua into my tight little bottom, in and out, in and out; the man was a machine softening the anal muscles, teaching them that their task of pushing down can be reversed to draw alien objects up, up into unknown forests of sensation and pleasure, the pressure from his tongue crossing the narrow bridge of my perineum to tease the demanding fires of my clitoris.

Boys. Boys. Boys. You have so much to learn.

Girls. Girls. Girls. Let yourself go with the flow.

There is in fairgrounds an amusement where strong men wield wooden mallets, striking down on a wooden peg, the force of the blow driving a marker up a tall column towards a bell. Ring the bell and you win a prize.

That was me, the bell was my clitoris and, as the marker rose higher and higher, Sergio withdrew his tongue and filled my back passage with his fierce cock, the probing, heavy-headed mallet driving up inside me until I exploded and all my bells rang out as in the finale of Tchaikovsky's *1812 Overture*. The cannon boomed. The percussion exploded. I'd been well and truly ass-fucked, actually for the first time, though not the last that night. I was a bottle of champagne and the Duc de Peralada had filled me to the brim with bubbles.

He collapsed and lay on top of me, sweating and quivering, totally spent. He had left his essence in my mouth and, revived, rejuvenated, he had left a fresh supply in the deepest part of my body.

'*Voy a comprarte de Simon,*' he whispered. '*Venga conmigo.*'

I lay there wondering what this implied.

Sergio Buenavista was going to *buy* me from Simon. I was going with him. He had power over me. But I now had a certain power over him.

That is the way of the gift, I thought, the exchange.

Should I tell him now that I spoke Spanish? Did he already know? I lay there thinking so hard for a suitable remark I didn't say anything. My breath slowly came back and my heart stilled. He rolled to one side, slipped from the bed and I watched him dress.

'You stay,' he said. Then he did something sweet. He leaned over and kissed me very gently on the lips.

He left me now and I studied myself in the mirrors above, my arms pulled back, my legs spread on the round bed with its white sheet stained with sperm trickling

154

warmly from my humming ass and juice from my dizzy pussy.

The room grew silent in anticipation. A few minutes passed and another man entered. I didn't recall having seen him before.

11

Being and Fantasy

Every man is different. They are like snowflakes. They
have their patterns and designs, their character and
temperament, flavour and tempo, their fantasies and
fervent thirsts. They are like boys with toys that have
moveable parts.

Some are big, so meaty and solid you feel in your belly
the pulse of their burning balls of fire. Others are petite,
slender as lolly sticks, and it needs all the cunning
vibrations of your thigh muscles and vagina walls to
remunerate their feverish efforts.

Some are in a rush. Wham Bam Thank You Ma'am.
In and out as if there's a fire on the first floor, or the last
virgin is about to be sacrificed. They impale you like
spear fishermen on the South China Seas, like javelin
throwers at the Olympics, like darts players in the pub,
leaving their marker in you or over you.

I'm in there.

I'm outta here.

You're just the quickie before more urgent things drive
them onwards and upwards. They scurry and they sweat.
They lose their hair. Their focus. They know there's a
secret. They feel it. Sense it. They calculate if they move
fast enough they'll get there, they'll win the race, they'll
learn the secret.

But they never will. Those men are the progeny of the
legendary hare. It is the tortoise who wins the race.

Unhurried, dogged, deliberate, the tortoise knows that life is a mystery solved with persistence. He's prehistoric. He has been among us for a million years and, when you sift through every grain of earthly promise, the seed that flowers into the brightest bloom is the slow-growing, seldom-seen erotic. The tortoise knows that.

The hares are narcissists, the alpha males, the ego-maniacs terrified that just around the corner there may be a better hole to bore, a new bit of stuff that's sexier, prettier, curvier, younger, more flexible, more intelligent, with longer legs, a longer tongue, bigger tits, a better ass, a better attitude. These guys are in such a hurry they have never found the time to learn that of all life's pleasures the erotic is at the peak, above the treeline and clouds, that what they give out will come back a hundredfold. A thousandfold. What a sad Neanderthal bunch of brain-deads they are. They've never grown up from being schoolboys. They are and will remain forever on the bottom field.

Other men are patient, ponderous, like a philatelist with a rare stamp, or a scientist with a new species of flora. Like a mathematician with algebraic puzzles, or a topographer surveying land, they want to analyse every angle and turn, every hill and dale, every curve and fissure with its moist secrets and inexplicable erogenous zones where a mere touch or a breath can set pulses racing and knees atremble. These connoisseurs of the female form want to smack you, spank you, whip and cane your white flesh until it is patterned with the geometry of their deepest lusts. Your body is an abacus and the maestro sets your beads flying.

Why does a man want to beat you?

He wants to beat you because in the thrall of domina-tion and submission you find the chemistry of sexual oblivion. You find your true self. You find the absolute: total sexual gratification. Weird, I know, but true and I would advise every girl to try it.

To the stamp collector you are the celebrated Penny Black. He wants you in his album below a sheet of tissue, in a display case, nakedly on show. He wants you this way and that: prone as a missionary spouse doing her duty to king maker and country, looming above like a harem concubine who reminds him oddly of mummy in those days when she peered down at baby in his cot and the love in her eyes stirred the little member sleeping in his nappy. He wants to see you on the floor balanced on hands and toes, breasts swinging like pendulums striking the hour in a grandfather clock, back at an angle, the pink feast of your pussy open like a rip in the universe, soft as velvet, sweet as rose petals below the dark gaze of your puckered anus.

Agh, the angst of choice: the dripping, sweet-smelling rose or the pungent fruit from the Judas tree?

Or both!

Like the tortoise.

I felt detached, freed from the chains of choice, my nerve endings keened with a desire for esoteric wisdom, for pleasures and experiences on the very edge of my imagination. I wanted to swim like a fish and fly like a bird. When you are young and naked with your life before you, anything may happen. Every girl fantasises about having a stream of lovers. I was living the fantasy. It was hallucinogenic, a drug trip on nothing more than a flute of champagne and a feast of fresh semen. My brain was humming, my body was bathed in perspiration. I was the perfect object, the guava hanging ripe and shiny from the Tree in the Garden of Eden, ready to be used, abused, defiled and worshipped. I was the virgin sacrifice.

With my wrists fastened to the bed and stretched above me, I could smell the almond scent of my underarms. My heart was beating fast, my stomach muscles clenching and unclenching. Being bound was a dance of conflicting emotions: arousal and acquiescence, and panic too, like the moment before the curtain rises and you go on stage.

After Sergio Buenavista left me with the aftershocks of that bell-ringing finale, the first man to come through the door immediately unclasped the bracelets from the rings on the side of the bed and set me on all fours. My well-tanned backside like a monkey's mating display was waggling in the air, my back bowed in a shallow curve, my breasts swayed and my nipples were pinging like fireworks.

Men like this position, this simian pose, down on hands and knees, my spread cheeks like open curtains revealing the treasure kept hidden within the neat nips and tucks of my pretty bum which I could see in all its shiny glory in the clever arrangement of the mirrors. The man said something in a language that made no sense to me, spat on his fingers, wet the mine shaft of my back passage and shoved his cock straight inside that innocent chasm. His trousers were about his ankles, his jacket slapped about like the sail of a ship and no sooner had he started than he stopped.

'Turn, turn about,' he said urgently.

I turned, dropped down on my haunches, took his thrusting dagger in my mouth, massaged his balls, and in two seconds he was pumping warm sperm down my throat, a stream of one hundred per cent protein. He took the back of my head in his two hands, pushed in harder. His blunt helmet tickled my tonsils and I could taste the sweet girlie secretion of my own bottom – and it wasn't bad at all.

He withdrew his withering apparatus and retreated from the room without a word, and I wasn't surprised when I was later told that he was the Prime Minister from one of those anonymous countries that used to be a part of the old Soviet bloc and would have remained forgotten if it weren't for their oil and gas, for the pipeline snaking its way underground to the new container ports built by the Americans on the Caspian Sea.

How judicious of the men of the New World Order, I thought, to draw these old communist apparatchiks into their complex game, this bacchanal of free market sex and global domination. And how fascinating that the delights of the flesh and the demands of commerce should be so manifestly intertwined, two lovers carved from the same block of stone.

It was an obvious market strategy, but not one that had occurred to me studying economics at Saint Sebastian. I had lived as most people live, like a horse in blinkers, and I felt as if the scales had peeled from my eyes. There is so much to this life that the man in the street doesn't understand and I felt honoured to have this glimpse of the secret. Like Milly, I could see suddenly that being a part of this world above the clouds was a privilege as well as a pleasure.

I sighed with contentment and wriggled like a fish. The room was warm. The round bed was huge, a pearl-white dais, and I lay there like a precious stone in the jewellers, my image passing endlessly from mirror to mirror. As I gazed at my dissociated form, my only regret was that there was no time for reflection among all those reflections. The door closed and the door opened. It was like a pub door, a revolving door that led to the tower room, and another man I didn't recall was making his way in.

He was plump around the middle and wore a clip-on bow-tie – *déclassé*, mother would have said, *nouveau riche*. He unceremoniously unclipped his tie and pulled open his shirt to reveal the lush coat of fur covering his chest. He tugged his black leather belt from the loops of his trousers with a saucy snap and doubled the length into his right hand.

'I'm Kurt. You want to play around?' he said; it sounded like a line from a Quentin Tarantino movie.

'Ooo, yes please,' I replied.

He was standing between the door and the bed. He approached, slapping his palm with the leather belt. I rolled backwards from my prone position and landed on my feet. He chased me around the perimeter of the bed, wielding the belt like a horse whip, but I was far too fast for him. The lash cracked the air behind me but the tongue never reached my wiggling bottom. He tried a new tactic and ran across the bed. I allowed him to get close and did a back flip, landing on my feet. His eyes came out on stalks and, as he continued the chase, I did front rolls round and round the circular room, Kurt whooping and shouting and splitting the air with the bite of his belt.

He was tired a long time before me. He made one last desperate charge, tripped over his shiny shoes and collapsed, crumpling like road-kill against the mirror. He sat up and watched, shaking his head in disbelief as I coolly stretched backwards, placed my hands on the floor behind me so that my feet were facing one way and my hands the other. I arched my body in a perfect circle, making the sign of Ω, the twenty-fourth and last letter of the Greek alphabet. In astronomy Omega refers to the density of the universe, as Pi is a mathematical constant which represents the ratio of a circle's circumference to its diameter.

God, would I ever leave school behind me?
Where was I?

Aah, yes. I walked very slowly towards him like some imaginary creature from the *Island of Doctor Moreau*, my hair a long mane dragging behind me, my open pussy like the eye of the Cyclops.

Kurt stood to admire this arrangement of enticement and suppleness. He dropped his belt, flipped his erection from his trousers and cautiously slipped it inside me. In this position I could do nothing but maintain my balance and use all my powers of pussy control to clasp the length of his cock, my vaginal muscles clenching and releasing with contractions.

I got the feeling that this guy was one of those speed jockeys, the wham bam off to the races type. But with my slippery young crack presented in this unique way, he

161

became a tortoise; he discovered his serene self. He took his time, filled me to the brim with his pudgy thick cock, withdrew and pushed in again, slowly, slowly, until I felt the spasm gripping his body focus like a laser beam around the head of his engulfed penis. He paused, as do the old on the stairs, or parachutists making their first jump, then released his sperm, pumping the stuff out in slow steady jerks as if wringing the last drop of water from a canteen in the middle of the desert. He was panting like an old cart horse.

'Very gut. Very gut. You very gut,' he moaned.

He slid from me and, pushing from my fingers, I straightened up in one effortless motion. He was spent, but I was relaxed, refreshed, re-energised. Sperm was oozing from me, creaming my thighs, coating my crotch with the aroma of lust, that mesmerising scent, that supernatural elixir that persuaded the Greeks to launch a thousand ships – it wasn't Helen's face that drove them to folly and war. How absurd. It was her allure, her looks, her mystery, her magic and, most of all, her smell. The Greeks understood the powers of Omega and Pi but not the whims of a woman.

I breathed in deeply through my nostrils. I could smell all about me the reek of lasciviousness, the matted copse of my glistening pubes sheltering the lips of my sodden pussy, that clump of fur I loved to stroke and fondle like a little pet or a stuffed toy.

I felt in my round room of many mirrors like a satiated little animal, like a red-assed monkey in the midst of a marvellous experiment, like a bird in a mirrored cage. I was the cocoon girl metamorphosed into the butterfly woman, ensnared by Simon Roche, yet free to be all that I am and all that I may ever be. I may with my nudity and bondage straps have lost facets of my individuality, the memory of who I thought I was, but the men who shed their seed in the dome of my vagina lost aspects of their individuality, too. Only through merging your self into the oneness of pure debauchery could you reach the heights of the erotic.

I realised, too, that I had been thinking along these libidinous lines for a long time. It wasn't sudden. Not really. Didn't I, in my quest to learn how to beat the casinos, allow Sandy Cunningham to take me on a totally licentious journey? I had told myself immediately before and immediately after that it was awful, shameful, a terrible trial, but, if truth be told, it came as easily as breathing. My clothes were off and his cock was up my bum on that hotel bed in about the same amount of time that it takes for me to swim two lengths of the swimming pool.

That was me. The real me. That was the girl who had begun to appear in the mirror during my last year at Saint Sebastian, the look in her eyes growing ever more knowing, more aware, more sensual. The girl in the reflection was replacing the inexperienced schoolgirl gazing into the long mirror in the shower room and, as her body changed, swelled, re-formed, the girl I had been slowly vanished to be reborn as the girl I am.

As I lay back on that round bed in that circular room aromatic with lust, it was obvious that I should have found my way into the New World. As people are born to be leaders, to win Olympic medals or to clean lavatories, I suppose, we are each one of us born with a purpose, a talent. We speak of talent as a gift. The secret of life is to discover who you are, to be the best you can be, to nurture your gift and share your gift as an artist shares the gift of his written or carved or painted work. When we are moved by an object of art, we are grateful that the writer or artist created that work, that he dug deep in the quarries of his gift and brought it to the surface.

The girls gathered at Black Spires were conscious of their gift. They found genuine pleasure in sharing their gift, and it occurred to me that unhappiness, depression and disappointment awaited those unable to explore and enjoy the miracle of their divine talent, that one special gift.

The girls were slender, ethereal, dainty, svelte, yet with perfectly round bottoms, lean waists and unusually full breasts. Even barefoot, they walked as if in heels, their naturally full hair heavy on well-defined shoulders, their eyes gleaming like stars in the sky. Naked, their bodies ingeniously cut by the six leather bands, they were a breed apart, a different species, and it was a relief and a strange joy to know that I was one of them. I had fooled myself into thinking I was born for a career calculating numbers, although I had, I recalled, begun to suspect as my bottom curved and my breasts filled out that my gift lay elsewhere, less in figures than my figure. Sister Benedict had known it, too. That bottom, her eyes informed me, had to be spanked.

Girls like Melissa and Sarah were not born for this life, as they were not born to taste the Sister's cruel cane. Melissa carried too much *avoirdupois*, big thighs, breasts like udders, objects of amusement more than desire. Sarah was anorexic with sunken cheeks and arms thin as matchsticks. Girls required slenderness, not thinness, a sense of grace without heaviness. Girls born with the gift were born blessed with the eternal, perfectly proportioned physique of the feminine ideal: the beauty that must be profaned at the height of the erotic in order to reach the erotic, the core of the gift that sleeps deep within and awakes in the chosen woman.

If we look at engravings of Helen of Troy on ancient coins and shields, or the maidens copulating with men and gods carved on the walls of caves in India, or at the girls offering up their bottoms to be thrashed and filmed on Far East Media, through three millennia they all have the same willowy-ripe busty innocence, they all have that ill-defined flawlessness men want to beat and adore.

There is a moment, a precise second, when a girl becomes a woman. It's that moment when you notice men looking at you and you know what they are looking for. They are measuring your breasts pushing through your high-buttoned blouse, the roundness of that saucy bottom wiggling by in a pleated skirt down the high street, the turn of your plump lips they want to consume, as the Duc de Peralada had done as soon as he got the chance. It's the time when Sister Benedict starts bending you over the desk so that she can lower your knickers and tan your backside, beat all that ripe sensuality out of her convent.

Whatever it was the Mother Superior hoped to achieve, beyond her own gratification, it didn't work. It never works. Girls like me have to be what they were born to be. There is in each of us the propensity for all extremes both good and evil, the escape valve that saves us from mediocrity. Are we that different from the kidnapper, the assassin, the thief? If temptation is put in your way, as it was put in mine, is it not natural to take the prize, slip the gold ring on your finger, the $100 bill into your palm, to transfer £3,100 from the company account into your own? If you were a fat cat banker with the prerogative to pay yourself a million-dollar bonus would you be able to resist?

The men who came into that room were tempted and lured by this eager young girl bonded to the New World Order, bonded by black bracelets and anklets, with breasts yearning to be touched and a lush-smelling crotch that grew wetter and more desirable with each coupling. Those men were doing what comes naturally to powerful men, to all men, I imagine, and it was both a surprise and a revelation to realise that it came naturally to me, too.

I felt no shame, no ignominy, no doubts. Heaven forbid! I felt good about myself. It was a pleasure parading around starkers. It was pure bliss being crowned the queen of the mirror room and taking those men whose names I didn't even know into my body without the bourgeois, time-wasting game of getting to know you, without preliminaries and foreplay. I was spring flower bursting with nectar and they were a swarm of hornets darting into my sticky parts with the gift of their juicy liquids. I was created, it seems, to spend time on my back, on my front, on my knees. I was born to enjoy sex in every possible form and position, and what better time to indulge this craving than now, at the age of eighteen, at my succulent best.

I stretched and sighed with a sense of wellbeing, feeling I hadn't really had since Daddy announced that he was selling the house in the country, our flat in Lowndes Square, the Andy Warhol print of Clint Eastwood he'd acquired in a moment's excitement in New York, his cherished Cessna SkyCatcher, Mummy's jewellery, my brother's future, my own. I had cried for a week. Mummy was still crying. Then I woke up. I dried my eyes. I applied to be an accountancy intern and I took Melissa's advice, and dressed to kill for that interview with fate. The path through life, it seems, is like helter-skelter and once you push off from the top of the chute you spiral round and round and down and down until with your head spinning you arrive at who you are.

We are, each of us, the master of our own ship. I felt positive, optimistic, more alive. Something had crossed over in me, perhaps it was the reality of growing up. When I strode naked through the Roche-Marshall building, it wasn't only my clothes that I'd left behind. I had left the child, the schoolgirl, the past, the fear. I would have to redirect my destiny, make my own future, and it started here, now, in this round room of many mirrors among the most powerful men in the world.

I had quite forgotten Kurt, the Quentin Tarantino extra. I lay there on the big bed enjoying my own smell, as all animals do, and watched as he pushed his belt back through the loops in his trousers.

'Very gut,' he said.

Then he was gone and another man appeared. The fourth, was it? Maybe the seventh? Perhaps the tenth? Was it an odd number or even? A prime or square root? It was hard to keep score, to keep count. And it occurred to me that under normal circumstances a girl might sleep with eight or ten men in a month, even a year. In that old Norman mansion in the aura of orgy, there need be no end to the number of men you could drain and entertain in one long night. I lay, spread like a starfish on that circular ten-foot platform staring at an infinity of Magdalenas in the mirror tiles of the dome above my head, each reflection a different angle, a different aspect, a different suggestion of what we might be in life.

The door opened. I watched the man whom I had first seen spanking the twins, before doing them as a pair, approach with another, quite similar-looking man in the same sort of dinner suit, the same swagger and look of confidence.

'The oyster in the shell,' said the first man, gazing at me spread out on the bed.

The other was removing his clothes. They both did. Beads of sweat were coursing between my breasts; there must have been under-floor heating and the temperature was rising.

Ravisher One licked away the sweat, tasting me, and started nibbling my nipples, his stiffening cock pushing gently against my hipbone. Number Two spread my legs and pushed his tongue into that discreet arch containing the firebird, that mythical creature men know is there even if they can't always find it. He found it.

This was nice, one above and one below, my body a playground for inquisitive teeth and tongues.

'Wow, she's wet,' said Number Two, an American.

'It's my hormones,' I whispered and he laughed.

Number One straddled my neck and tapped my closed lips with his mauve helmet, knock, knock, knock. I opened the door, allowed it entrance, this salty, fishy thing that had been locked in his underpants with a vague hint of the emerald twins, and I wondered if the two girls had the same smell, or if all girls were different, that like fingerprints we are blessed with an individual scent. It was something I thought I might study when I got the chance.

Number One's silky cock slithered down my throat and I did my trick as it drew back again. I stippled the tip of my tongue around the indentation. Then, I pressed down with my teeth before opening my gullet once more and drawing it down, down, deep inside the sensory cathedral of my gaping mouth.

Number Two had given up invigorating my clitoris. Sitting with legs spread for balance, he lifted my thighs over his torso and his cock went scurrying like a hungry serpent up inside my insatiable pussy.

They were like two men rowing a boat, getting into a steady rhythm, two cocks gliding inside me at the same time, one in my mouth, the other in my vagina, and I knew before the night was through I would know what it was to take a third, to be filled with cock, and honestly couldn't wait.

It was deep-rooted in me to want to overstep the limits, to sell my soul in the surreal frenzy of orgy. Mummy believed a woman's role was to be obedient, something she taught me but never practised herself. It made me sad that my beautiful mother had never learned that discipline and corporal punishment weren't humiliating and undignified. *Au contraire.* All fleshly pleasures are empowering, emancipating. Those black leather bands decorating my naked body were a symbol of freedom, a sign that I had broken the chains of an imposed and artificial respectability, a morality that belonged to that part of society that was deadly dull and really not for me.

A woman is fulfilled by being filled. We are born with wet vacant places designed to be plugged. This is a truth, an axiom, and understanding that is at the heart of female liberation. We are taught to be ambitious, to shatter the glass ceiling, but this I thought was bogus and wrong. Our role as animals is to continue the species. Our role as women is to seek the quintessence and core of our sexuality. Knowing that, feeling it on my skin, was like opening a safe door and finding the key of life.

As the man with the cock in my mouth stiffened, the spasm clanged the bell on my vibrating tonsils and the echo travelled through my gut, into my belly, ricocheting over the walls of my vagina and gripping the cock delving down inside me. As the first released a gout of semen, the second answered as if it was a tennis ball to beat back over the net. He tensed, he paused, and let go his load. They were shivering and trembling, but I felt relaxed, fed, nurtured, in control of my gift.

They rolled away, panting for breath, and a third man appeared through the revolving door. He threw off his clothes as he dissected the room, dived in among the sweating bodies and began kissing me violently, grabbing my hipbones, squeezing my breasts until they tingled with pain, biting down into that part of my neck just above the collarbone that sends tremors of pleasure shimmying down your backbone. He was grunting and panting like a wild dog with fresh prey. I wriggled from his grasp and, as I was about to vault from the bed, Number One caught me in a rugger tackle and swung me over on to my stomach.

On seeing my red bum, the new arrival buried his head between my cheeks and drilled his long tongue deep into the hidden valley. He came out panting.

'Delicious,' he yelled.

His cock soon followed, jabbing into me, a young boxer in the ring leading with a series of swift rights. His arms coiled under me, filling his palms with my breasts. He took my nipples in the thumbs and first fingers of both hands and squeezed down so hard I squealed in ecstasy, in that peculiar pain sensation that isn't pain in any normal sense.

In one swift movement, he rolled on to his back, and kept pushing into my tight bum with me spread-eagled across his broad chest. Number One, who had just climaxed in my mouth, had found enough vigour to join the fray and climbed on top, pushing his cock limply up into the pool of semen left by Number Two. Number Two straddled me and the guy below me in order to push his pussy-juiced member into my gaping mouth.

Your wish is my command. Ask and it shall be given. Knock and the door shall be opened.

It seemed as if the moment I imagined taking three men at once, the universe answered my call and I lay there, as lucky as any girl can be, our quartet like the jazz musicians in the grand hall finding harmony and rhythm, our bodies joined like a machine mining precious substances.

I could see fully now the benefit of the many mirrors. I was facing the ceiling, my mouth filled with cock, but I could see in a long series of reflections a fourth man enter the room with Milly. They were holding hands like lovers. When they reached the bed, the man stepped from his clothes and lay down on his back. Milly straddled him, took his cock up inside her, and the alpha male with his cock in my mouth removed his member and transferred it to Milly's mouth.

What did I taste like? I wondered.

We were four men and two girls.

A sextet.

I smiled as I stretched my aching jaw. I am an instrument in a sextet, a high note in the New World Order. It occurred to me that these men of big business spilling their seed together were united in a way that a thousand board meetings could never achieve. They needed no contracts, no handshake. Their naked body was their bond, their signature, and I and Milly and all

170

he girls at Black Spires were the links in the chain that held them together. The glue, the gum, the gluck. They needed us. We were a part of something bigger and more important than I understood, perhaps more important than I could understand.

This, I thought, is what life is. This is how it works. People want to let go, strip naked and follow their base instincts wherever they may lead them. The masters of the universe understood this: when you have everything, wealth, power, respect, achievement, connections, what remains?

The orgy.

All the people out there reading their newspapers and watching their TV sets were listening to politicians and pundits with about as much power to intervene in events as the captain of the *Titanic* when his ship struck that fateful iceberg. Everything that Milly had said earlier made sense now on that round bed with our stripped bodies magnified to infinity.

The man below me shot a cannonball of hot spunk up my bum and a little squirt, small as a tear, was released by the man in my vagina. He'd done well. I'd done well. Our bodies collapsed in a boisterous pile. There were lips and mouths everywhere, kissing, licking, biting, and I'm sure I saw Number Four, the man who'd arrived with Milly, take Number Three's cock in his mouth, and I thought, why not, they are probably partners. I found myself kissing Milly and realised that kissing men would never have quite the same appeal. Girls' lips are soft, tender, sugary, plump and taste of heaven. They are made to be kissed and being kissed was a pleasure every bit as great as having three cocks filling my three orifices.

As our lips parted and another cock wound its way into my mouth, it was impossible to know who it belonged to, and this lack of a face and name, of the man's persona, his character, his being, made it all the more pleasurable. There was an equality on that circular

171

dais, that lozenge of white linen. Our individualities were consumed in the pure sweet decadence of the orgy, an almost spiritual ritual that allowed my soul to grow wings and fly.

Others were appearing in one and twos, the emerald twins like Siamese twins, the links of their bracelets and anklets joined left to right so that they walked in step swinging their arms like soldiers. The girl with the panorama of tattoos led the older man with snowy hair by his small erection. He looked dazed and boyish. watched another girl I hadn't seen before appear on all fours, the rings on her choker linked to the belt of a Cabinet Minister who had recently resigned 'to spend more time with his family'.

Now I knew what the euphemism meant. This was his family. We were his family. In the photographs of him in the newspapers he had looked tense and anguished. In the mirror room he was naked, relaxed, content, the belt like a dog lead in one hand, his free hand nursing his erection. He paused and shot a stream of spunk over the girl's back. She had reached the edge of the bed and another man immediately shoved his cock in her pretty mouth.

The tattooed girl had reached the side of the bed at the same time. She was shuffling the wrinkled flesh of the older man in one hand and in her free hand another man had found his way into her palm; her arms moved like the beams on an ancient spinning jenny, up and down, up and down. The Maasai was performing a belly dance around the Arab sheik, the bells about her ankles ringing her spiralling hands finding their way into the folds of his jalabah to unleash the serpent, as the notes from a flute encourage the cobra to rise from his basket. She began rocking the monster up and down to the same rhythm as the tattooed girl, and those men, at the same time, as if linked on a circuit board, launched their stuff over the writhing bodies of those on the bed, great spurts of semen

172

that blinded my eyes, went up my nose and in my mouth. It was like being baptised.

Someone opened a magnum of champagne with an explosive pop and the bubbly stuff cleared the gunk from my eyes and slipped deliciously into my mouth. With my lips stretched open for more, the great heaving mound of the older woman, the one without bonds, lowered over my face. It was like being a bear in a cartoon putting your head in a jar of honey, the sweet sticky stuff covering my chin, my neck, my breasts. She tired of me and moved on to Milly, bending forward at the same time to nurse a stray erection emerging from the mass of limbs and torsos, male bodies and female bodies in one erotic display like a painting depicting the bacchanal that emerged in Rome 200 years before Christ and in which it was the female who ruled. As it should be. And would be again, I thought. It was the best time ever to be alive and better still being born female.

Girls everywhere were growing more comfortable and confident about exhibiting their curves, their chic, their nudity. Heels were higher. Clothes were tighter. Breasts were everywhere, and thighs, too, and backs and bare tummies. Even newsreaders are chosen for the cut of their cheekbones, the mystery of their cleavage, their unreserved sensuality. The pretty young blondes are easing out the grey men in grey suits with their deep, doom-laden voices as those in charge of the media, those masters of the airwaves, come to see that news of war and chaos is sweetened when read through cupid lips.

What the men of the New World understand, what I was beginning to understand, is simply this: that nothing matters. Nothing. Just this one moment in time and how you best spend it. People are born, they live, they die and the wheel keeps turning. Banks crash and people starve. Empires rise and empires fall. Our time is brief and fragile. If we strip away our garments with our self-doubt and self-imposed morality, what's left is a round room with many mirrors where people can be themselves.

The bacchanal was banned in Rome by the petty politicians who had not been invited to take part. People loathe seeing others enjoy themselves, and condemn others for the very things they most wish to do themselves. For 2,000 years, our sexuality has been repressed. For 2,000 years, women have been made to feel ashamed of their natural urges, their natural instincts, their desire for multiple partners and that inimitable freedom only found in the hedonistic heat of the orgy. That was going to change. It was changing. There was a revolution going on and I wanted to be out in front of the charge waving the banner.

I heard the shrill ripping of the air behind me and turned my head to watch as two men brought their leather belts down on the perky bottoms of the twins, their wrists hooked to rings set invisibly in the mirror walls. Their bodies moved like sublime snakes as the pain and pleasure blazed up their long spines. The men beat them mercilessly, the girls cried in ecstasy and the two men like rampant fauns set about filling their backsides, their fiery cocks demanding attention after the stimulation of the beating.

Other girls, girls I hadn't seen before, were leaning across the mass of bodies on the bed, their legs spread, the masters of the universe piercing them back and front. More champagne showered over me. Over us all. We were one. I was drunk and delirious. Time was suspended. The temperature had risen. Every space in the round room filled, the white bed raised above the black carpeted floor in an eruption of naked flesh. I sucked and I fucked. I took one cock and two and three and four. My skin was alive and electric with new sensations, coated with semen, girl discharge and sweat.

For a girl, sex is at the heart of our nature, it is our pleasure and deepest desire. For a man, more than

174

leasure, more than a sense of conquest, sex is a fantasy. The moment a man vanishes inside a woman, he is free from the chains of squalid reality. If he is going to stay one step ahead of reality, he must emerge from that woman and disappear into the next. The fantasy must be kept alive by changing constantly, changing partners and having partners adapt and change through costume and mask, something I had yet to see in Black Spires but felt intuitively would come before I had served out my thirty-one days.

In that marvellous mirror ball where you didn't know which body belonged to whom, your sense of self was lost in a whirlpool of sweating, throbbing flesh, each sensation fading into a new sensation and taking you deeper and deeper, higher and higher, until you became one with the whole. In a world of theories, equations and maths, small amounts of matter can contain vast amounts of energy. The orgy is the centrifuge that refines and enriches the life force. Your own pleasure and energy is multiplied to infinity by the vicarious pleasure of those around you.

The temperature had gone up a few more degrees, the lights were low and the moon's silver glow through the high arched windows gave those tumbling, frolicking bodies the look of ghosts and spirits, of satyrs and elves. I watched the men and girls matched in every conceivable way, and in ways beyond conception, exploring and exploiting the supreme pleasures of each other. Men were spanking girls. Girls were spanking girls, kissing girls, licking out girls in one orifice while the other was filled by a passing cock still with enough energy to stay upright. When it comes to group sex, women have far greater capacity than men; men grow flaccid and tired while women just get more randy.

The men in the mirror room could do anything, and what they wanted to do was be with each other and be with us, the girls with the gift in the house of mirrors. I was overcome with a sense of unfettered joy. Any girl can be an accountant. Any girl can get a first at the LSE. Any girl can get a boyfriend, get engaged, get married, be like the cows and zebras and continue the species. You had to be special to be there at Black Spires and I felt special taking part in that carnival of euphoria and delight. The round room was a circus ring without a ringmaster, anarchic, debauched, perfect.

Every scene in every act unwound and ended. The men in the room were exhausted, drunk, slowly losing themselves to sleep. I, on the other hand, was fully awake, my body burning like a bright light. I had, as Milly had said, been born with the gift, and I realised at that moment that everything I might achieve in my life would be less from my own efforts than from nurturing that gift.

I had watched through the hours for Simon Roche to appear in the round room and now he did appear, fully dressed, tall and stern, his dark eyes finding me where I had been all that time, in the centre of the large bed, in the centre of the room, in the centre of the activity.

He remained in the doorway and, as he beckoned, I realised that this was the moment I had been waiting for.

12

The Olson Ranch Brand

t was difficult to extricate myself from the twisted knot
of limbs and make my way through the obstacle course
of couples and trios still copulating about the floor.
Everywhere you looked, in every direction, reflected in
perpetuity and multiplied in the mirrors *ad infinitum* were
the naked bodies of masterful men and willing girls
satiated in the dying embers of the bacchanal.

The scene was mythic, glorious, almost spiritual, and I
could see both why the Greeks and Romans in pagan
times had revelled in this strain of human excess and why
early Christians with their teachings on renunciation and
the virgin birth had brought it all to an end. That is, I
thought, until now. Sodom and Gomorrah had fallen.
We were living in a post-apocalyptic, bankrupt and
broken new millennium. Just open the pages of any
tabloid. Watch cable TV after midnight. Put 'orgy' into
your search engine. What people want to do most is fuck
and fifty years of free love was taking us full circle back
to classical times. The orgy was back.

How many men that night had left their sperm in me
and on me? It was impossible to calculate and that, it
seemed to me, is the difference between the purely
promiscuous, the wife swappers, gang bangers, the nervy
stab at group sex, and the sublime, wholly decadent gift
of the orgy. The orgy is not about base numbers, it's

about that place in the mind beyond numbers, beyond definitions, that place where body and soul are one with our primal urges and natural instincts.

To take part in an orgy, you must forget who you are, who you were, who you thought you might one day become. You cease to be an individual with a history, a culture, dreams and future plans. You go beyond morality, beyond philosophy, beyond rational thought. The purpose of meditation isn't to *think* about something. The purpose is to *still* the mind, think about nothing, enter the void. The orgy has the same abstract yet mystical quality. At the heights of ecstasy you are merely a body emptied of all things except animal instinct, the way man was before the guava grew on that twisted tree in the Garden of Eden.

My mind had been still but it wasn't still now. It was filled with thoughts, and images as my tummy was filled with butterflies. A faint smile touched my lips as I made my way towards Simon Roche, a shoe in each hand. He didn't return my smile. Standing there on the edge of that sea of hot flesh in his suit, he was a stranger peeping in on paradise, I thought, his bow tie and crisp shirt a masquerade, while the nudity on all sides of the circular room was wholly natural, unaffected, a representation like in an art gallery where he, dressed, was the spectator, the uninvited guest, and we, the celebrants of the orgy, an oil painting of man's innermost desire. We had created a *tableau vivant* of the sort the great surrealist Salvador Dalí staged at his Spanish home in Cadaqués, a gathering of perfect strangers who, after sufficient pink champagne, stripped and performed for his sexual and artistic gratification.

Dalí didn't like to touch or be touched. He liked to look.

The smile slipped from my lips. Simon's dark eyes were on me, but as I crossed the room my own eyes strayed continually towards the wall of mirrors. I had been conscious since that moment when I first discovered myself in the long mirror in the bathroom at Saint Sebastian that wherever I went I was accompanied by my own image of myself, that I had got into the habit of observing myself being looked at. It was a form of vanity, I suppose, at least to Sister Benedict, but more, I now thought, the sign of someone glimpsing the seeds of the gift, or rather the ghost of the gift growing corporeal.

Simon stood to one side. The door closed behind me, and there was silence except for the whisper of the wind whistling under the eaves and the pounding beat of my heart. I felt as if I had just run a marathon.

I slipped into my black shoes. My back curved in an imperceptible bow as if tensed for action and, in the cool air of the corridor, my nipples popped out, hard and inquisitive. The warm pony smell rising to my nose made me feel quite giddy. Simon scrutinised me in the same way as he had studied me that day at the interview. Then, it was my breasts rising and falling over the line of my blouse that held his attention. Now, it was difficult to know what intrigued him most.

As I thought about that, I was again aware of seeing myself as he must have seen me, and the picture brought that faint smile back to my lips. Every inch of my body was smeared and streaked with discharge, semen, sweat, saliva and champagne. The cocktail was in my hair, thick and lush over my stomach and thighs, sticky and matted in my pubes, sunk in the wells below my collarbones and embedded in my bellybutton. Female fish leave their eggs in vacant places and male fish cover them in sperm. That was me, a living, moving, breathing depository of male and female essence, a *tableau vivant* to be called *All Life Begins Here*.

'Are you enjoying yourself, Magdalena?' he asked, and I paused before answering.

'No, I'm having an awful time,' I said.

He tried not to smile and failed. I'd got him.

'Come,' he instructed.

As we moved towards the stairs, he patted my bottom in the same way that he'd patted his poodles when I first arrived at Black Spires. It made me feel like one of the family. I was at my piquant best, a salacious little creature fit for nothing but fucking, and I assumed as we descended the stairs that this was Simon's fetish, to have me finally after everyone else, after he could have been the first, with me covered in spunk and as smelly as a goat house.

Another flight of stairs went down to the main hall, but we continued through a vestibule and turned into a wide corridor with flowers in vases on walnut tables. The passage had an arched ceiling like a tunnel and it seemed to go on and on as far as I could see.

'Where are we going?' I asked, forgetting myself.

His brow rippled. 'Isn't it more interesting not to know? he asked.

I thought about that and nodded. 'Yes, I suppose so,' I replied, and then added, 'Thank you.'

He slowed his pace. 'For what?' he asked.

'I don't know,' I said. 'For everything. For giving me the chance to, you know . . .'

'Make an honest woman of you?'

'Yes,' I said. 'I will never do anything like that again.'

'I know that,' he said darkly and we came to a stop outside an oak door that was wide and arched like the entrance to the chapel at school.

'Good luck,' he said.

He knocked and, as he turned and made his way down the passage, I shivered and my perky breasts stopped showing off.

'Come,' boomed a voice from inside.

We all want to know what it is that waits behind closed doors but, naked and smelly, still flying like Icarus in the slipstream of the orgy, I suddenly felt as if the sweat and perm holding my wings were melting and gravity was pulling me back down to earth.

I turned the metal ring and entered a large room with a vaulted ceiling supported by beams and the same narrow arched windows as those in the mirror room. It was a bit like the chapel at school, but without the altar and pews. Instead, there was an enormous bed, a sunken bath in a recess edged by leaded windows and, across one wall, a display of whips with one and two and three and more tails, canes long and short, phalluses, harnesses, gags, clamps and things I had no names for, implements more of torture than passion, it seemed to me. I chewed my lips and waited.

Sitting in a wingback chair reading what looked like a financial report was the Texan. I remained where I had entered, just inside the door, while he read on for several more minutes, this drawn-out delay reminding me of my role. He finally placed the magazine on the table beside him and knitted his fingers across his chest. I stood immobile, shoulders back, hands gripped in front of my smelly pussy, and the way he looked at me recalled the way people look at abstract paintings at the Tate Modern when they are not entirely sure if they should be deferential or if they are being made a fool of. It was a questioning, sceptical study through pale-blue eyes with a hint of cruelty and madness, the eyes and the look of Sister Benedict.

'You're Magdalena,' he finally said.

'Yes, I am.'

'How old are you, girl, fourteen?'

I almost corrected him but stopped myself. 'Just about,' I replied and a fleeting smile ran across his thin lips.

'You're a busty girl for your age,' he added.

'It's my hormones,' I explained and he laughed.

I had said that once already tonight but I had learned from theatre that, when a line works for the audience, it works even better when you repeat it.

'You know who I am?' he now asked.

'You're the man who decides on world oil prices,' I said.

'That's me. Ben Olson,' he continued. 'You get the initials: Ben Olson, Big Oil.'

He found this amusing and laughed to himself as he stood. He was tall, well over six foot six, and about sixty, I guessed; at least he looked a lot older than Daddy, who was forty-two. Ben Olson turned on the large mixer tap that rose like the neck of a swan from the floor over the bath, took a jar from a shelf and emptied a generous helping of blue crystals that foamed as the hot water splashed into the pale-pink porcelain.

'You're about as rank as a mare that can't be broken,' he remarked and glanced across the room at the torture garden of whips and canes.

'I'm already broken, Ben,' I said as I stepped into the water.

'Let me tell you something, I've never come across a filly that didn't race better after a spot of discipline,' he replied, the icy look in his eyes making it clear that the subject was now closed.

In the corner there was a three-way mirror and, when he pulled his chair closer, I could see more clearly his lined face with strong features and, in the mirror's reflection, the shiny dome of his bald head with a fringe of iron-grey hair. I lay back in the bubbles trying to relax and he watched as I soaped my limbs and washed away the glaze of semen. His face was old but his eyes were as sharp and shiny as diamonds. He didn't seem to be looking at me but into me, into my hidden fears. He loosened the turquoise clasp holding the bootlace tie tight to his throat and crossed one long leg over the other.

'Now tell me about you, Magdalena,' he said. 'People always fascinate me.'

'All people?'

'No,' he replied and his voice grew as icy as his eyes. Always remember this, I'm the one who asks the questions.'

I was lying in hot water but a chill ran up my spine. I finished washing my face, added more hot water, took a breath and settled back under the quilt of bubbles. I told him everything. How I had gone to work in a casino as a hostess as well as becoming an accountancy intern. How I had got into problems gambling and stolen £3,100 from the Roche-Marshall account.

'They caught you with your hand in the cookie jar,' he remarked.

'I've never done anything like that before.'

'That's because you haven't had the opportunity.'

I flushed. I explained that I had only done it because I was desperate, because my father had lost his money in a publishing deal with the Chinese man, and that elicited a sudden look of sympathy.

'He should have known better than get into bed with those guys,' he said.

Poor Daddy, I thought. Poor Mummy. Poor Rafael. Would my brother ever survive sixth-form college? He was small like Mummy with Father's heavy features, while I was much bigger like my father, with Mummy's hair and Spanish looks. Rafael had an angel's name but he was never going to become a master of the universe.

'Daddy's trying to start a company selling second-hand aeroplanes,' I murmured, more to myself.

'That right?'

'In the Middle East,' I added.

'Good market for it,' replied Ben Olson. 'Does he know anything about aircraft?'

'He's a pilot,' I replied. 'He sold his own little Cessna. Now, I'm not sure, he's making contacts, talking to people . . .'

'What's your name, again?'

'Magdalena.'

'Yeah, I know, the rest of it.'

'Magdalena Maria Manzano Wallace.'

'That's a lot of names for a little girlie,' he said as he leaned over to pull the lever that drained the bath.

I stepped out, glancing round for a towel, but there wasn't one. Big Oil removed his jacket and placed it over the back of a chair with his bootlace tie. He stretched his right shoulder.

'Don't grow old,' he said. 'You get problems. And I've got a problem.'

'I'm sorry . . .'

'You know what my problem is?' he asked, and as I shook my head he tapped the area of his crotch. 'It's finished, lifeless, dead as a tree stump, dead as the European Union.'

He shrugged. I shrugged. I was dripping over the wooden planks of the floor, but the room was hot and my being there naked and wet like this, with the Texan towering over me in his Cuban-heeled boots, underlined both his absolute supremacy and my complete loss of freedom and free will. I was his prisoner, a bird in a cage. I was wet clay: he could shape me and make me into anything he wanted, and this sudden realisation added to my sense of fear, but also to the sexual tension. The leather straps, wet from the bath, made me feel for some reason more vulnerable, more naked, but my nipples were prominent and a spasm stirred in my womb. Even after the restless excitements of the tower, I remained an eager student in the house of the erotic.

Ben Olson glanced at the torture garden, and I followed his eyes as they roamed over the display.

'It's a hobby of mine,' he explained and turned with a lopsided smile. 'If this don't wake the old fella, nothing will.' He removed a bull-whip from a spring clip. 'You like the look of this one?'

I wasn't sure what to say, but my knees were trembling

and my voice when it came was a whisper. 'It's quite nice.'

'Quite nice! I love that. You English are always so . . . understated,' he said. 'I'm going to beat you with this whip, Magdalena. You going to be able to take it?'

'I'll do my best.'

'Good for you, girl. That's how the Pilgrim Fathers built America, whipping their wives and doing their best.'

He fondled the whip, running the long plaited leather through his fingers as if he were waxing a bow before playing the violin. 'I'll tell you something I learned from my daddy,' he said. 'When one of these is used in the right pair of hands the tip of the whip moves at over 700 miles an hour. It's hard to imagine. You're going to hear a crack as the whip slices the air. That crack, girlie, is what's called a sonic boom. A long time before men built airplanes, whips were the first tools to break the sound barrier. What's the name of your daddy?'

His question caught me unawares. I was mesmerised by his long white fingers stroking and caressing the whip, as the length of that whip was soon going to be stroking and caressing the poor little mounds of my bottom.

'Gordon,' I finally said.

'Well, that's nice. Let's make him proud of you.'

At the foot of the bath there was a sturdy double wooden rail bolted into the floor. It was designed for towels, but I could see as he crossed the room and ran his palm over the top rail that it would serve as a useful prop for his particular fetish: pretending I was fourteen and beating the living daylights out of me. I approached and he tugged on one of my bracelets. The rail was equipped with two perfectly spaced ring clips that he attached to the rings on my leather bracelets. With my hands gripping the rail and my wrists held steady, I shuffled back my feet and presented my backside.

'Cute ass,' he said. 'That's something I like in a girl, a cute ass.'

'Thank you.'

I didn't wonder for a moment why, if my ass was so cute, it had to be beaten, but I knew it had to be done, and just bit my lip and waited.

'Now, Magdalena, I don't want you to hold back. I want you to cry out long and loud, the louder the better. A lot of the guys in this place are halfwits who shouldn't be here. They've done themselves in fucking you women. Let's see if we can wake 'em up and put the fear of God into 'em.'

I now caught out of the corner of my eye the sight of Big Oil removing his shirt, his trousers, his cowboy boots and boxers. He had the longest penis I had ever seen, and I'd seen quite a few that night. It hung halfway down the inside of his long white thigh, completely inert. He could see me watching and he demonstrated just how unresponsive it was, weighing the monster in his palm, bobbing it up and down.

'If you can wake him up you'll be the first girlie to do it in a decade,' he said.

I gave a shrug and held my breath as he seized the bull-whip. He uncoiled the tail, playing out its length in a series of swift, jerking motions, three, four, five times, the leather biting the air. He looked magnificent standing there, white as marble, naked as a Greek god. He beat the air one more time and I heard the crack, the sonic boom; it almost split my eardrums and I wondered if the sound travelled through the halls and corridors to wake the masters of the universe from their slumbers in the tower.

He was ready. I was terrified.

'This is going to hurt, girlie,' he said. 'But it's the only way.'

He got in position behind me. I tensed, my palms gripping the rail, legs spread for balance, feet steady, breasts motionless, nervously poised, my nipples itching with fear and expectation.

186

I heard the whip slice the air and as the tongue flicked swift as lightning across my backside I didn't at first cry out. I was in shock. I was stunned. Bewildered. I gasped. My knees trembled and sweat broke out across my entire body. A message ran through my cerebral cortex. It said: this is pain. This is pain such as you have never known before. This is pain that you will remember always.

Then I screamed.

The taste of that whip was an experience beyond my imagination, beyond the range of my senses, something I had no name for, a throbbing, pulsing ache that spread out in every direction as if my body had been plunged into a furnace. As the fire burned at its brightest, I screamed again from the depths of my lungs, a scream that made the glass in the arched windows vibrate, its echo hammering over the vaulted roof and bouncing across the strip of sea that ran those twelve miles down the coast to the convent in Westgate where Sister Benedict lay in her little bed dreaming about the girls of the upper sixth across the quad innocently tuning into YouPorn.

This was not the same as being spanked by Simon Roche, being smacked by the stray hand at Rebels Casino, even enduring the bitter taste of the cane in the Sister's office. The whip uncoiled once more, the crack split the air, and the finely woven thread of plaited leather found an unsullied target just below the curve of my bottom, the heat touching my pussy like the devil's kiss. I screamed again as the second strike of the whip turned into a streak of sheer agony that encouraged the first to glow more brightly.

I panted for breath. I could hear Ben Olson panting behind me. I heard that terrible sonic boom a third time and the leather tongue took another taste of flesh from my bottom, turning it into a raised welt like a migraine pain engulfing body and mind, a pain that if it had had a colour would have been the deepest black. Tears ran in

187

streams down my cheeks. Snot fell from my nose and landed on the floor below me. Sweat dripped from my armpits.

New sensations were racing through my body as my voice, in a scream that could have come from a wounded animal, filled the room and rattled the wooden beams supporting the roof. With my limited experience, I had come to think of spanking as an enigmatic pleasure, a naughty, well-kept secret. The pleasure in corporal punishment was all one-sided for the man who decided the world's oil prices and, even in the midst of the beating, I couldn't help wondering if a bad performance by the girl being flogged would cost the motorist at the pump the following day.

Did I deserve a thrashing? Did I push out my bottom arrogantly, as Simon had said? Was I in love with the mirror, as the Sister once told me? Was I going to be a better person after the beating? I bit my lip and snivelled. I took a firm grip on that wooden rail and tensed my burning flesh as I heard that fearful crack break the air above my head once again.

Ben Olson was clearly an expert, a connoisseur, a master. He knew how long to wait between each stroke and where exactly to lay the line of leather, picking out the space just below the third stroke, closer to my poor little pussy cowering between my legs satiated with pleasure and terrified by the mere thought of pain. That fourth whiplash sent a ricocheting series of vibrations through the pleats and coils of my vagina and back passage, resonated through my womb and stomach and came up through my throat in a wail to waken the dead.

The feel of that fourth stroke was painful, of course. It was agony. But I sensed a certain numbness. I screamed, and kept screaming, but this was part of the procedure, it was expected. But I knew, too, for the first time, that I could take the flogging, that, in the sadomasochistic interplay between Mr Big Oil and little Magdalena with

188

her wrists bound and bottom so hopelessly bared, I was an equal partner.

I waited for the fifth stroke of the lash and, when it came, my body jerked forward and vapour rose in a mist from my skin. I screamed, but it was more for effect, theatrical. The worst thing about a beating is the fear, the fear of pain, the fear of the unknown. Once you get over the fear, the pain becomes a companion, understood, something you can absorb and make a part of you. It still hurts, it hurts like the flames of hell, but you know you can take it and you know that it will soon come to an end.

The sting from the fifth stroke roared like fire and, like the first four, faded to an ember. I could feel those five scorched welts running in lines from a fraction above the lips of my pudenda to the top of the crease in my bottom. Was there room for another? Where would he place it? Was six going to be it, as I had thought? Or was it going to be more? I didn't know why beatings and canings were measured by the duodecimal system, in sixes and twelves, but the English had long favoured it for their currency and wasn't spanking known as the English Disease?

Please make it six.

The pause stretched. I was countering the pain by running through the different counting systems I could recall. The fact that we have ten fingers made 10 the basis of most systems, but there were some odd variations, the Babylonians using 60, the Arabs 80, and the binary system of computers was founded on the base of 2 rather than 10, requiring just the numbers 1 and 0 for their immeasurable calculations, those numbers beyond numbers like the reflections in the mirror.

Big Oil was flexing his shoulder muscles, building up his strength. I was trembling. My breasts swayed below me, that shiver of my own tanned flesh oddly soothing. My distended nipples, immune from pain, were actually enjoying themselves, and I could smell the faint musky aroma of my shameful arousal. My pubes were drenched and my tummy was sucked up in a hollow below my ribcage, the bones defined in a sheen of sweat. I could not imagine any position more exposed and, in a way, more erotic than this, legs stretched, arms stretched, toes pushing down into the floor, my damp hair in a veil across my face, my tanned bottom pushed out as arrogant as ever. What man could resist such a provocative display?

I had tensed the cheeks of my bottom before each lash. Now, I tried to relax. I counted in sixes, 6, 12, 18 . . . I got as far as 19×6 when the sonic boom exploding above my head broke my concentration. The wet tongue of the whip flashed across the small of my back just above the crease of my bottom and the scream that left my lungs was not in any way theatrical. The sum total of those first five lashes was equal to the pain inflicted by the sixth. That last lash made me feel as if I had been cut in two but, as in the trick of putting a lady in a box and sawing her in half, I was still in one piece, still standing, the embers from the first five strokes blazing again so that it felt like a forest fire running from the top of my skull down to the tips of my toes.

I wailed and screamed. Tears rained from my eyes. I was only vaguely aware of Ben Olson unhooking my bracelets from the bar and, when I stood straight, my bottom closed like a concertina and the pain was all the greater.

'Come here, girlie,' he said.

He crossed the room to the three-way mirror. I joined him, each step a separate torment, the lines on my bottom jiggling up and down. I stood before the mirror in such a way that I could see the six crimson welts. They were perfectly spaced, like steps, like a grid.

'The Olson Ranch Brand,' said Ben Olson smugly 'Now you belong to me.'

190

I wasn't sure what he meant and remembered how Sergio Buenavista had said he wanted to 'buy me'. Had the Texan pre-empted the sale? Was I in the world market a piece of merchandise? Were we all? Did it matter? I had taken six strokes from the bull-whip he was now hooking lovingly back on the display. I knew I had done well and knew by the set of Ben Olson's craggy features that he thought so, too.

He found a jar on the shelf and came back to join me, unscrewing the lid. I couldn't tear my eyes away from those six gorgeous red lines. I would wear the Olson brand invisibly for the rest of my life. The welts would go down and heal, the fine scars would fade, but on nights when I was naked in the moon's waxen glow those lines would come to life and shine in the dark. I was and would always be a creature of the night, a slave to my senses, and it would all have begun that night in Black Spires.

Ben took a large dollop of cream from the jar and gently smoothed it across the welts. It was arnica, the same as Lee-Sun had used after Simon's smacking, and it was surprising how quickly the fire died down to a gentle and pleasant glow.

'What do you have to say for yourself now, girlie?' he asked.

I swallowed. I didn't know what he expected me to say.

'Well, nothing, really,' I replied.

'It's always best to say nothing when you've got nothing to say. Is that the first time you've been thrashed?'

'Well, like that, yes.'

'It won't be the last, but girls always remember the first time,' he said.

I do declare, there was a faint stirring in the tall Texan's blue-veined and flaccid length of wrinkly cock. The moment he finished spreading the arnica on my bottom, I went down on my haunches and fed it like a lollypop into my mouth, sucking hard, moving slowly back and forth, pausing to stipple the big smooth helmet before swallowing it down once again.

He stood with his feet spread, his hands locked against the sides of my head, and I kept going for a long time, sucking and licking, using one hand to jerk off the creature, pausing to give my jaws a rest and using two hands, one above, one below, as if climbing a rope. It was getting harder, easier to manage. I plunged it back down my throat again, gagging momentarily, taking it all, the entire length pushing beyond my clanging tonsils, and back out again, up and down, up and down.

I could take six lashes from a bull-whip. I could do this too: I could make Ben Olson's cock respond for the first time in a decade.

His grip grew tighter. I thought he was going to come prematurely and expected ten years of accumulated semen to pour down my throat. But he stopped suddenly, grabbed the back of my hair and pulled me to my feet. He kept hold of me this way, like a caveman grasping me by the hair. We crossed the room to the big bed where he tossed me across the sheets of white linen.

'You've got a mouth that could suck oil out of the Texas desert,' he said, and I felt inordinately pleased with myself as he lay back, his enormous cock like a lighthouse rising above his nest of pubic hair.

He spread his legs and, on my knees like a believer at prayer, I continued sucking him off, sliding my hands under his buttocks and pumping them up and down. His body was tense, but he stayed hard and I worked on that giant phallus, sucking, swallowing, stippling, licking its entire length, chewing on the bulbous head. I was like a dog with a bone, or a thirsty creature lapping away at a salt-lick, my dribble keeping the monster well oiled, my throat expanding and contracting as I swallowed it down once again.

As I came up for air, he again dragged me by the hair and, crablike, I swivelled round, took his cock back down my throat and wriggled with satisfaction as his tongue parted the cowling about my clitoris and pressed down on the magic button. It was weird but, after the beating, the little bulb was hot, electric, desperate for some action, and that big wet tongue was just what she needed. Now that I was getting some attention, and from this angle above the Texan, I was able to take the entire length of that astonishing cock down into the darkest depths of my throat and down, it seemed, to the place where my heart was beating faster and faster.

A spasm gripped me and, as if this was a sign, he pushed me sideways, rolled me over and plunged into my wet pussy like a battering ram breaking down the doors to the castle keep. I arched my back, pushed down with my heels and gasped as his long cock plunged up into those places never reached before, the membranes vibrating with unfamiliar sensations, my gymnast muscles firming and softening like a sea anemone swallowing a fish.

He had been silent all the time I was sucking him off, but now he started to pant like a runner at the end of a race, his breath coming faster and faster. I could feel the tension across his shoulders, in his loins. I could feel myself coming and wanted to hold back for him but couldn't. Those places that had never been reached before were just too energised, too stimulated. The feeling started in my chest, ran down through my tummy into my womb and I roared as I'd roared being flogged, as a climax like a tidal wave gushed through my body.

The spasm overcame Ben Olson. He tensed and withdrew the monster as he was about to climax so that he could pour the creamy stuff like milk from an urn over my belly, my breasts, my face, a great stream of sperm ten years in the making, sticky as glue, hot and tasting of bitter chocolate. He held on to his cock as if it was the short handle on the bull-whip, pumping out every last drop of semen, and almost immediately he was flaccid again.

I was on my back. He dropped to one side, snuggled under my arm and lay there panting, fondling my breasts.

'You see, Magdalena, you never know what you can do when you try,' he said.

I wasn't sure if he was referring to himself or me but didn't think it wise to ask. He seemed content running his hand over my breasts, turning my nipples in his fingers, rubbing them with the flat of his palm. We were quiet for a long time, dozing, lost in our own thoughts.

'You know something, I never felt any love from my mother and I never felt any love for her,' he then said, his voice soft as if he was speaking in a confessional. 'The only tits I knew as a baby belonged to Mammy. Then, they sent her away. I never knew why, but it was a good lesson. I learned I could never trust nobody, that the things you love will always be taken away from you.'

He was quiet again. The sperm across my body and over my face had hardened and gone cold. I shivered.

'You cold, girlie?'

'I am a bit.'

'Then why don't you turn out the lights and pull the covers over us. You've got a big day ahead of you tomorrow.'

We lay close like spoons and in seconds he was sleeping. Sleep for me came slowly, my nerve endings were tingling so, and I lay there as a storm moved across the channel and rain lashed the leaded windows.

13

The Hunt

In my dream I was a mermaid with a shiny green tail swimming in a warm sea. There were other girls like me with long hair gliding behind them as they moved towards me and around me, their breasts bobbing above the surface of the water.

'Shush, shush. Time to wake up.'

As my eyes fluttered open, I wasn't sure if I were a girl who had dreamed she was a mermaid or a mermaid now dreaming she was a girl. I'd read that somewhere, or something like it, and smiled trying to recall where.

'Come. Come.' Lee-Sun was standing beside the bed, a finger to his lips.

'No rest for the wicked,' I said.

'Shush. Is time,' he whispered, and I uncoiled myself from Ben Olson's circling arms. The Texan was sleeping like a baby.

The sun through the leaded windows lit the display of canes and whips, the glass and rubber phalluses, the metal clips and clamps. My gaze was drawn to the bull-whip, the fine leather glossy with memories in the refracted light. My smarting bottom reminded me that I wore the Olson brand. I had been whipped and serviced in ways girls can only imagine. I had been at the heart of an orgy, my first, and while I felt as if I should be vaguely ashamed, on the contrary, I was inordinately pleased with myself.

I had no idea of the time or how long I had slept, but felt refreshed and fully awake, primed for adventure. Perhaps all the semen I'd swallowed had given me fresh energy. I slid from the sheets, took Lee-Sun's hand, and left Big Oil murmuring in his sleep, deciding on the day's price of oil, I assumed.

We raced back along the corridor and down the stairs to the grand hall, empty now, the candle wax melted into grotesque carvings, wedding dresses for headless brides, the light through the windows like crossing swords. We climbed the staircase of the far wing and, on the top floor, I returned to the boudoir where I had learned the art of making love with a dildo from Milly. I had since coupled and trebled in every way and felt momentarily sad that in this house of love there was so much to learn and I had learned so much in so short a time. I showered and then followed Lee-Sun to a long chamber, like a dressing room in a theatre, and, like a theatre, it was filled with voices and laughter.

There were about fifteen girls in various stages of applying make-up and dressing in masks. Everyone was chewing toast and drinking coffee and fresh orange juice, and I realised that there was a kitchen somewhere with staff to care for us, that behind our pleasures others were working, cleaning, carrying the bags. I was content to be up above with the gods, not labouring in the basement below.

Several girls turned to wave. I recognised Milly, though barely. Her face had been painted in a palette of yellows, ochre and umber, and her body was dyed a dark coppery red. She was lacing up a pair of gold Nikes. I hurried towards her and we kissed cheeks.

'Hello,' she said.

'Hello.'

'Well?' she asked.

I shrugged and grinned.

'What if Sister Benedict could see us now,' Milly continued and we broke down in a fit of giggles.

196

As my eyes ran over the other girls, from one to the next, I was reminded for some reason of making flick books as a little girl with my *abuelo*, my Spanish grandfather; he was quite the expert, drawing figures slightly different on the corner of each page of a notebook, then flicking through the pages to reveal the illusion of motion, a running bull or a flamenco dancer. As the newcomer, I was stark naked, but I could see the final image in the flick book, how I would appear when the costume was complete.

I was starving and stuffed myself with toast and jam. Milly combed my hair and helped me dress. It was a costume of sorts we would be wearing, but it amounted to merely the head and tail of a fox, a real head and a real tail, she told me. She started with the make-up, painting my face that dark-ochre colour before adding yellow streaks to highlight my eyes. I was still eating toast.

'Careful, you'll get crumbs smeared across your face.'

'I've had a lot more than crumbs smeared across my face,' I replied and we giggled once more.

It was like being in the showers at school after hockey, especially when we'd won a match and everyone was in good spirits.

By the time Milly had finished making up my face, I had stopped looking like me and had that haunted animal quality I'm sure foxes feel. That was the plan for the day, she explained. Now that fox hunting had been banned, our masters had devised their own variation. Milly used a large brush to paint my body in that coppery colour, down my arms and sides, my tummy and legs. She turned me round and paused to admire the six scarlet lines raised across my bottom.

'Big Oil?' she asked and I nodded. 'Did he make it?'

'What do you mean?'

'You know exactly what I mean, Magdalena,' she said and I blushed through the sunny shades of make-up.

'For the first time in ten years,' I boasted, and Milly brought me back down to earth.

'He always says that, the old devil.'

'No . . .'

'You can't trust a thing they say.'

She carried on painting and I carried on eating. There was fruit salad and hard-boiled eggs. I hadn't eaten a thing the previous day and I had a feeling I was going to need all my energy. When she had finished with the painting, she sprayed me from head to toe with a fixer that made my skin feel tight, as if I was covered in sperm again.

There were numerous boxes containing new trainers. I found some that fitted and slipped them on. Milly attached the tail to my belt and it hung down all tickly between the tender cheeks of my bottom. Poor little fox, I thought, and stopped stuffing myself to put on the mask. It fitted over the top and back of my head, leaving a gap for my eyes and providing me with a long snout – to sniff out what, I wasn't sure. Milly hooked the rings on my collar to the clips on the mask so that it fitted snugly and felt more comfortable. I helped her do the same and we turned to the mirror. I was ready. A foxy little fox identical to all the other girls, in fact so identical I'm sure our mothers wouldn't have been able to tell us apart.

Just like in the theatre, now we were in our costumes and make-up, we had to wait an age before Lee-Sun reappeared.

'They are ready,' he announced.

'And we are ready for them,' said the Maasai, recognisable as she was the only one among us barefoot.

We ambled down the staircase, out through the double doors and down the steps into the raucous gathering assembled in the courtyard. It was an astonishing sight. There must have been about thirty, perhaps forty men on horseback, quad bikes and motorbikes, some in jogging clothes limbering up ready for the chase. Among the horsemen I recognised the Duc de Peralada dressed in riding pink. Ben Olson looked refreshed in a cowboy outfit, a whip coiled in his hand, silver spurs attached to his boots. The sheikh was on a tall black stallion with an ornate saddle, magnificent in white robes that danced on the breeze.

Riding bareback, naked as ever, was the woman who had lowered her cleft over my face during the orgy, poised, back straight, awe-inspiring. It was difficult to tear my eyes away from her and I only did so when Simon Roche approached with his two giant poodles on leads. The waft of our scent was driving the dogs wild. They were slobbering and barking, their jaws a hair's breadth from our slippery parts.

Sandy Cunningham looked like a Hell's Angel in an ensemble of chains and black leather. He revved his Harley Davidson and drove towards me, then swerved to a stop.

'Is that you, Magdalena?' he asked.

'How did you guess?'

'You're wearing the brand, girl,' he replied, and glanced at the Texan. 'We had a little chat about you this morning.'

I turned to look at my bottom. The red lines were visible through the thin layer of copper paint, a raised grid I was strangely proud of, though I wasn't entirely sure why. I wanted to ask Sandy what exactly he and the Texan had been chatting about, but he dragged on the accelerator and shot off again.

Two butlers in black appeared with silver trays balancing sherry in crystal glasses and the men raised those glasses as you do before the hunt. I noticed the butlers never looked in our direction, at this gallery of decorated girls, and it occurred to me that, just as there were workers in the kitchen, there must also be grooms in the stable, cleaners, maintenance staff, chauffeurs and pilots. Serving the masters of the universe was big business, almost certainly well paid, and I was sure it was only men who were offered those jobs.

That would explain the glass ceiling, but not the fact that among the men gathered in the courtyard was that solitary woman. Was she just a token, the exception that proves the rule? If she were equal to the masters, why was she naked?

I turned to Milly, and pointed. 'That woman . . .'

'I'm told she's a Minister in the French Government,' she whispered in reply. 'And, by all accounts, more powerful than the President.'

'But why hasn't she got any clothes on?'

'She likes it that way, I suppose,' she answered. 'She was one of us once, you know.'

'Really?'

'She has shared her gift,' said Milly.

I looked back at the woman on horseback through the slits in the mask. Our eyes met and I was sure I saw in them a look of complicity. The ties binding the powerful and the erotic were many and subtle. I had thought I had learned so much at Black Spires, but realised now that the more you know the more there is to know, that I was setting out on a long journey and had barely taken the first step. My old life was fading from my mind like the mist over the trees. The sun pressed through the clouds, warming my skin, and now that the fumes from Sandy's motorbike had gone, I could taste the tang of the sea. The land smelled primal and verdant after the storm the previous night.

Milly pointed at the tower standing above a low hill on the horizon to the south of us, in the direction of Saint Sebastian.

'That's our destination,' she said. 'The first girl to reach the tower is the winner.'

'What will she win?' I asked her.

'Mmm, I've never thought of that. The men are all rogues. I don't think there's any chance of anyone winning.'

'That's not fair,' I said, and she shrugged philosophically.

As I looked round at the gathering once more, I was stunned to see Jay Leonard, the TV actor fond of smacking my bottom at Rebels. He wasn't a master of the universe, surely? He was just a soap star. He was wandering round with a notebook writing down figures.

'Bets,' Milly explained. 'They love gambling, all of them. They're betting who will get the furthest.'

'But he's just an actor,' I said, pointing at Jay.

'Well, yes, but his father owns the rights to half the casinos in the world, and Jay runs Jabber TV, the cable company. It's all multi-tasking now,' she added and we broke down in a fresh bout of giggles.

When I was able to get control of myself, I glanced from Jay Leonard to Sandy Cunningham to Simon Roche. They were all in on it, tricking me on to the road to Black Spires, to my standing here outside this big house this July morning in nothing but a fox's head and tail. I tried to feel angry, but I wasn't. I was determined. I would show them. Show them all. They on their quad bikes and fine horses weren't going to catch me.

Someone blew a hunting horn. The dogs barked excitedly and Simon came back towards us.

'To the tower,' he yelled dramatically, raising a whistle to his lips and blowing. 'You have ten minutes' start.'

The Maasai didn't delay for a second. She sprinted out of the courtyard, crossed the gravel driveway and bolted into the woods. She looked as if she knew what she was doing and I followed, Milly close behind. The rest of the girls spread out in a fan, picking their way through the wet undergrowth, the sound of their footfall like a whisper through the trees. The Maasai was loping along, shoulders forward, her long legs moving mechanically. In no time she began to pull away from me and almost immediately I could feel the burn in my thighs.

In ten minutes I could run about two miles. I calculated

that it was ten or twelve miles to the tower. By the end of the third mile, we would be tired and the horses and vehicles would have caught up with us. Like all games of chance, this was weighted on the side of the bank, the house. If we had a chance it was slender, hardly a chance at all.

We had left Milly behind and the Maasai had gained a hundred yards on me. I could hear the rev of those motorbikes and quad bikes, the horns, the dogs, the beat of hooves. The pack was coming. It was impossible to outrun them.

I could see patches of sea through the undergrowth to my left. I imagined most of the land to my right belonged to Simon Roche, but where the woods of Black Spires ended there was real life, country lanes, isolated farm houses, the small hamlets we had passed through on our way from London. If I could cross the boundary from Simon's land without getting caught, I would stand a better chance. It was going to be embarrassing if someone from the outside world saw me, a naked girl disguised as a fox, but it was the only way.

Milly was far behind me now. Two other girls had gone off to the left. Perhaps they intended to try to swim to the tower. The hoof beats were like a war drum pounding louder, getting closer. I paused to look back. The mask gave me tunnel vision and it wasn't easy to focus across the breadth of the landscape. I couldn't yet see, but I could hear the riders coming and at that moment I felt like a hunted animal fleeing for my life.

I took off at a right angle away from the sea, away from the direction of the tower, and pelted as fast as I could, swerving through the undergrowth, leaping small bushes and puddles, the slight slope of the land adding to my momentum. When I had first entered the trees, it had seemed as if I were in a dense forest, but in a matter of minutes the trees thinned out and I could see below in the distance a golden field of rape seed edged by a stone wall.

Where the ground was no longer in shadow, it was thick with brambles and blackberry bushes whose thorns tore at my legs. I slowed to pick my path more carefully and, as my heartbeat stilled, I heard the pack drawing closer. Glancing back, I caught a glint of silver on a horse's bridle and imagined for a moment that I was an Apache brave running naked out of the past, the US Cavalry hunting me down with their long rifles.

Now I really knew what it was like to be hunted. I searched for an escape. There was nowhere. The trees were sparse, mostly saplings, a few ancient specimens with gnarled bark and long memories. The brambles grew thick all the way down to the yellow field still a half-mile away. I stopped completely. I could hear one of the quad bikes revving loudly. I could smell the exhaust. Tears welled in my eyes, but I gritted my teeth and I wiped those tears away. I wasn't a fox. I was a gymnast.

I sprinted flat out towards a big old oak tree with a low-hanging bough that I reached in one flying leap. I swung my legs up and was thankful for all the hours I'd spent on the parallel bars. I clung to the bough, catching my breath, hanging there like a little monkey. I then crawled upside down, hand over hand, until I reached the thick trunk with its blisters and knots that formed a ladder and allowed me to climb into the heights like Jack on the Beanstalk. I kept climbing until the ground below me was out of sight.

From my bird's-eye view, the forest was a narrow strip edging the sea and stretching as far as the tower. It was impossible to run those ten miles through the trees without getting caught and it was only by standing back, or rather by being up there in the crow's nest, that I could see the whole picture and really work out how to reach my destination.

Behind me, beyond the trees, there were fields with ripening crops, and in the distance I could just make out what looked like a tractor moving leisurely on a country lane half hidden below tall hedgerows. My best chance was going to be out there in the open, in the unknown: more frightening, for sure, more dangerous, but more of a triumph when I reached the tower.

The sound of the quad bike grew closer. I saw one of the girls running for her life and two masters of the universe gaining on her, the Arab on his black steed, the other on his roaring machine. The little fox hadn't seen the muddy pool coated in leaves in the clearing just in front of her and, when she did, it was too late. She stumbled and fell face first into the mud.

The quad bike braked, swerved and fell on its side. The sheikh reined in and the horse trotted into the muddy pool. By the time the quad rider had scrambled out from under his machine and made a dash for the pool, the sheikh had already slipped from his saddle. He lifted the girl by the back of her belt and unhooked her tail, which he waved exultantly in the air.

Now that her tail had been won, the girl stood and unhooked the clasps holding the fox's head in place. She shook her head, releasing her hair. It was Milly. Of course. Even from the distance she was unmistakeable with those red flames dancing in the sunlight. I wondered if she had decided on the same ploy, to escape from the confines of the woods, or whether she had seen me taking off in a new direction and blindly followed.

It didn't matter. The race for her was over and the men who had captured her, all sweaty and covered in mud, claimed their prize. The sheikh, the fox tail in his teeth, turned her over on the edge of the mud pool, pulled his erection from his robes and took her with the careless haste of a ravening beast, of a boy on the bottom field, and I wondered if there was something about the great outdoors that gave men such urgency.

Milly pushed up on her hands and knees. The sun gleamed on the copper paint coating her hide. She was like a little animal, covered in dirt, doing what animals

204

are meant to do, her rolling motion harmonious like poetry, like the jazz musicians who had played in the grand hall. The sheikh was slipping in and out of her wet places, faster and faster, his white robes in the mud turning as black as the oil he pumped from the desert and sold at prices he and Ben Olson decided upon. The quad-bike rider, who had been slowly masturbating, slid his cock between Milly's gorgeous lips.

Two things went through my mind: how enjoyable it was to watch others making it, especially in the open, and how, if I had not stolen that £3,100, I would not have been there now on top of the world.

I probably should have climbed down the tree and continued through the brambles to the field of rape, but I couldn't tear my eyes away from Milly and her lovers. I adored sex in its array of colours and varieties, doing it, seeing, imagining it. If there is a battle between the sexes, that battle must logically end in union, in possessing and being possessed. It follows to my mind that it is the female who, after losing every battle, wins the war. Possessing leads always to disappointment, while being possessed is eternal. I remembered a visiting bishop at prize-giving one year saying that everyone is born with one gift and his was to serve. Mine, too, I thought, and watched as the two men changed positions. The quad-bike man took Milly in the places moistened by the sheikh and the sheikh cleaned the juices from his cock in Milly's agreeable mouth.

Satisfied, satiated, her tail tucked into the sheikh's belt, the fox mask swinging from her fingers, Milly climbed up behind the horseman, her long white legs like zebra stripes against the horse's back, and the sheikh trotted off behind the quad bike he had beaten to the prey.

When they vanished from view, I climbed back down from my perch and continued picking my way through the undergrowth. The brambles cut my legs, but the blackberries were big and juicy, that shade of blue like a

205

bruise, like a raven's wing, and there was something oddly sensuous being naked in the middle of nowhere eating fruit ripening in the wild. I ate my fill and pressed on, away from the woods, until I reached a tall barbed-wire fence impossible to climb over, which I imagined marked the edge of the Black Spires estate.

I followed the fence until I found a place where the land dipped and I dug out the leaves and wet earth until I had made a hole big enough to crawl under the wire. Once I had crossed to the other side I would have reached the point of no return, the point we should always try to reach.

There were more brambles on the other side, but beyond, fifty yards on, was the stone wall I'd seen from the treetop. I made my way to the wall, climbed over and entered the field, a golden fox invisible among the swaying blooms of rape. Rape was a strange name for a beautiful plant. It was being grown as a renewable energy source, and I wondered if the sheikh and the Texan and their cohorts in the New World Order fixed the prices of crops and food as well as petroleum, if everything was fixed, the stock market, the banks, the government.

The sun had grown hotter. I was tempted to remove the fox head, but thought that went against the spirit of the chase. I was not supposed to have left the woods, of that I was certain, but the rules and the spirit are not the same thing, as those alpha males and masters of the universe I'm sure would have agreed.

After crawling under the fence, I was covered in mud and, where I had sweated, the mud had turned into a sticky paste that was oddly pleasant and made me feel less naked. Little flies were buzzing around my head, and I had the shock of my life as I looked down and saw a rabbit standing at my feet washing behind his ears. His nose twitched and he looked up at me as if to say, 'I've never seen a fox like you before.' Then he went jumping off.

206

On the far side of the field the wall was higher and ran alongside a dense hedge. I found a five-bar gate, which I climbed, and dropped down to the lane I'd seen from the oak tree. The vehicle I'd seen earlier was indeed a tractor and at that moment it turned the corner and skidded to a halt.

'Bloomin' heck.'

The tractor driver was about my age, a young lad with a shock of scruffy blond hair, lots of muscles and eyes as big as dinner plates. His mouth had dropped open and the fag in his mouth dropped on his bare chest. He started fluttering his hands about, slapping his chest, flinching and dancing in his seat. That over, he looked back at me, his mouth still open.

'Bloomin' heck.'

'Hello,' I said. 'I hope I didn't frighten you.'

He swallowed and managed to recover his composure. 'Nah, we're used to seeing girls without any clothes on wandering round these parts,' he said, and I wasn't sure if he was being sarcastic or whether the locals knew what went on behind the walls of Black Spires.

'It's just a game. I've got to get to the tower.'

I pointed, but he didn't bother to look in that direction: his eyes were fixed on my bristling nipples, the mud over my breasts and down my tummy to the sticky patch of my pubic hair.

'Still got a long way to go,' he finally said.

'Will you help me?'

Again he paused and a calculating look gripped his features. 'I might,' he answered. 'What are you going to do for me?'

I paused. A smile came to my lips – a smile of recognition. I was getting to know myself.

'Anything,' I said.

He climbed down from the tractor, opened the gate and backed the vehicle in. I followed and he closed the gate again.

'How come you haven't got a stitch on?' he asked.

'I thought you said you were used to seeing girl running round in the nude?'

'In my dreams.'

He grabbed hold of me and I tensed up. I gripped hi arms. 'Not like that,' I told him. 'The way to make love to a woman is the way you would cook a small fish.'

He thought about that for a moment and then tried to kiss me. It wasn't easy with the fox's head in the way. He pawed at my breasts, my bum, my hipbones, and I calmed him down, unbuckling his belt, lowering the zip on his jeans and unleashing his hard cock. I drew the loose skin backwards and forwards and he let out a long sigh of relief.

'There, that's better,' I said.

I went down on my knees, popped it in my mouth to make it wet and leaned back to take a closer look. It was beautiful, glistening in the July sun, the white skin soft as silk, smooth as glass, the helmet as pink as my own wet parts. His cock smelled like fresh milk, young and full of energy, and slid like a greyhound down my open throat. He soon started to pant.

'Bloomin' heck,' he said, and I let it slide from my mouth, teasing it with some nips and nibbles, rimming the groove.

He pulled his trousers over his muddy boots and I turned, going down on my hands and knees, country style. He paused for a moment; men always do faced with the choice, my slippery wet crack or the dark pulsing ring of my anus. He was too eager to think about lifting the pleated cape about my throbbing clitoris and giving her some action first and rushed in one swift charge through the pink lips of my labia into the moist warmth of my pussy. I pushed back on my hands and knees, my position reflecting exactly that of Milly and the sheikh on the edge of the mud pool, but my rider was young, bounding with health, his cock like an explorer conquering new worlds.

208

He climaxed quickly and as the sperm oozed out of my pussy, I remained in the same position, waggling my bum until he got the message and fed his oiled cock into my back passage. I stretched my thighs, taking all of him – he was hard still – and we got into a steady rhythm, tango dancers moving as one until we reached a grand finale, an orgasm of biblical scale, a seismic shift that must have changed the tectonic plates below the Garden of England.

'Agh, agh, agh,' I screamed.

'Agh, agh, agh,' he echoed.

And we collapsed in a heap laughing.

'Bloomin' heck,' he said once more, and I fed his shrinking cock below the snout in the fox's head and sucked it clean.

'There, is that better?' I asked.

'Blimey, I wish there were more girls like you.'

'I don't,' I replied. 'Come on, I've got a race to win.'

'You haven't told me your name,' he then said.

'I know.'

He pulled his trousers up and buckled his belt. He drove out of the field, back in the direction he'd been coming, and I closed the gate behind us.

'Here we are, jump up here,' he said.

I climbed up and balanced on the big mudguard, the metal hot on my tender bottom. The vibration as we bounced along the lane loosened the sperm inside me and it oozed out in a continual stream like honey being poured from a jar. I was muddy, spunky, sweaty, totally satisfied, and really at that moment wouldn't have wanted to be anywhere else in the world.

'I shall call you Foxy,' he said.

'And I shall call you Blondie.'

He patted my head and I looked up at him through the slits in the fox mask. 'Here,' he said, 'how come you've got those red lines across your bum?'

'I beg your pardon?'

'Looks like someone's been having a go at you.'

'It's nothing. Just a little whipping,' I said in the hope that that would shut him up. It didn't.

'Bloomin' hell, fings you lot get up to,' he continued. 'Where you from, anyway? You've got one of those funny accents.'

'Kensington, if you must know,' I replied, and screamed. 'Look out!'

He'd been looking down at me instead of the way ahead and almost drove off the road into a ditch.

'Oops a daisy,' he said and got back on course.

The lane followed the field, turning to the left, and from my position above the hedgerow I could see the barbed-wire barrier cutting across the landscape as if fencing in a secret. Blondie had a wide grin on his face and the muscles in his arms and chest were golden like ripe apples, tempting me to take a bite.

Suddenly we stopped. A car was coming in the opposite direction and the lane was too narrow for the two vehicles to pass. The tractor pulled up close to the fence, the camber tipping me an angle so that I almost slipped off, my legs shot out and I grabbed on under the big mudguard as the car inched by. The window was down and, as the driver leaned out to wave in thanks, he almost got a mouthful of pussy.

I waved back. The tractor started up again. We followed the fence, the road climbing steadily. As the lane curved to the left, the tower loomed up like a standing stone above a low conical hill, like a giant phallus, and I could appreciate why primitive people were drawn to these sites to make offerings.

'There it is,' he said.

As we drew closer, I could see the gathering, the horses, the riders, the quad bikes, the girls who had been caught, the men in jogging clothes doing stretches. I could hear the dogs barking and could just make out Sandy Cunningham going in circles round the tower on his motorbike.

'Can you stop?' I said, and the tractor ground to a halt. 'I've got to get through that lot without being caught.'

Blondie looked thoughtful as he climbed down from the vehicle. Under the seat there was a metal box and from the box he pulled a filthy blanket which he gave to me.

'Hide under that,' he said. 'Try not to make it dirty.'

'What are you going to do?'

'I'll just drive through the lot of them. They won't stop me,' he replied.

'It's worth a try.'

He climbed back in his seat. 'Where's Kensington, anyway?' he asked.

'Next to Chelsea,' I said, 'where they play football.'

'Load of fairies,' he remarked, and put his foot down.

As the tractor went hurtling along, I pulled the blanket over my head. I wrapped it around my body and peeked out through a narrow gap. Blondie turned off the lane through an open gate and as we bumped over the grass I was terrified of being tossed off the bouncing mudguard.

Everyone turned in our direction. Some of the men were waving away the tractor as you wave away flies, but my blond companion just kept going, weaving around the motorbikes and quad bikes. He shouted at a couple of girls lying on the grass sunbathing. 'Wanna lift?' but he didn't stop and they came to their feet and ran along beside us. I saw Milly and the Maasai, the emerald twins, the girl with her tattoos like bronze reliefs over her painted skin. I saw the Duc de Peralada, the Texan, the oil sheikh in his muddy robes. Simon's two dogs had got my scent and were barking and jumping up at me as we drove along.

Sandy Cunningham had stopped at the foot of the tower. He must have guessed it was me sitting on the tractor wrapped in a blanket, because all the other girls had been caught and were there in the field.

'It's her,' he shouted, kick-starting the Harley and skidding down the hill headlong towards us.

Blondie had the tower in his sights now and just kept on the same course. Sandy had to swerve out of the way and crashed in a heap. Now I'd been seen, I threw off the blanket and stood up, balancing on the mudguard and steadying myself holding on to the shoulders of my driver, my charioteer.

The dogs were barking louder, biting at the tractor wheels, jumping up and rolling over as they fell. The other girls when they saw me joined in the chase and formed a cordon around the big wheels of the tractor making it harder for the men to break through; the foxes turning on the hounds.

One of those athletic men, the American, I thought, did manage to charge through the barrier and made a grab for my legs, but I slid out of his grasp and he fell to the ground. Another man pushed through the foxes and vaulted up on the other mudguard, but, as he tried to cross over towards me, Blondie gave him a good hard push that sent him flying.

The ground rose steeply around the base of the tower and the tractor slowed as it climbed. I could smell the old stone in the hot sun and I could see a gap between those stones a couple of feet above my head.

'There,' I said and pointed. 'Aim for that gap.'

Blondie nodded and pushed on. He swerved right and left, this swaying action making my balance precarious, but it did stop the men breaking the cordon and getting a hold on his tractor. He pulled finally to the right, almost hitting the tower. I used his shoulder as a stepping stone and tucked my foot in the gap between the stones, grateful that I was wearing trainers, not high heels. As he swerved away, my feet found footholds and step by step, just as I'd climbed the oak tree, I climbed the tower.

When I reached the top I punched the air with both hands and a great cheer went up from the crowd below.

The girls danced, the men clapped and at that moment I felt like the master of the universe. The sky was blue and cloudless. The sea was lit by the sun, calm now after the storm. The woods of Black Spires stretched out to the north, and to the south I could see along the jagged line of the coast all the way to Westgate, where Saint Sebastian stood out above the white chalk cliffs.

14

The Ball

That night we peeled off the black straps and roamed th
wardrobes in the long changing room. There wer
hundreds of dresses with labels from the best couturier
shoes by Jimmy Choo and Manolo Blahnik, little dream
of silk and satin panties in their swaddling sheaths o
tissue, in boxes and shiny black envelopes. In a world o
hunger and want, no expense had been spared.

I had taken my bag into the changing room and whe
my mobile rang it was like hearing a sound from anothe
lifetime. I answered eagerly and was disappointed that i
was only a message.

It's your dad, call me soon as you can.

He sounded far away and I could hear in the back
ground the chatter of an airport or a hotel. I calle
straight away, but there was no answer and I tagged hi
message with my own.

'I'm here, Daddy, call me,' I said.

I slipped my phone into the gold link bag I'd foun
packaged in a soft leather case. I was wearing a strapless
Balenciaga gown and shoes with towering heels and letha
points, all in gold like an Olympic medal winner.

As I descended the stairs with Milly, I felt let down b
the pleasure that arises from a challenge realised. I ha
climbed to the top of the tower. Like a racing greyhound
for me there was no prize, winning was the prize, and

214

couldn't help wondering: what next? Would my long gown and fragile puffs of golden underwear be torn from my body as the night turned into another orgy? It had been so gloriously decadent, such fun, but I imagined it was going to become tiresome if that was all that lay ahead for the next thirty days. Once you reject convention, you don't want to keep repeating yourself, become the reflection in the mirror; you find pleasure in constant change and novelty.

An orchestra was playing themes from Tyler Copic films. Lee-Sun and the butlers were passing flutes of champagne and *tapas*, as the Duc de Peralada explained.

'*Si, yo sé,*' I said. '*Hablo español.*'

If he was surprised, he didn't show it. 'I have a very nice castle, quite small, you must come one day soon,' he said.

'I would like that,' I replied, and we touched the rims of our glasses.

'You were . . . *una maravilla* today.'

'Was I?'

He didn't reply. Other men, shiny after their showers, girded in dinner suits, came up to congratulate me.

'She's too foxy for us. Just like a woman,' Sandy Cunningham remarked.

'Is that sour grapes?' I said

'Not from my vineyard,' said the Duc.

The woman, the French Government Minister, magnificent in red latex and long boots, pushed through the men, leaned towards me and our lips met in a leisurely kiss.

'One day, *chére*, they will walk naked and we shall hold the whip,' she said, and the men roared with laughter.

'Not if I have anything to do with it, they won't,' said Ben Olson, his big voice breaking through the noise. 'Come, you might bring me some luck,' he added.

We wandered as a group through the hall to the adjoining annexe where some roulette and blackjack tables had been set up. The croupiers, severe men in black suits, made columns of chips and pushed them across the green baize, the players signing for the amount they required with Jay Leonard, everything done on trust among the men of the New World Order.

The lights were low. At the next table, the ball danced over the grooves of the roulette wheel, tapping and clicking, tempting fate. The cards slid across the black-jack table as the dealer shuffled three packs together before lodging them in a shoe face down, their arrangement a narrative of good luck and ill fortune. I could smell those cards, like cotton growing in the sun, like fresh linen. My underarms were tingling, my fingers prickled with pins and needles. A bead of perspiration ran down between my breasts as the dealer turned the cards across the playing field, each snapping into place like a bolt into a lock.

The Texan placed a £1,000 chip on the six of hearts; it was joined by the seven of hearts. He asked for another card, a 10, bringing him to 23, and I watched the £1,000 chip being scooped back into the dealer's pile. I watched Sandy lose £1,000 and double up, following the system. Sergio Buenavista, the Duc, won with his £5,000 stake and left the two black-ringed chips to ride on the next deal. He won again, a total of £15,000 to the good in a few minutes, so quick, so easy, so painless. Money attracts money, money likes money, that's why those men at Black Spires enjoyed each other's company, why they could bare their bodies and souls and deepest desires and primitive instincts.

The cards turned, the chips moved back and forth like a tide, though more in the direction of the bank. I noticed Simon appear on the other side of the table, watching me as I watched Sandy Cunningham double again, £4,000 now riding on the two of diamonds.

'You're not playing, Magdalena?' Sandy asked, grinning, his blue eyes sparkling with the light from the chandelier.

'I don't have any money,' I replied.

'That never discouraged you before,' said Simon, and they all laughed.

'Here,' said Sandy, 'you make it last.'

He rolled a red £100 chip across the table. It slowed, shivered and fell in front of me.

'Hey, don't encourage the girlies,' said Ben Olson. 'You'll lead them on to the path of wickedness.'

That red chip felt comfortable in my hand, as a ring feels comfortable on your finger. I didn't sit. I remained aloof as I leaned over to place the chip on the last available playing site at the table.

I was back.

Ten of hearts. Ten of clubs.

Jay Leonard had taken over the dealing. 'Split?' he asked, and there was another rumble of laughter.

To have split the two tens I would have needed another £100 chip to place an equal bet on each, managing two hands instead of one. Most players do split tens, but I couldn't and, calculating the odds, I didn't consider it a good idea anyway: I already had 20 and the banker was sitting on a seven. He drew a 10. I'd doubled my money.

There was a little round of applause that I didn't acknowledge. I was deep in thought and what I decided was to take Sandy's system and stand it on its head. Instead of hoarding my winnings and doubling when I lost, I thought I'd let it all ride. Play to win. In for a penny. All or nothing. I placed the two red chips on the table and drew the seven of spades. The King of Spades came to join him and Jay Leonard bust with a nine, a six and the enigmatic Jack of Diamonds.

I let the money ride again. I won again. The four red chips became eight.

On the fourth hand I drew the Ace of Hearts and the Jack of Clubs: blackjack.

From just one red chip, I had 16 chips, £1,600, and around that table the king makers, the masters of the

217

universe, the politicians and media moguls, the oil men and the men who matter, were silently watching. I had won four hands in a row. Losing five in a row is almost impossible. That's what Sandy Cunningham had told me. I imagined winning five in a row must be the same, a challenge to the odds, an affront to the law of averages. You needed the luck of the devil. The men knew that, too. They had watched me on that tractor with Blondie cross the field and climb to the top of the tower. They were waiting now for me to fall.

'Place your bets,' said Jay Leonard.

I hesitated.

And I remembered something Sandy had once said. *Never trust anything but your own instincts.*

I placed those red chips in four neat piles on the table. The other players idly pushed their £1,000 and £5,000 chips out into the playing arena. They weren't watching their hands, they were watching me. The cards cracked from the shoe and there was something musical about the way they fell crackling to the table, the notes slipping across the scale as if scored by Mozart.

I drew a two followed by a three. The bank sat on a Queen of Clubs, juicy as a ripe blackberry, every inch a winner. My heart sank and I tried not to show it. I drew another card and when Jay Leonard turned over the six of diamonds my spirits lifted again. I had 11 and drew the King of Hearts: the perfect 21. I flushed with pleasure.

Jay Leonard adjusted the position of his Queen, pausing before turning his second card. If he turned over an ace, he would have a blackjack and I would be finished, bankrupt, an example of Sandy's system. But it wasn't an ace, it was the nine of diamonds, giving him a score of 19, enough to rake in thousands from the other players but not enough to beat my 21.

I had won five in a row. I had accumulated £3,200 and for a moment I was in shock. My heart was pounding and beads of sweat broke out on my brow. I looked up and the eyes that met mine belonged to Simon Roche. I studied those eyes and those strong features for any emotion his expression might betray. He studied me, too.

What now?

The amount I had won was magical. The perfect number. A sum chosen by providence. I returned the one red chip worth £100 to Sandy Cunningham and I pushed the remaining £3,100 across the table to Simon Roche.

He looked at those chips. He looked up at me and, at that same second, my mobile rang. For some reason it sounded urgent.

'May I?' I asked, and Simon nodded.

'Oh my God, hello, Daddy . . .'

The game had ceased. Everyone was listening.

My father spoke hurriedly and excitedly for two minutes and I'm sure my mouth must have fallen open as I listened. He told me that he was in Dubai where he had met at the hotel a director from CunniLingus who had *heard on the grapevine* that he was in the business of selling second-hand aeroplanes. The low-budget airline was updating and needed an agent to unload 400 craft surplus to its requirements. Daddy would make about $100,000 on each, a total of $4 million.

'Everything's going to be all right,' he said.

'I always knew it would.'

'So, what are you up to, Madge?'

I paused before answering. 'Playing blackjack,' I said.

'Listen, a word to the wise, run with your luck and quit when you're ahead.'

We hung up. I stared in turn at Simon Roche, Sandy Cunningham, Ben Olson. They all wore that complicit, vaguely condescending look of teachers and elders, of people who think they know you better than you know yourself and perhaps they do.

'Happy, now?' asked Ben.

I nodded.

It was the perfect Hollywood ending.

219

The orchestra was playing dance music and Simon Roche led me away from the gaming tables to waltz in rather old-fashioned way. I danced with the Texan that night, and Sandy, and Kurt – *very gut, very gut*, he kep saying. I danced with the American, the diplomats an politicians, the kings and king makers. I drank cham pagne. I ate blini, lush with caviar and sour cream. I wa like Cinderella in my golden heels and at midnight danced up the staircase with Simon, my tormenter, m master, my lover. I was free now. I had paid my debt. would, as I had planned, go to the LSE and work a Rebels to pay my way if I had to.

Simon's room was decorated in gold, black and white modern and minimalist like the Roche-Marshall building The windows were open allowing the sound of the sea t enter with the briny smell I remembered from the dorn at Saint Sebastian, just a tractor ride down the coast.

Heathcliff peeled the golden gown from my body an lowered my knickers over my heels. I was naked again Not because that was the rules for the girls who came t Black Spires but because that's what I wanted. I lay bacl on the white silk sheets.

'I hope you're not going to give up being an intern, Simon said.

'Will you trust me with the secret codes?'

'Of course. Girls should always be tempted,' he replied as he pulled his leather belt from his trousers.

nexus

The leading publisher of fetish and adult fiction

TELL US WHAT YOU THINK!

Readers' ideas and opinions matter to us so please take a few minutes to fill in the questionnaire below.

1. Sex: Are you male ☐   female ☐   a couple ☐?

2. Age: Under 21 ☐   21–30 ☐   31–40 ☐   41–50 ☐   51–60 ☐   over 60 ☐

3. Where do you buy your Nexus books from?
☐ A chain book shop. If so, which one(s)?

_____

☐ An independent book shop. If so, which one(s)?

_____

☐ A used book shop/charity shop
☐ Online book store. If so, which one(s)?

_____

4. How did you find out about Nexus books?
☐ Browsing in a book shop
☐ A review in a magazine
☐ Online
☐ Recommendation
☐ Other _____

5. In terms of settings, which do you prefer? (Tick as many as you like.)
☐ Down to earth and as realistic as possible
☐ Historical settings. If so, which period do you prefer?

_____

☐ Fantasy settings – barbarian worlds
☐ Completely escapist/surreal fantasy
☐ Institutional or secret academy

- ☐ Futuristic/sci fi
- ☐ Escapist but still believable
- ☐ Any settings you dislike?

_____

- ☐ Where would you like to see an adult novel set?

_____

6. In terms of storylines, would you prefer:

- ☐ Simple stories that concentrate on adult interests?
- ☐ More plot and character-driven stories with less explicit adult activity?
- ☐ We value your ideas, so give us your opinion of this book:

_____

_____

_____

7. In terms of your adult interests, what do you like to read about? (Tick as many as you like.)

- ☐ Traditional corporal punishment (CP)
- ☐ Modern corporal punishment
- ☐ Spanking
- ☐ Restraint/bondage
- ☐ Rope bondage
- ☐ Latex/rubber
- ☐ Leather
- ☐ Female domination and male submission
- ☐ Female domination and female submission
- ☐ Male domination and female submission
- ☐ Willing captivity
- ☐ Uniforms
- ☐ Lingerie/underwear/hosiery/footwear (boots and high heels)
- ☐ Sex rituals
- ☐ Vanilla sex
- ☐ Swinging
- ☐ Cross-dressing/TV
- ☐ Enforced feminisation

☐ Others – tell us what you don't see enough of in adult fiction:

_____

_____

_____

8. Would you prefer books with a more specialised approach to your interests, i.e. a novel specifically about uniforms? If so, which subject(s) would you like to read a Nexus novel about?

_____

_____

_____

9. Would you like to read true stories in Nexus books? For instance, the true story of a submissive woman, or a male slave? Tell us which true revelations you would most like to read about:

_____

_____

_____

10. What do you like best about Nexus books?

_____

_____

11. What do you like least about Nexus books?

_____

_____

12. Which are your favourite titles?

_____

_____

13. Who are your favourite authors?

_____

_____

14. Which covers do you prefer? Those featuring:
(Tick as many as you like.)

- ☐ Fetish outfits
- ☐ More nudity
- ☐ Two models
- ☐ Unusual models or settings
- ☐ Classic erotic photography
- ☐ More contemporary images and poses
- ☐ A blank/non-erotic cover
- ☐ What would your ideal cover look like?

_____

15. Describe your ideal Nexus novel in the space provided:

_____

_____

_____

_____

16. Which celebrity would feature in one of your Nexus-style fantasies
We'll post the best suggestions on our website – anonymously!

_____

THANKS FOR YOUR TIME

Now simply write the title of this book in the space below and cut out the
questionnaire pages. Post to: Nexus, Marketing Dept., Virgin Books,
Random House, 20 Vauxhall Bridge Road, London SW1V 2SA

Book title: _____

NEXUS NEW BOOKS

To be published in October 2009

The Girlflesh Captive
Adriana Arden

The Shiller Company's secret slavegirl business is ruthlessly exploited by its archrival Harvey Rochester when he has an entire truckload of their beautiful and highly trained slave girls abducted. The girls will be forced to work in his own cruel slave houses and also serve as hostages guaranteeing Shiller's will replace them with a fresh batch when they are exhausted.

Vanessa Buckingham, happily working for Shillers as a slave reporter for The Girlflesh News, has suffered torture at Rochester's hands once before and knows this state of affairs cannot be allowed to continue. She is further motivated by the fact that her slave lover Kashika will be in the next batch of girls to be handed over to Rochester.

Rochester must be stopped for good, his slave business destroyed and the captive girls rescued. But how can his elaborate security precautions be bypassed? To succeed Vanessa must risk all and enter a secret world of depravity and suffering.

£7.99   ISBN 9780352345417

If you would like more information about Nexus titles, please visit our website at www.nexus-books.co.uk, or send a large stamped addressed envelope to:
Nexus
Virgin Books
Random House
20 Vauxhall Bridge Road
London SW1V 2SA

NEXUS BOOKLIST

Information is correct at time of printing. To avoid disappointment, check availability before ordering. Go to www.nexus-books.co.uk.

All books are priced at £6.99 unless another price is given.

NEXUS

☐ ABANDONED ALICE	Adriana Arden	ISBN 978 0 352 33969
☐ ALICE IN CHAINS	Adriana Arden	ISBN 978 0 352 33908
☐ AMERICAN BLUE	Penny Birch	ISBN 978 0 352 34169
☐ AQUA DOMINATION	William Doughty	ISBN 978 0 352 34020
☐ THE ART OF CORRECTION	Tara Black	ISBN 978 0 352 33895
☐ THE ART OF SURRENDER	Madeline Bastinado	ISBN 978 0 352 34013
☐ BARE, WHITE AND ROSY	Penny Birch	ISBN 978 0 352 34505
☐ BEASTLY BEHAVIOUR	Aishling Morgan	ISBN 978 0 352 34095
☐ BEHIND THE CURTAIN	Primula Bond	ISBN 978 0 352 34111
☐ BEING A GIRL	Chloë Thurlow	ISBN 978 0 352 34139
☐ BELINDA BARES UP	Yolanda Celbridge	ISBN 978 0 352 33926
☐ BIDDING TO SIN	Rosita Varón	ISBN 978 0 352 34063
☐ BLUSHING AT BOTH ENDS	Philip Kemp	ISBN 978 0 352 34107
☐ THE BOOK OF PUNISHMENT	Cat Scarlett	ISBN 978 0 352 33975
☐ BRUSH STROKES	Penny Birch	ISBN 978 0 352 34072
☐ BUTTER WOULDN'T MELT	Penny Birch	ISBN 978 0 352 34120
☐ CALLED TO THE WILD	Angel Blake	ISBN 978 0 352 34067
☐ CAPTIVES OF CHEYNER CLOSE	Adriana Arden	ISBN 978 0 352 34028
☐ CARNAL POSSESSION	Yvonne Strickland	ISBN 978 0 352 34062
☐ CITY MAID	Amelia Evangeline	ISBN 978 0 352 34096
☐ COLLEGE GIRLS	Cat Scarlett	ISBN 978 0 352 33942
☐ COMPANY OF SLAVES	Christina Shelly	ISBN 978 0 352 33887

NEXUS CLASSIC

NEXUS NON FICTION

- - - - - - ✂ -

Please send me the books I have ticked above.

Name   ....

Address   ....

              ....

              ....

              .... Post code ....

Send to: Virgin Books Cash Sales, Direct Mail Dept., the Book Service Ltd, Colchester Road, Frating, Colchester, CO7 7DW

US customers: for prices and details of how to order books for delivery by mail, call 888-330-8477.

Please enclose a cheque or postal order, made payable to **Virgin Books Ltd**, to the value of the books you have ordered plus postage and packing costs as follows:
   UK and BFPO – £1.00 for the first book, 50p for each subsequent book.
   Overseas (including Republic of Ireland) – £2.00 for the first book, £1.00 for each subsequent book.

If you would prefer to pay by VISA, ACCESS/MASTERCARD, AMEX, DINERS CLUB or SWITCH, please write your card number and expiry date here:

....

Please allow up to 28 days for delivery.

Signature   ....

Our privacy policy

We will not disclose information you supply us to any other parties. We will not disclose any information which identifies you personally to any person without your express consent.

From time to time we may send out information about Nexus books and special offers. Please tick here if you do *not* wish to receive Nexus information.   ☐

- - - - - ✂ -